Pudel & Cie
Problems Solved

CASE # 1 MORONEY BOLONEY

A.R. Donenfeld-Vernoux

Published by Curmudgeon Gal Productions

This book is dedicated to:
Petite Four, Peaches, Aka, Baby,
Lucy, Lexie, Humphrey, Duffy,
Tommy, JoJo, Myrtle, Heidi, Pink,
Calvin, Tug, Irving, Josie, Sammy,
Lorenzo, Gertie, Henry, Daisy,
and all the other 4-paws who have
passed through my life, either
as my owners or owners
of friends and family.
I always knew how smart you all were,
how well you train your humans,
even as you chose not to be obvious,
your way to kindly not embarrass us.

A special thank you to my favorite writers:
Dirk and Gregg, who once again offered
support, great ideas, insight, and have
put up with me for years at the
Orange County Advanced Fiction Group,
and to Melinda Bates for editing patience
I couldn't have done it without you all.

Magnus' Magick

Once upon a long time ago, at least three hundred years before the present time, there lived a man named Magnus Pudel.

Magnus was the local wizard of a small village perched precariously on the side of a high peak on the French side of the Pyrenees, the Basque Country.

A man way ahead of his time, Magnus experimented with chants, spells, chemicals, potions, mirrors, and all forms of magic.

Since he wasn't a farmer, shepherd, blacksmith or knight, in order to support his family he became expert at removing warts, birthing stubborn calves and babies, making love potions and getting rid of pesky spells cast by black magicians.

Magnus only believed in white magic, as he called it. But in fact, he was a healer. Knowledgeable in herbs and roots, natural medicines, setting broken bones, reducing fevers, he did whatever was needed to keep his patients healthy.

The local priest was his uncle, and turned a blind eye when the Catholic Church frowned on the sort of skills Magnus was famous for. He knew Magnus was a man of good intentions and shouldn't be punished for his kindness. The people from the neighboring farms and villages were sorely in need of his medical skills.

But Magnus had a motive hidden behind his medicines, potions and spells. He was sure he could create a magic elixir to prolong life. It would bring him untold riches to help support his family.

One night he had a dream. A deep voice spoke to him, saying, "Your name is the clue to what ye seek." It seemed strange to him to believe 'Pudel' could be the key, but he was willing to try.

Magnus read every book he could find that might mention the word or name 'pudel.' He finally found a reference to 'pudelhunds,' German hunting dogs with curly coats perfect for retrieving game from cold waters.

Gathering up what little money he had, he made the long and dangerous journey across the Pyrenees and the breadth of France, all the way to Germany. After months of searching, he returned home with four healthy and playful pudelhund puppies.

He raised the puppies into beautiful strong dogs, then bred them again and again. To keep the breed strong, he added in other dogs with qualities he liked, such as strength, endurance, intelligence, and kindliness of disposition.

The dogs were so funny and sweet, he wouldn't harm them, he only took tiny samples of their blood and small skin scrapings to use with his spells, elixirs and magic.

His family fell in love with the good tempered animals. Then the villagers and farmers saw how smart the dogs were and wanted them too. Soon Magnus found he could support his family only by selling the puppies. In a few years, he had many dogs, and a booming business. People were willing to travel miles to buy Magnus' pudels.

Still, he kept on his quest. After years of unsuccessful experiments he finally had a breakthrough. One of his concoctions actually worked. But not quite the way he expected.

He drank some of his latest attempt, a truly foul smelling liquid, and said a chant in Basque to complete the spell. *Auto bikoitza naiz, ispilu aldatzeko me nire beste auto bat.*

An odd feeling came over him—his legs changed. Something began growing in his back nether parts. His nose and mouth elongated together, his sense of smell became more acute, and curly hair grew on his bald pate. When he looked in the mirror, a very large grey muzzled poodle looked back at him, and wagged its tail.

CHAPTER TWO

A New Client—Now

My name is Antonio Pudel—problem solving is my game. Adjusting my Panama hat, I'm on my way to meet a new client, one in the upper stratosphere of the many billion dollar range.

I'm wearing a cream colored linen Armani suit with a black silk open necked shirt, black Gucci loafers, no socks. My hair is white blonde in long waves, almost brushing my shirt collar. I always like things well styled, and I don't go for ragged, whether it's my hair style or a shave.

As a man, I'm six feet two inches, and both women and bitches think I'm handsome. I admit I'm also a dog, and like the description no matter what form I'm in when it's applied. Not bad for a problem solver. I'm not a detective—don't like chasing errant spouses or violence if I can avoid it.

My sister, Belvidere, is almost as tall as I am. She doesn't say much and she's one tough bitch you don't want to cross. My little sister, Callista, is another story. I'll get to her later.

The three of us inherited the family business, 'Pudel & Cie. Problems Solved'. 'Cie.' is an abbreviation for 'compagnie', or 'company' in French. Since the business is global, we keep the name intact.

We've also inherited a genetic anomaly caused by an ancient ancestor's magic spells—the ability to flip between human and dog. Flipping is a dominant trait with our family.

The odd part is, when we flip, our dog persona appears complete with whatever collar or sweater we were wearing the last time we flipped. When we flip back to human, our clothes are the same as before we flipped to dog.

Some of our family believe Magnus' spell causes travel between two dimensions. Others of our family couldn't give a rat's patootie how it works. Sometimes it can be useful. Other times...not so much.

Belvidere and I flip to standard poodles, our sister Callista flips to a Pomeranian. Don't ask me how Callista happened. As soon as my puppy eyes opened, I remember seeing a tiny orange ball of fuzz snuggled up against my curly black poodle sister. As we grew, I discovered

Bel and I looked alike except for our color. The orange fluff...we don't know how she got there. Both parents refuse to say a word. We've accepted her as just another mystery to add to the Pudel family tree.

Our parents have taken off on a yearlong round-the-world cruise. Their parting words as they walked out the door—"Don't call unless you're in jail or the emergency room. Good luck!"

Fair enough. Bon Voyage!

This will be our first case on our own. Thinking about it makes me puff out my chest with pride while at the same time I stifle the worm of anxiety in my gut. Time to prove we can handle the family business all by ourselves. We have big paw prints to fill.

The long entrance leading to the Freedhoff estate overlooks the costal bluffs of Orange County, giving a panoramic view of the Pacific Ocean out to Catalina Island. I stop for a moment to stare at the mansion. I'd seen opulent before, but this was so far over the top I wanted to look twice to make sure it was actually resting on the ground. My first thought was Versailles had been cloned and moved to California.

Personally, I'd have gone for something more modern, maybe the Bauhaus school, impressive, but open. This mansion crouches on the grounds behind a topiary menagerie as if ready to leap up and snarl at all intruders. The rampant green-leaved horse and slinking bear do nothing to detract from the effect.

I park my ten year old BMW M-5 under an arch that could give the Arc de Triumph a run for its money. Smoothing seatbelt creases from my jacket, I climb the marble steps to the equally impressive door— bronze bas relief commemorating Charles Martel's victory repelling the Umayyad at Tours. Interesting place, I think as I gauge my surroundings before rapping the trunk of a brass elephant against a plate on the center of the door. The elephant's in no hurry, and neither am I.

Coming from behind the house, the sound of surf murmurs like a contented lioness; the front of the house offers a glimpse of distant mountains glowing white from the recent dusting of snow. California living makes it always hard to believe winter is so close when you're bathed in sunlight and warmth.

Off to the side of the porte cochère, a dapper youth energetically shines the chrome on an antique Rolls Royce. The Roller sparkles brilliantly in the early light. It clearly enjoys the ministrations.

The door opens before I have a chance to knock, disturbing my reverie. A tall, dark skinned man stands behind the door—his body and most of his face, other than a black eyebrow and one startling green eye—obscured.

"Mr. Pudel, I presume?" His deep basso profundo voice resonates.

"Yes, Antonio Pudel." I hand him my card, 'Pudel & Cie, Problems Solved'. He opens the door wider.

The entrance is graced by a domed rotunda. A portrait of a somber man, bald, double breasted pin striped suit, portly, black wispy hair parted in the middle, and a Clark Gable mustache, hangs in prominent position to my right. I assume this must be the ancestor who made the family fortune. Who else would deserve such a place of honor?

A round marble table, inlaid with a mosaic of flowers in every imaginable color perches on an Aubusson in the same brilliant tones. On top, a Ming Dynasty vase overflowing with fresh blooms, dominates the center of the room.

"If you would be kind enough to wait, I'll advise Madam you have arrived." Stepping out from behind the door, a Sikh, at least six feet six inches tall, bright turquoise turban, long beard and cheekbones so steep only a mountain goat could climb them, greets me with a broad smile. His black handlebar moustache and beard frame blinding white teeth, while eyes black as the contemplation of eternity survey me over a hawk nose. A beige raw silk kurta is immaculate over a matching pair of slim fitting dhotis, a long silver and gold chain with carved jade on a silver background edged by a rope design in gold around his neck.

Impressive, I think, and my mind reviews what I knew about Sikhs—never cut their hair, fierce warriors. Mrs. Freedhoff is obviously discerning in her choice of servants.

The Sikh drops my card in a silver salver on the table. If Callista has trained me correctly, I recognize the salver—Paul Revere.

I nod in return and wait, happy with time to study the portrait. Blue eyes, colder than polar ice, chill my soul to look at them. The firm set to the pronounced square jaw, topped by aquiline nose a bit too thin for my taste, all confirm the first impression. This was not a man to be trifled with.

I assume he was Madam's father. The brief research I had done on the family refresh my recollection from the scandal rags. The man whose portrait I'm perusing had two children, a boy and a girl, the boy was infamous for scandalous escapades—too much money and not much sense had marred that generation's son. He wanted no part of the business, preferring to squander money rather than make it. Dying young from an overdose, his sister inherited their father's estate.

The girl, now the Dowager Freedhoff, was quite an interesting case in herself. At the age of twenty-three, she took control of the family holdings, ruling the empire with an iron fist. An anomaly at a time when women were supposed to be pregnant and barefoot in the kitchen, she surprised everyone by multiplying the family worth time and time again. After doing a little calculation, I reckon she had to be pushing ninety by now. If one believes the sparse current articles, she is still quite a vibrant old gal.

Meanwhile, her feral family gets all the press. The old guard made the family fortune, a current generation intent on frittering it away.

At quite an advanced age for a woman, the Dowager married for a short time and gave birth to fraternal twins, a boy and a girl. Her husband died several years later in a boating accident. Both of their children died under scandalous circumstances, the son found dead in his suite on a cruise ship, cause unknown or never revealed. The daughter was a drugged out mess who died in an automobile accident, leaving her mother with two granddaughters to raise. A family rich in money and poor in luck.

Not an easy task, inheriting two teenage girls at the age of eighty. In my opinion, teens are unpleasant under any circumstances. The idea of two of them under the same roof appeals to me about as much as training pit bulls to be therapy dogs.

Instead of twiddling my thumbs and speculating, I continue looking around. Two closed doors on the sides of the entrance I imagine lead to halls branching into the wings of the mansion. A long staircase behind the table winds up to a clerestory windowed gallery running around the base of an overhead dome. I look up to see a vision of cherubs with nasty faces grinning at an old man with a long beard and a flowing robe. An expression of mortal pain shows on his face. Must have been contemplating the idea of teen girls.

The door to the left of the staircase opens and a female apparition flies through. Somewhere in her early twenties, she's Goth to the max—black and aubergine spiked hair, combat boots and a plaid hip-hugging mini skirt. A tee-shirt, at least two sizes too small, crudely cut into a deep V at the font, reveals white orbs a grapefruit could envy, and is so short her belly ring shows over the top of the skirt.

Her eyes are obscured by long false lashes punctuating black eye shadow on top and bottom lids. All in all, a disturbing sight, especially when she begins to hum a toneless melody. I'd seldom seen a face so devoid of emotion. One of the granddaughters? And is she on something? I silently watch and let the scene play out.

She walks up too close, her eyes level with my third shirt button, strolls around me once, and then again. Something about her smells unpleasant, like a mixture of unwashed hair, sweat and old sex. Even in human form, my olfactory perceptions are heightened. It takes all my self-control not to recoil or flip.

Stopping at my right arm, she leans close to sniff me. Loudly. Then she sniffs again. Seeming satisfied, she walks back a step and looks up. "You smell good. Vetiver, Givenchy? I like the classic colognes better than the new celebrity driven ones." Her voice is deep and husky, unexpected in such a young woman. It would have better suited a throat used to plenty of scotch and several packs of cigarettes a day over a few decades. If the voice had come from anyone else, I might even think it was sexy. But not from this broad. Something about her makes the hair on the back of my neck stand on end. I've enough dog instinct in me to know when danger is near.

Her intent gaze bores into my face, eyes blank, filled with nothing. I feel my neck turn red. I don't like her so close to me. "You're handsome too. Strange coloring with such white-blond hair—but I like it...a lot." She reaches a hand to touch my hair and I back up. Lunging forward, as if to grab me, she stops in mid grab. Beginning toneless humming for a moment, as if it is how she collects herself, she asks. "What's your name?"

"Murphy. Cathouse Murphy."

"I don't believe you." She looks down and adjusts one of her breasts in a way that make it look like an ostrich egg about to tumble out of its nest. "What do you do? Are you a bouncer in a cat house?"

"Not quite. I'm a problem solver."

"You're shitting me?" Her expression turns from playful to sulky and she isn't as pretty as I thought at first.

"Actually, I'm not. My calling—Professional Problem Solver."

"Huh?"

"That's it—all you get."

"I really like you...more than a lot." Her face strains into a mask, the skin over her cheekbones whitening with the tension and her eyes narrowing into slits, like a wildcat ready to pounce on its prey. This is one bitch I definitely won't return the favor of sniffing.

Twisting her arm behind her back, she grabs her elbow with her other hand. It forces the egg to almost fall off the wall, but gravity doesn't always have its way. I see the tiny blue veins behind the white skin of her breast and imagine them pulsing in terror of falling.

She looks up in my face again. "You have big shoulders." Standing on her toes, she tilts towards me. I back up again. If she tries to get any closer, she'll fall flat on her face.

When she sees I'm not going to play her game, her face clouds over and she shows her teeth in the rictus of a snarl. Yes, I think, feline, and no house tabby.

Just then, the Sikh comes back into the hall, looking unconcerned. Her humming rises to a thrumming crescendo as she turns and struts away.

I notice I'm sweating, even though the air in the house is cool and I hadn't been warm ten minutes before.

"Who was that?" I ask.

"That was Miss Moroney Freedhoff. Madam will see you now, Mr. Pudel."

"Has anyone thought to house train her? She seems like she could use it."

He says nothing, but something behind those black eyes squirms as he points me towards a hallway to the left of the staircase and repeats that Madam is ready to see me. The blankness of his eyes is enough of an answer for me.

That sunny California day has since been indelibly stamped on my memory.

And so began the saga of our first problem to solve.

CHAPTER THREE

The Interview

I followed him down the hallway and outside to what appeared at first to be a small, rustic shed. Upon closer inspection, it was a much larger structure than I had thought.

Partly hidden by dense foliage, a large screened porch overlooked the cliffs and the ocean. Inside, bundled under a faux fur ermine throw and a large brimmed soft grey hat, was a tiny woman; shrunken and wrinkled like a mummy someone had only partially wrapped. One hand, veins blue and prominent, beckoned me to come closer. When I did, I saw the traces of real beauty, the bones of her face showed a perfect oval, large round blue eyes, and skin marred by the spotting that comes with very old age. The frame was still there, but the upholstery had slipped, discolored and frayed.

When she smiled, her teeth were yellowed like old ivory, but her eyes danced with vivid blue fire. She must have been a real stunner in her day.

I introduced myself and handed her a business card. She reached for a gold colored lorgnette and intently studied the tiny print. I guessed the gold was real.

"Interesting. Problems Solved. Tell me, Mr. Pudel, do you generally solve all the problems presented to you?"

I smiled my best smile, one I hoped didn't show too much long canines, and was welcoming rather than predatory. Sometimes it's hard to make warm and fuzzy come across clearly. Especially after meeting first with Moroney.

She continued without waiting for my answer. "I see you've met Gupta already. Has he taken good care of you Mr. Pudel?" She nodded and smiled at the tall man standing silently at attention. At the mention of his name he nodded and performed a small intricate twirl of his left hand as if in agreement.

"May I bring you some tea, or perhaps a beverage—Madam, Mr. Pudel?" Gupta asked, nodding in turn to each of us.

"Yes, please bring me a tisane, you know, the usual, and perhaps

Mr. Pudel might enjoy something stronger?"

"A mineral water would be nice, thank you."

Gupta nodded his head again, performed his hand twirl and walked out the screen door.

As I looked around the porch, I noticed it was situated to shield its occupants from the prevailing winds while presenting a perfect view of the ocean. The lazy swell of the waves moved the kelp bed below, slowly undulating in the ebb and flow of the tide. I thought I saw the fin of a dolphin, but maybe it was only wishful thinking.

Mrs. Freedhoff studied me intently. Blue eyes picked at my features the way a bird pecks seeds. I could almost feel the quick sharp touch as she moved from one place to another, first on my body, and moving up to my face. Then she stopped, and slid a fragile hand holding a lace handkerchief up to her eyes. I could swear she was wiping away a tear. But when she looked directly at me, those eyes were clear and demanding immediate attention. "Well young man, you are certainly an intriguing specimen of masculinity. If I was fifty years younger and in better shape, I'd be boffing your socks off in a heartbeat!"

I'm sure my mouth dropped open far enough to swallow a Great Dane. It was certainly not what I expected as a greeting. Perhaps the actions of her granddaughters weren't so outrageous after all—apple falling from tree and all that.

"Oh don't look so surprised. Just because I'm old doesn't mean I'm stupid or don't know a good looking stud when I see one."

I began to understand how she was able to control a large financial empire on her own. Clearly, little evaded her scrutiny, and she didn't mind letting you know it.

Gupta returned and put a silver tray on the rattan table off to the side of her chair. It contained a cup and saucer, a silver ice bucket and a glass. All as expected. Unexpected was the frosted bottle of vodka sitting next to the Perrier. He handed me a glass of sparkling water with ice and a small linen napkin. He then poured the vodka into the tea cup and handed it to Mrs. Freedhoff.

She winked at me and smiled, "The doctor says I'm not supposed to drink—it will kill me." She laughed with a dry coughing sound. "As if I'm worried about it at this time of my life."

I sipped the Perrier, she held the teacup to her lips and took small sips, her pink tongue slipping in and out of the cup like a cat lapping milk. There was some feline traits about her I found disconcerting. This was no housecat. But was she a cougar, or a lioness, or maybe a jaguar? Cats can't flip to my knowledge, but if they could, my money would be on Mrs. Freedhoff.

"So Mr. Pudel, tell me about you and your business and how you came to get into it. You were suggested to me with very high recommendations by my attorney, and I'd like to know why."

"I run Pudel & Cie. with my two sisters, Belvidere and Callista. Our family has been problem solvers for generations; a profession my ancestors brought with them from Europe. Pudels have solved problems for over three hundred years."

"It's a very strange occupation, if I may say so. Exactly what do you do that an attorney, or a private detective can't?"

"The restrictions are much less. As consultants, all we need is a business license, we take no bar exam and we do not have a private investigator's license. We have more freedom to operate in ways some might consider unique, but they are well within the purview of the law. You can rest assured, nothing we do is illegal, but I admit sometimes our techniques can be just a bit...shall we say...unorthodox?"

"Can you explain yourself?"

"I prefer not to, Madam. We give our clients results, not platitudes, and we do not disclose our process. As you noted, we were recommended by your attorney, with whom we have worked on many different problems. Please feel free to check with him again, and let him assure you our services were most satisfactory."

As she sat back in her chair, I could see she was not used to being rebuffed. A woman who always got her own way. But she leaned forward. "I will check your references again, be assured of that, but in the meanwhile, I would like to discuss a matter with you that needs an immediate solution.

"My youngest granddaughter, Moroney, has gotten herself into another mess. That child has neither sense nor discretion, and I admit I've been lax with her. The demands of business took too much of my time away from my family and I'm afraid the result has been disastrous. The child has run wild and is the target of yet another scam." She reached beneath her robe and brought out an opened envelope, a folded letter protruding through the slits.

Odd, I thought, no one writes letters anymore; everything is done electronically. This was done on purpose to not leave a digital trail. I took rubber gloves out of my breast pocket and put them on before taking the letter from her. She looked at me quizzically.

"Forensics can lift fingerprints if necessary." I said. She nodded her head.

The content was simple, virtually untraceable. It was a copy of a promissory note printed with an inkjet printer on cheap paper. "I, Moroney Freedhoff, agree to pay the bearer of this note the sum of $100,000 in full payment." It was signed with a childish scrawl, almost illegible.

I pointed to the signature. "Is this the handwriting of your grand-daughter?"

"Yes, it is." She looked away for a moment, and when she turned back, her face was paler, the grayish color of winter ice in a country pond.

"Have you spoken to her about it? Asked what it's for?"

"No. There is no point. The girl lies to me, or starts that infernal humming and runs away. Even if she answered, I wouldn't believe a word she said."

"The sum is substantial, but, from your reputation, I don't think paying it would be much of a hardship for you. What do you think this is for? Is she a gambler? Does she use drugs? Blackmail? I'm not sure what it is you would like me to do for you?"

"I've paid blackmail for her escapades before, and yes, she gambles. I'm sure does drugs and has sex with any available male. This could be for a cover-up of any one of her many excesses."

She brought the handkerchief up to her face again, and shook her head. The hand with the handkerchief trembled and I saw this conversation had tired her considerably.

"Have there been efforts to collect this so-called debt?"

"Yes. I had a call yesterday afternoon. It was a man with a deep voice who said he wanted his money, in cash, old hundred dollar bills. He would call today at the same time to give me the instructionst for when and where he could get his money. The odd thing was, he sounded very polite, and added that he hoped he had given me enough time and I wouldn't be too inconvenienced by the short notice."

"Has he called back yet?

"No. He said he would call today, I assume around two o'clock this afternoon."

"Do you have the money on hand?"

"Yes, Gupta went to the bank this morning and collected it. I called the manager as soon I hung up with the man...to make sure it would be available." She pointed to a bright red gym bag resting at the base of the table next to her.

"Do you mind?" I pointed to the bag.

"No, go ahead, suit yourself."

I opened the zipper and saw stacks of neatly banded used hundred dollar bills tucked inside.

"Do you want me to deliver the money? Is that your problem?"

"No, Gupta will take care of that. What I want is for the blackmail to stop—to find out who is behind this, and make sure they get the message it won't continue. Since I gave in once before, and will pay now, whoever is behind this thinks I'm an easy mark...just like a cash machine whenever their funds are low. Whatever Moroney is doing to cause this has to stop, and the blackmailers must learn I'm not their PayPal."

Her voice was firm and her hands had stopped shaking. "I will record the call when he calls back. Unfortunately, I was not prepared yesterday, and he's left me with no time to get a tracking device for the money."

I began to like the old gal more and more. She was someone to be reckoned with, and I'd like to help her out, but Pudel & Cie. might not be the right place for her.

"We don't deal in violence, so don't expect us to put the arm on anyone. Our company doesn't work like that. Finding out who is behind this, as well as tracking your granddaughter is one thing, but threatening with anything more than legal action is beyond our purview. We have, in the past, done protection duty when required, and been called in to consult with the police from time to time when the matter was international. Our company has branches around the world, quite a few in Europe."

I looked around, past the glass barrier that kept the ocean winds off the covered deck where we sat. Seagulls lazed across the sky in search of some small fish swimming too close to the surface. The predators are always on the alert, I thought. No matter how deep or shallow the waters were, someone was always on the lookout to swoop in for an easy meal. I wanted to help Mrs. Freedhoff, but our position had to be clarified.

"Mr. Pudel, I'm not interested in violence. I want reconciliation and closure. Please, what do you charge for your services?"

"We get two thousand five hundred a day plus expenses. That covers the cost of one operative and office support. If more than one of us is required on a full time basis, then the cost is increased accordingly." As I spoke, one of the seagulls dove into the crest of a wave and took flight with a fish dangling from its beak.

She nodded at Gupta before turning towards me. "I've already prepared an advance against your services. I hope it will be satisfactory."

Gupta handed me a check and I glanced at it. Twenty-five thousand dollars. I put it in my pocket. "Thank you. I'll get on the problem right away. Don't you think you should also advise your granddaughter of the situation?"

"That girl has never been quite right. She does what she wants, runs wild and behaves like a feral cat in heat." She sighed deeply. The tremble was back in her hands and I saw the whole discussion had left her exhausted.

"I'll go back to my office and get to work on this immediately. If I don't think I can be of any assistance, I'll return your payment."

"That won't be necessary. I feel sure you are the man to get the job done."

I turned to leave, but as I stepped on the walkway, I turned back. "Mrs. Freedhoff, there is something else. You have another granddaughter, don't you?"

"Yes, her name is Felicity, in case you haven't seen it in the papers. Both girls are quite open in their shenanigans. Felicity less so, thank goodness for small favors. She is married, but her husband disappeared recently. He went out one morning and we never heard from him again. Felicity and I reported it to the police. They investigated and found nothing. It was as if the winds carried him off."

"He was famous, wasn't he?"

"Infamous would be more like it. Remember Carlos Etcheveria? The baseball player they suspended? About six months ago, an investigation was started concerning his use of certain enhancement drugs. After some damming evidence was alleged, he was put on suspension and fined, but after all, it resulted in nothing. No wrongdoing was ever found. He disappeared practically at the end of the suspension. It all seemed odd to me. He could have gone back to his team last week, but never appeared."

Sadness filled her eyes. She looked down again into the hand with the handkerchief and began twisting it.

"I get the feeling you liked him."

"I did. Very much." She had a wistful smile. "He was a bit of a rogue, a big fellow with a bigger heart. We spent many hours together. I reminded him of his grandmother...she was the one who brought him up. His mother was a junkie, never home, sold herself for drugs. I'm sure you've heard the same sad story time and again. They found her in an alley, two kids in a flop house almost starved to death, wondering where their mother was. He and his sister were sent to different foster homes. Carlos was the lucky one. Social Services found his grand-mother and she took him in.

"His sister got lost in the system, ended with an abusive family and ran away. He didn't find her again until she saw his name in the papers when he was drafted by the Dodgers. By then, it was too late. He paid for her to go to rehab, but as soon as she got out, she overdosed."

I understood. Some people are so damaged by life, there is no sal-vation for them.

"Felicity and Carlos fell in lust and married, but they were never a good match. Felicity's very different from Moroney. I love her, she's my granddaughter, but she's a cold fish at heart. Once the excitement wore off, she went her own way and so did Carlos, but they remained married and friends. They had an odd relationship that seemed to work for them.

"Carlos always felt this was his home. When he wasn't training or playing, he was here with Felicity and me. He had plenty of money in-telligently invested. He had no material wants. All he wanted was our company. We'd all have dinner together, I'd listen to him talk about baseball, not that I'm much of an enthusiast, but I liked him. He'd leave after dinner and a brandy and I'm sure he was out with other women. Felicity didn't care, she also went her own way, but she liked the fact Carlos still lived here.

"Carlos was a lonely man at heart and we were all the family he had. Leaving Felicity without a word wasn't surprising, but I thought he would at least have said goodbye to me."

As I turned and left, I heard her sigh again. The old woman must be very alone with Carlos gone, the one person who seemed to have genuinely loved her. It was curious she hadn't asked me to find him. It would have been the obvious problem to be solved. I'd have to think about that on the way home.

When I rounded the mansion to get into the Beemer, the young man had finished shining the Rolls. The big car languished in front of the open carriage house in all its brilliance. I looked back one more time as I opened the Beemer door. Did a shadow move behind the curtains or was my overly active imagination at work?

CHAPTER FOUR

Home & Office

After parking in the garage behind our house, I walked around to the front entrance rather than coming in through the back. Both my sisters were sitting on the front porch. I wanted to discuss my meeting and had also planned a little surprise for them.

Our Victorian house sits on a quiet street in Orange County, California. Plopped smack in the middle of gentility, it sticks out like the festooned madam of a colorful whore house.

A wild English flower garden spread a riot of pinks, yellows, purples and blues along the walkway. Two steps lead to the deep porch wrapping around three sides.

Carved wooden cobwebs decorate deck-to-roof post corners. Pale lavender siding, and glossy white trim highlighted with bubblegum pink complete the image of...perhaps a brothel left over from the 1890's?

The front lawn sports a large white sign with gilt Edwardian scrollwork proclaiming "Pudel & Cie. Problems Solved."

Our office has been in this house since the turn of the last century. Built by our great-great-grandparents, it was declaration of stability. They had emigrated from Germany, well before the beginning of the First World War. We are now the fifth generation of Pudels to live here.

Great-Great-Grandfather, Eldred Pudel, was the favorite duck hunting retriever of Bismark, First Chancellor of the German Empire. Eldred's wife and sons ran the problem solving business while he stayed by the side of the Chancellor. The family business thrived by selling the information Eldred was able to glean.

While the Chancellor was a dog lover, treating his animals kindly, Eldred distrusted his plans for world domination and was alarmed by the violent spread of the newly declared Empire.

One night Eldred slipped out of the hunting lodge, flipped, gathered his family together and left. He wisely chose to immigrate in America and open a Pudel & Cie. branch in the fast growing infant country.

The far west appealed to him. He knew gold was being mined, and people were swarming across the plains in the new transcontinental railroads built after the Civil War. A country and area with such rapid population growth had to have growing pains. A perfect place, rife with problems to be solved.

Eldred knew what he was doing.

The front lawn was guarded by a picket fence, each upright painted in a different color—jewel tones, pastels—like a line of new crayons. The horizontal fence supports and the crossbeams on the gate were stark white in contrast.

The porch beckoned with comfortably worn wicker chairs and loveseats pillowed in a plethora of floral chintz dating from sometime in the 1930s.

In a moment of extreme madness, Belvidere and I had agreed to leave the décor to our sister, Callista. It was a mistake we realized too late to correct. While inviting, her selections gave new meaning to 'shabby chic.' It wasn't my taste at all, nor that of my sister Belvidere.

Taking a deep breath, I opened the latch, and entered our property. My first reaction was always to imagine Callista impaled on the pickets, but I gave it up. I love my sister, no matter what decorating horrors she foists upon us.

A poodle almost the size of an Irish wolfhound reclined on one of the love seats. Its jet black fur was fluffed, shining, and clipped in a neat kennel cut. The dog bent over, gave a few desultory scratches to its neck, stretched out all four legs and yawned. A pink tongue flashed a spot color flicking over its muzzle.

Sitting next to the poodle was a tiny orange Pomeranian with perky black tipped ears. Bright obsidian button eyes shifted back and forth as the Pom tracked a small lizard in and out of the plants edging the porch. Both dogs stopped what they had been doing to watch me intently as I came up the walkway.

Once on the porch, I reached down, and in turn, ruffled the fur on their heads in greeting. With a sly smile, the hand I had held behind my back reached front to give each dog a long stemmed, blood red rose.

The Pom took it in her mouth and ran a victory lap hopping around the porch. Smart me, I had all the thorns removed at the florist. My sisters knew exactly what the roses meant.

It was a Pudel family tradition, or at least our branch of the family. When Father brought home a new problem to be solved, he always brought Mother a long stemmed red rose with the first check and he gifted her with another rose at the solution of the problem. The roses were symbols, a token of love and respect from the alpha male to his mate. Our American male ancestors were too civilized to lay a dead hare at the alpha females' paws as ancient tradition had dictated. The roses were less messy stand-ins, not to mention a lot more fragrant.

Now it was my turn to keep the tradition alive. Since I don't have a permanent mate yet, my sisters get the roses. Belvidere took hers with solemn dignity while Callista was still hopping around the porch with glee.

My sisters', Belvidere, the large black poodle, and Callista, the tiny Pomeranian, greeting was typical dog. The first thing was to sniff me all over.

"You smell like an old woman, Chanel No. 5 and Lily of the Valley talcum powder, no one else uses that combination any more, and something else...unpleasant...and...nasty?" Belvidere wrinkled her long nose in disgust. "Where on earth have you been to pick up such awful odors? It makes me think of back alleys and death all at once."

She nailed Mrs. Freedhoff first, and confirmed what I had thought about Moroney. "I was meeting with our new client, Mrs. Freedhoff."

Callista sat down in front of me, her paws resting on the tips of my shoes. Her bright eyes glowed with interest. "You mean the Mrs. Freedhoff with the two horrible granddaughters who are always in the newspapers? The ones famous for scandalous escapades?" Callista likes scandal almost as much as she likes money...almost, but not quite.

"That's the one. She wants me to do a little problem solving for her."

"How much is she paying?" Typical Callista—straight to the point.

"Just wait, I have a check for you in my suit pocket. Just a little advance."

They followed me inside. I put down my briefcase, took off my jacket, stretched my arms above my head and said the ritual Basque chant in my mind, *Auto bikoitza naiz, ispilu aldatzeko me nire beste auto bat.* As I looked, the mirror image changed from my usual dapper self to a large white Poodle in a neat kennel clip, with a little fluff on the topknot and long full ears.

We Pudels can change at will. I use the mind chant once in a while. It amuses me to feel a link to our ancestor who created the spell and our condition. Stress, fear, any strong emotion, can cause an unexpected flip, and not always under the most convenient circumstances. Flipping can be a problem unless the 'flipper' is well trained in how to control the event. My sisters and I have been schooled in flipping since early childhood but even we get taken by surprise occasionally.

I know it sounds strange, but it's the curse, or maybe blessing, I'm not sure which, of the Pudel family, as well as those we have interbred with over the centuries. Three centuries to be more precise. We are 'flippers'—as our family calls our ability to change back and forth from dog to human and human to dog. We are not shape-shifters, we can't change into other creatures.

The trait appears to be dominant, even though caused by a spell. Flipping can be passed to our offspring, but with the inconsistency of all genetics, there is no way to rely on who or when it will appear.

That's it. Our story in a nutshell. Odd, yes. Useful? Unimaginably so, if you are clever about it. The skill has allowed our family to amass a decent fortune through solving problems for the powerful and rich for most of the three centuries we've been around. Our ancient relative who started everything was French Basque, but now flipping Pudels are all over the world. We are experts at keeping secrets or we'd never have lasted this long.

Think about it. Dogs can be places humans would never be allowed, especially if they are intelligent and housebroken poodles, perfect companions for those who can afford them. Remember the many paintings of world leaders with their loving pets by their sides? Just Google '18th Century portraits with dogs' and see what you get. None of those aristocrats had ever imagined their faithful companions might be collecting both information, and secrets, undeniably the most valuable coin worldwide. But that's enough history for the moment.

"Where's the money? Can I see it?" Callista's favorite mantra is 'show me the money'.

"Just give it a rest for a moment, will you please?"

Her ears flattened back against her skull and she skulked over to a corner. But it didn't last long.

"Did you say it was an advance? I like advances, and that family can afford them. What's the advance against? How much is it? I remember hearing on TMZ one of the sisters, Felicity I think, has a missing husband. Is that what you were meeting about?" Callista is our resident expert on the latest gossip.

Belvidere moved closer, her interest piqued. She does like finding things, and is very good at it. Everyone has their strong points.

"No," I said, "that wasn't the problem at all. It seems the younger sister, Moroney, is being blackmailed and Mrs. Freedhoff wants to not just make the payment, but also find out who the blackmailer is and put a stop to it."

"Why doesn't she contact the police?" Belvidere asked.

"I think she wants a little discretion. The girl is a real handful. She's the one who smelled so nasty." I went on to tell them about the rest of my afternoon.

Both of them were interested, but Callista's ears perked up when I flipped back to man to pull the check out of my briefcase and hand it to her. She grabbed it in her mouth and scampered for the office to stash it in her desk for safekeeping. Tomorrow, early morning, she'd put it in the bank.

The doorbell rang. "Are we expecting anyone?" Callista was back already. We all looked at each other and shook our heads—no. "Okay, I'll look out the sidelights and see who's there. But I think Belvidere should flip back too."

Belvidere glanced into the hall mirror for a second. An imposing and handsome woman appeared where the black poodle had been standing. Callista went to peek out the front door.

"A very tall guy in a turquoise turban is with a witchy looking broad." I couldn't help but notice Callista's switch to gangster slang when we were in detective mode. It always made me laugh inside, but I never told her. If I did, then she'd stop.

"I know who one of them is, I'll get the door. You stay as you are and sniff around while Belvidere and I see what they want."

As I opened the door, the woman struck a deliberately seductive pose, hand on hip, breasts thrust forward. The 'girls' weren't as big as her little sister's, but her complexion was much better, a soft cream with a hint of coffee. This one at least was out in the daylight enough to get a little Vitamin D on her skin. I heard a soft snicker from Belvidere as she caught the pose.

Gupta was the first to speak. "So sorry to disturb you at your home Mr. Pudel, but Madam received what she was waiting for. There was no call, but this was slipped under the door. She wanted me to give it to you with a personal message." He handed me an envelope, one of those square ones engraved invitations usually come in. I could feel the weight of the paper, heavy and expensive, like an invitation to a tête-a-tête with the queen. I'd bet anything the envelope belonged to Mrs. Freedoff. Before I opened it, he continued. "May I present Mrs. Etcheveria, Madam's other granddaughter. Mrs. Etcheveria insisted on coming with me. She would like a few minutes conversation with you in private.

"I believe, if you read the message, you will have time to speak with her. We will drop her at Bloomingdales before our meeting. The chauffeur will pick her up later if I'm not available when she calls." He was frowning under the turban, and moved to do his little hand twirl before smoothing his moustache. It looked to me like he found Mrs. Etcheveria an unwelcome intrusion, but was too diplomatic to fend her off.

I nodded at them both. "I'd like you to meet my sister, Belvidere. She will show you to our office area." Mrs. Etcheveria gave no indication she heard me, nor did she lower her nose to look at any of us. Ignoring everyone, she strutted past us into the house without a word. Screw her, let her find her own way. Belvidere snorted behind me. My guess was Bel would disappear in the ninja way she used when she wanted to make herself scarce.

I turned to read the letter, but Gupta interrupted me.

"If it's all the same to you, sir. I'll leave Mrs. Etcheveria with you and be outside waiting in the car."

"Okay, that's fine with me." I went back to the letter as he left. It was short and to the point.

Dear Madam: Please have the parcel in question dropped off at the bicycle stand on the north-east corner of Third and William Street at precisely four o'clock. Have whoever is leaving it go north on William and not turn back. I will know if there is anyone else there, or if my messenger is being followed. Thank you in advance for your kind assistance, Your Friend

I read the letter over three times. Certainly the strangest blackmail note I'd ever heard of...signed 'Your Friend?' What was he or she thinking?

It was written on the same plain computer paper, printed on a cheap inkjet, nothing to distinguish it other than the envelope, which I placed on the hall table to examine when I had more time. I nodded at Callista who was standing quietly at my feet. She knew the signal to tag it and bag it when they left. There might be trace we, or the police, could use if necessary.

Tucked into the same envelope was a note on the kind of memo paper people keep around for lists, this one written in pen with a slightly shaky hand.

Mr. Pudel, please go with Gupta and see if you can find who is doing this. I leave the method up to you. This must stop.

Nodding to myself, I headed to our office and Mrs. Etcheveria.

Oak double doors engraved with griffons and peacocks were half-way slid into pockets opening to a ballroom size room, oriental carpets delineating five different seating areas—four with sofa, coffee table and chairs, the fifth in the center on a round carpet dominated by an odd piece of furniture—a series of conversation chairs rotating off a center hub like a wheel. On top of the wheel, a tall Art Nouveau vase with an arrangement of dried flowers and pussy willows. Our round table and vase were dwarfed by the ones I had just seen at the Freedhoff mansion. I better not tell Callista, I thought to myself.

Off to one side, a large alcove housed our desks, computers and office equipment—where the actual work was done.

Felicity Etcheveria had found her way to the office, but was standing in the doorway. Looking around in what I could only call a state of shock, she tried to figure out where to sit.

There were plenty of seats available, but hard to select which area to park yourself in. She started to move to the center monstrosity when I stopped her. "For heaven's sake don't sit there. Just the dust from those damn weeds will have you sneezing for days. We can't figure out what to use the god-awful thing for, but it's the favorite piece of one of my sisters. She insitss it's a rarity, and we don't dare touch it."

"Why don't you come join me? Over here?" Belvidere's voice was light, purring, a soft, ethereal quality wafting from across the room.

She unwound from a loveseat. My sister is six feet two inches tall, and the look on Mrs. Etcheveria face was obvious lust while she gazed at the dark-haired woman in a shiny black leather and spandex unitard, high black boots, all set off by a vivid blue silk scarf and a large smile.

Belvidere's face, while exotically feminine, has a similar bone structure to mine. Broad shoulders and narrow, almost masculine hips are belied by generous breasts. As she stood to welcome our guest, her muscles flexed and relaxed, the tight fabric highlighting every movement. Felicity's mouth fell open at the vision of, well, maybe a new female super hero?

When I watched Felicity take a good look at what she had missed during the earlier introductions, it was clear she'd like to rip off the spandex and leather to see exactly what was moving beneath it. On second thought, she'd probably rip it off with her teeth.

She must have caught me watching her, because she then turned a brilliant smile in my direction before sitting down in a graceful swoop ing motion that opened the front drape of her wrap-around dress all the way up to her crotch. Obviously, she wasn't choosey about what gender she wanted to seduce.

I took my eyes off the intended target and directed my gaze to her face. "A pleasure to meet you. I had a very nice talk with your grandmother earlier today, as I am sure you know."

Her face was a cream colored oval beneath flamboyant, and wiry, mahogany hair. Hazel eyes fixed me with a hard stare, wrinkled commas bracketed her tightly pressed lips that looked like they might crack if she moved them.

I wondered if she could release the tension enough to speak. She did, a little, but her words came out as tight as her face. "Cut the crap! Of course that's why I'm here to speak to you. What did the witch want from you? What did she hire you to do?"

"Mrs. Etcheveria, or should I call you Felicity? I have been retained by your grandmother, so I suggest, if you have a question—ask her."

Her lips tightened more, if that were possible, and two red spots began to grow on her cheeks. This was clearly another woman who was not used to being refused. Like her grandmother.

"Don't give me any of your roundabout bullshit. I want an answer from you. Did she hire you to find my husband, Carlos?"

"That I can actually answer without a breach of client confidentiality. She did not.'

"Does it have to do with business? What else could she want?"

"Again, I suggest you have this conversation with your grandmother."

She leaned over to reach into her handbag, squeezing her shoulders together to give me a full on view of cleavage and the girls before she came up with a cigarette and lighter. I could see a light dusting of freckles on both breasts before she sat back again.

"Sorry, but we don't allow smoking in the house." The admonition came from the other side of the room. Belvidere.

Felicity shot a death look in her direction. The gaze quickly lapsed into what looked like yearning as she caressed Belvidere's spandex again with hungry eyes. She was so intent on slithering muscles beneath black leather and stretch fabric she ignored the little dog pawing and sniffing in her handbag. I caught Callista's attention and shooed her away. She turned and gave me a 'talk to the tail' swish and left the room.

Felicity angrily smashed the pack of cigarettes into her handbag. "How about this. I'll hire you. I can offer as much as grandmother. Can you then do what I tell you?"

"Thank you for the offer, but it would be a conflict of interest. Can't be done."

"Well, if that's the case, and you both are being so rude and uncooperative, I'll just leave."

"Whatever suits you." Belvidere and I both got up to escort her to the door. She gave us one last look at her cleavage, and a pronounced hip swivel as she huffed out.

I walked her to the car and handed her over to Gupta. I stuck my head in the passenger side of the door. "Give me a couple of minutes, I have to get some items before I go.

He checked his wristwatch. "You have ten minutes before we have to leave. Remember, we'll drop off Mrs. Etcheveria before our other errand." I nodded, sure he was going to be grilled like a t-bone steak before I returned. He probably had plenty of practice and could handle it so I stopped feeling sorry for him.

I had already made my plan.

Once back inside, I handed Callista the note. "Here's the address where the drop off is to be made, and all the instructions. You should leave now to get in place while we drop Felicity off at Bloomingdales. One of you flip and the other walk her on a leash. Then trade places."

They looked at each other in glee and nodded assent. I knew there was nothing they liked better than field work. Sick of complaints from them that, as front man, I had all the fun; this was their chance. "I'll have Gupta let me out of the car before the drop off point and find a place to flip. Then I'll sniff around outside, and wait in front of one of the bicycles as if waiting for my owner. I'll be able to see who makes the pick-up. As soon as someone shows interest in the bag, whoever is in human form, run to the car and be ready to tail, the other help me. If the pick-up is on foot, I'll track them and whoever was on leash can spell me. Between the three of us, we should be able to find out where the money is taken." It's a simple plan and a lot can go wrong, but with such short notice, it was the best I could come up with.

The car ride was silent. Felicity was obviously not pleased with me. She hunched in a corner texting incessantly; a sour expression on her face. When Gupta pulled into the passenger drop-off in front of Bloomingdales, she flounced out of the car before he even had time to get out and around to open the door for her.

He almost was shouting after her. "I'll be busy for about two hours running errands for your grandmother, but afterwards, if you want me to pick you up rather than the chauffeur, just call and let me know." She didn't even turn to acknowledge his offer. As rude as an aristocrat in a flophouse—no need to be polite to the riff-raff. Still, not as bad as the younger sister, but both of them had manners like they were raised by wolves. On second thought, maybe not. Wolves were pack animals and obeyed their Alphas. These women climbed the ladder of self-obsession to new levels .

CHAPTER FIVE

The Drop Off

When Gupta neared our destination, he slid over to the curb and came to a stop. "We're about two blocks away. What would you like me to do next?"

"First, give me five minutes before you leave here, then drive slowly to the corner. Stop the car with the motor running; get out and leave the bag. Don't look around, don't stop for anything or if anyone calls to you. Just get back in the car and drive away. Think casual. Don't speed, don't look in your rear view mirror. Just pretend you do this every day. I'll take care of the rest."

"As you say, Mr. Pudel. If Madam has faith in you, then I do also." His dark eyes were serious beneath the bright turquoise of his turban.

When I got out of the car, I saw a gas station with a convenience store. The kind that almost always has bathrooms I can slip into. The men's room was both clean and empty, a perfect place to flip. As a pup, my father had taught me how to open doors with my paws and mouth. Not easy without opposable thumbs, but possible when you know how. The customers were uninterested in a large white poodle sauntering out of the men's room, through the store, and out the door.

I loped to the drop off, arriving in time to watch Gupta park next to the bicycle rack, get out and slip the red bag between two bicycles. Passersby seemed intent on their own business, no one showing any interest. Gupta walked back to the car and moved on. Good man. He never looked around. I sat on my haunches in front of a bright blue woman's trail bike and, tongue lolling, gave a good impression of seriously guarding the bike for my owner.

Callista and Belvidere came by, Callista on the leash. They paid no attention to me. No one even looked at either me or the bag. Ten minutes went by. I began to worry someone would steal the bag, but it was an upscale neighborhood. It must have been our lucky day. Maybe the thieves were working the malls?

Out of nowhere, a young guy on a skateboard whizzed by, reaching down and snatching the bag without slowing down. Callista pulled the leash out of Belvidere's hand and ran after the skateboarder, yapping for all she was worth. I took off after her and the two of us chased the kid for two blocks before Belvidere took over.

The kid looked back once, saw he had ditched the white poodle and the noisy Pomeranian. He paid no attention to the large black poodle sauntering across neighboring lawns on the other side of the street.

Belvidere kept him in sight, loping between bushes while Callista and I sped back for our car.

It was easy to find Belvidere through the GPS tracker implanted on her collar. We caught up with her as she was about to pass from the upscale neighborhood across a heavily trafficked main artery into an older area. Once filled with manufacturing and small business storefronts it was now run down. A few businesses hung on amid drug dealers and empty buildings, now a refuge for addicts and squatters. Dejected looking homeless panhandled on the corners. Not a great place for an elegant poodle. I was worried about Bel, she could be grabbed and sold, or worse, eaten.

The skateboarder was still ahead of us, the red gym bag clutched tightly under one arm as he artfully dodged the human debris cursing at him from the sidewalk. He made an abrupt right turn and upended his board to stop in front of a dingy storefront.

A lopsided and torn plastic banner sign announced "Computer Repairs." In the flyblown window, another sign proclaimed in smaller letters, "Corrupted Disks, Hard or Flash Drives? We can retrieve your information." From the street, the place looked closed up tight, as if it had been for years.

The skateboarder picked up his board, tucked it under his other arm and rang the bell next to the door. Within seconds, the door opened an inch or so to the limit of those metal loops used in hotel rooms.

The door closed for a moment, then opened to let the gym bag in first, followed by the skateboard and its owner. As the door closed, I heard the snick of a lock and a click as the loop and hook were put back in place. On closer inspection, the door was made of metal. Not a place one could easily get into.

I nodded to Belvidere and she padded around to the back of the building. When she returned we reconvened in the car. "There's a back alley and another door, but just as secure as the front. I saw a surveillance camera in the alley, but couldn't be sure which store it came from.

When I checked the garbage, there were fast food bags, but nothing out of the ordinary for computer repairs. The garbage seemed to have been there a few days, the food remains were stale. I did find packing boxes and receipts for several cartons of thumb drives. Seemed a lot of drives for a small place in such an out-of-the way area."

"Yes, but they could be selling stuff on the internet. You never can tell how much business places do by their looks if they have an on-line store." Callista, an eBay and Black Friday addict, loved to buy on-line and was always looking for new merchants.

"I think we should stay and keep an eye on the place. I'd like to see who comes out. The kid has been in there a while. He must be talking to someone. Callista, can you hide under something in the alley and watch the back door while Belvidere flips? We'll stay in the car and survey the front."

"Sure. If someone comes with me and upends a carton and puts a hole in it so I can see, I'll stay there as long as you want."

When I got out, I heard the sound of a car with a bad muffler pulling away from the alley behind the store.

Belvidere touched my shoulder. "There was a car parked in the alley a few stores down from the computer store. An older Ford Fiesta a little worse for wear. Probably had a worn out muffler to make that sound. Want me to check?"

"Let's all go, I'd like to scope out the place."

Callista trotted at our heels as we walked behind the store into the alley.

Belvidere looked in both directions. "Yep, the Fiesta left. It was parked down there." She pointed three or four stores to the left. "I hope it didn't belong to anyone in the computer store." She shrugged. "I'm going back to the car and watch the front entrance."

In the one of the dumpsters behind the stores, I found an empty carton. Perfect Callista-sized, I took out my pen knife, cut out three sides of a small rectangle I then bent into a flap. A perfect make-shift awning to hide her eyes.

I settled her next to a pile of garbage off to the side of the door where she had a line of sight to both the door and direction anyone coming outside might go.

As I walked away, a small African-American boy ran up to me waving his hands. "Mister, mister, don't throw the dog away, I'll take it." His face was lean and earnest, and he couldn't be more than ten or eleven years old. This was an unexpected wrinkle.

"Son, I'm not throwing her away, just finding an empty carton to make a little house for her."

"Oh, I saw you putting her in a box and I thought..." He looked very disappointed.

"See, this one is just her size." I turned the carton over and Callista obligingly jumped in, standing with her front paws on top of one side as she perked up her ears and looked like she was smiling at the boy.

"I really love dogs, but my Pa is out of work and says we can't afford to feed another mouth, so...no pets." He walked to Callista and bent down to stroke her fur. "She's so small I thought I could feed her from my food—she couldn't eat too much."

I watched as his hands gently scratched behind her ears. She moved so he could reach the places she wanted him to scratch. Sometimes she was such a pain in the ass, I was almost tempted to let the boy have her, but Belvidere would kill me! I quickly squelched the thought.

"How about we make a deal. I wanted her to let me know if anyone goes in or out of the computer store. She's an excellent watch dog, even if she is small. She barks like mad when she wants to tell me something. Tell you what, why don't you keep her company and you both let me know if anyone leaves. Those guys took my computer to repair and I can't get it back from them. I'll pay you five dollars and you can play with her while you wait...and by the way, her name is Callista."

"That's a funny name for a dog. Callista." He said it a few more times and laughed each time. "Okay mister, you got a deal." Callista seemed delighted to be left with her new friend. He must have the secret to a good ear scratch.

"What's your name son, and where do you live. I have to know in case you get any funny ideas about taking my dog."

He looked crestfallen and stopped his petting. "Just 'cause we're homeless doesn't mean we steal. I wouldn't do that. My name is Jonathan Rosemont and we live down there."

He pointed in the direction of two large refrigerator cartons pushed together at the far end of the alley. "My dad was head of sales for a big tech company, but when business dropped off, they replaced him with a younger guy at half the salary. He couldn't find a new job that paid anywhere near as much, and we lost our house. Now he's a short order cook until he finds something better, but at least we eat okay."

I was still reluctant to leave Callista, but she sniffed the boy while I watched, then wagged her tail and settled down in his lap while looking at me. If she was all right with him, I guess I could be too.

"Sorry Jonathan, I didn't mean to insult you, but Callista is like part of my family, she's even named after my sister, and I wouldn't want anything to happen to her. And by the way, my name is Antonio Pudel—everyone calls me Antonio." I handed him one of my business cards and he put it in his pocket.

"Okay Antonio, I get it. If she were my dog, I'd want to protect her too." With that, he bent down and put his face right next to hers. Callista is no dummy, her pink tongue darted out for a friendly nose lick and I knew they'd be all right guarding the alley.

He boy looked thoughtful for a minute. "Antonio, I don't know if you care, but the owner left a few minutes ago. He had his Ford Fiesta parked in the alley, as usual. But he usually doesn't leave the store so early."

"Did he have anything with him you could see?"

"I don't know. I didn't see him, I just recognized the noise his car made—kind of a growling rumble sound."

"That's good information, Jonathan. Thanks." It was clear Jonathan was both bright and observant. Assured Callista had a suitable stakeout partner, I went back to our car.

We spent the next three hours figuratively twiddling our thumbs. Belvidere and I sat in the car listening to audio books. When one of us needed to stretch, we checked in on Callista and Jonathan, amusing themselves playing games of fetch in between back rubs and ear scratches.

When I was about to give up, the door to the street opened and a man came out. He was tall and thin, surreptitiously checking to see if anyone was on the street. I hadn't seen him enter, but he could have been there before we arrived, or snuck in when we were checking the alley.

Belvidere and I ducked down in the car. He satisfied himself the coast was clear and tucked a small parcel in his coat pocket, pulled a cap on, and took off on foot, looking around furtively from under his cap every few minutes. I got out and followed him, making no move to hide the fact. Belvidere stayed behind to see if the guy with the skateboard came out.

I knew the man I was tailing didn't have the cash. The parcel he had was far too small. But I wanted to see what the store was peddling, guessing it wasn't something legit. The place smelled off, like something skanky was going on inside.

At first I matched his footsteps, then I decided to make him uncomfortable and walked loudly out of rhythm with him. This made him nervous and he turned around several times; the last time I looked him straight in the face. As he turned the next corner, he picked up speed and started to run. I kept right up with him.

After turning several more corners, I let him get further ahead until I lost him for a moment, then caught a glimpse of him, inside the tree shaded central courtyard of an industrial park, a place for employees to bring their lunch or take a break.

He darted behind a tree, then into the dense foliage surrounding the court. After crouching behind the hedge for a few moments, he stood up, and walked straight towards me as if he had nothing to hide. Whatever was in the parcel, he'd already ditched it.

I nodded to him and smirked as he went past. I could see rivulets of sweat running down his cheeks, and he was puffing from the exertion of the run. Yeah, the guy was guilty all right. I just didn't know of what. He wasn't afraid I was going to mug him or he wouldn't have walked past me so brazenly. That was the action of a guy thinking 'screw you, I've got nothing to hide.'

I sat down at one of the tables in the courtyard until he was out of sight. Then I went to the spot where he had hidden, and flipped. Within a few minutes I sniffed out the parcel. Once it was in my mouth, I sprinted back to the car.

Belvidere opened the door when she saw my snout at the window. As I jumped into the back seat, I dropped the parcel in her lap and flipped again. "Has there been any action at the store?" I asked.

"Nothing. No one in or out, and not a sound from Callista other than the growling she makes when she plays tug of war with one of her toys." I love my sister, but sometimes she forgets how small she is. I've installed both a GPS and a microphone in her collar. This way, I can keep tabs on her... just in case.

Belvidere opened the parcel with the all purpose Swiss blade combo she always carries. Wrapped tightly in small bubble wrap was a tiny leather drawstring pouch that held a thirty-two gig micro SD card. No markings.

I wanted to see what was so interesting on the card someone was willing to run away just to ditch it. But we had to stay longer and follow Mrs. Freedhoff's money. My curiosity had to wait.

Belvidere gave me a slight lip twitch, reached under the front seat and came up with a small tablet in a black leather case. "Thought we might need this." That woman astounds me. She is always prepared, and to my recollection, never was a Girl Scout.

When she slipped the micro SD into the slot, up came an image. It was a girl, no more than seven or eight years old, naked and crying. An older man, also naked, was in the act of doing unimaginable things to her.

Belvidere slapped her hand over the image. Her face went white. For a moment I thought she was going to be sick. Not much upsets her, but this was clearly one of those things. "I don't want to see this. I got the picture—don't need or want to see more." Her hand was shaking as she pushed the tablet at me.

I agreed with her. It was beyond sickening. No wonder the guy had run from me. He probably thought I was the police and didn't want to get caught. Child pornographers or pedophiles do not do well in prisons and just possession of this SD card was a crime. But the porn didn't solve the problem of why a pornographer was blackmailing Mrs. Freedhoff. Or did it? I took the tablet from Belvidere and turned it on again.

"You don't have to watch, but I have to see what's on it. Maybe this is what Moroney doesn't want made public." But then, the more I thought about it, I didn't think Moroney would give a rat's ass about anything being made public. The only one who would suffer was Mrs. Freedhoff.

"Go ahead, I understand. Just keep it away from me."

Reluctantly, I turned the tablet back on. The contents of the SD card, while disgusting, might be evidence.

As the images kept scrolling across the screen, the only thing I was happy about was that Callista wasn't with me. The photos and videos were not something she needed to see. Callista might be well over twenty-one and far from innocent, but she has an ingenuousness that lets her enjoy the world without needing to face all its grimy underpinnings. Better for her to play with Jonathan.

At the first possible moment, this SD card was going to go to the police. Maybe at least one kiddie pornographer would bite the dust.

Moroney In Her Glory

For the next half hour I was subjected to some of the most horrific images humans could concoct. I stopped when I came to Moroney. She was naked in the video, holding a whip in her hand and beating a man lying face down on a bed. She couldn't have been more than eleven or twelve in the photo, and the man, by the looks of his flaccid gluteus maximus, was in his middle to late fifties. His back was welted and bleeding, Squatting over him, Moroney's whip rose and fell, continuing the flagellation.

If the act itself wasn't disturbing enough, the expression of ecstasy on her face was beyond chilling. It reminded me of medieval biblical illuminations of hell. Hieronymus Bosch could have modeled one of his scenes after Moroney in ecstasy, her mouth stretched in glee like images of the devil. My stomach lurched and my head felt light. This time, I was the one slapping my hand over the screen.

"My god, what happened to you? Your face just crumpled." Belvidere was shaking my arm and looking concerned.

I took a deep breath and tried to collect myself. "I'm all right, just was shaken by one of the images. It was of Moroney, the youngest granddaughter." It took another second to breathe again. "I never thought I'd actually see evil, but I just did."

"Was she being abused by someone?" Belvidere looked concerned.

"Not really, she's the abuser. It's..." I took another breath, but still had the punched in the solar plexus feeling. "While the other perversions were disturbing, since I've recently met Moroney...just knowing a participant..." I shook my head. "This was really gut-wrenching...it made me feel...like a voyeur...somehow...dirty." My subconscious took control of my hands, rubbing them continuously together like Lady Macbeth to cleanse them.

There was no way I was going to describe the scene, and I was sure I'd never be able to erase it from my mind. There are some things in life you can't un-see. All I could do was sigh.

Client be damned, the SD card was definitely going to the police, and as soon as possible. Shows you how things can go sideways when you least expect them. If this is what they were selling in the computer store, the djinn was out of the bottle and Moroney's exploits were out in the world for all to see. I just didn't know for how long they had been in circulation and how many copies might have been made. All I could think of was our pillow fights as kids, our mother punishing us by insisting we get all the feathers back inside when the pillows ruptured. Not a chance in hell.

The door to the store opened and the kid with the skateboard emerged, followed by a tall blonde with one arm around his shoulders. As they got closer, I saw he wasn't a kid, but a guy at least in his mid-twenties, dressed like a kid in baggy pants, oversized rapper-style sweatshirt, and baseball cap with peak pulled to the side. Under his arm, the skateboard. No red bag in sight.

Belvidere and I ducked down in the car, but I opened the window and barked three times. I can even do that as a human. Cool, huh?

Callista came running around the building with Jonathan behind her. I didn't want the woman and man to see me, but I wanted to give Jonathan his five bucks. Instead, I pulled out a ten, opened the door enough to let Callista hop in and pushed the ten at Jonathan. He looked surprised. "Hey, that's too much, you said a five and I don't have change."

"Don't worry, you earned it by entertaining Callista. Keep the change and thanks for helping out."

By then, the woman and man had gotten into a grey Hyundai and were backing out of a parking space. It was getting close to rush hour and I didn't want to lose the car in traffic. "Sorry Jonathan, but we have to leave, see you another time." I pulled out from the curb to follow the Hyundai as he yelled "Say goodbye to Callista for me," and waved as we left. Callista jumped up on the back window ledge and put her paws on the window. A doggy version of goodbye.

CHAPTER SEVEN

The Tale Of The Tail

Following the Hyundai was a snap. The woman was a very cautious driver with no idea she was being tailed.

My sisters kept up a constant chatter but I was deep in thought about something altogether different.

My mind spins like a carousel once in a while, and often to our family's genetic inheritance. It's not easy to live a life caught between two species. Dog and human have been natural allies since the beginning of time, but the psyche of each has its own characteristics. We might be companions, but responses are often very different. The canine part of my brain sees evil as black, something to automatically put an end to. Rip out the throat and be done. Evil can't be cured or justified, it just exists. Like a rabid dog, evil must be put it down without giving another thought. Any creature capable of harming the pack must die.

As a human, I still find all the rationalizations for allowing evil frail and unwarranted. So what if someone had a damaged life, so did a huge percent of the world population. Many grow above the pain and try to do better for those around them. Human forgiveness is something I know exists—but for obvious evil, it's an idea that doesn't mesh for me.

What I wanted to do to those involved in the making of the videos on the flash drive was definitely not human, but then, I am one of the few who have that luxury.

My musing ended when the Hyundai pulled off the 101 Freeway in Thousand Oaks, an upscale city north of Los Angeles on the way into Ventura County.

Following two car lengths behind, we turned onto Lynn, a main thoroughfare, then onto a smaller street with no traffic. I didn't want the woman to see our tail—no pun intended—so I pulled into a driveway a few houses down from where she had parked. After making a U-turn, I drove past her to a curve in the road where we wouldn't be seen. By the time I'd parked, Belvidere had flipped, and Callista opened the door for her.

The neighborhood was one of the Eichler designed developments popular in the '50s and '60's. A quadrangle with oversized entrance doors onto the street, an open center courtyard, rooms with sliding glass doors on three sides. The mature trees and later renovations hid the usual cookie-cutter suburban community look. An old Ford Fiesta was in the driveway.

Belvidere was about to get out just as another car whizzed around the corner and stopped in front of the house. One tire was up on the sidewalk, the others on the street. A Rolls Royce, highly polished and shining. I had seen the car only that morning.

The driver's side opened. A small figure wearing a baseball hat and sweatshirt with hood pulled low, walked up to the doors and rang the bell. The door opened a crack and the figure slipped in sideways. I was guessing it was a woman from the lithe movements, small waist and curved hips, and as she turned, I saw breasts outlined by the hoodie. I couldn't see who opened the door, the figure was in shadow, all I saw was colorful fabric swish behind the door as it closed.

The couple in the Hyundai remained inside their car.

"What next?" Belvidere didn't want to stay in the SUV. "I don't care about the people in the Hyundai, I want to check this place out. No one will pay any attention to a neighborhood dog."

Before I could say a word, she was out of the car and trotting across the front lawn, poking the grass at anything interesting.

She chased a squirrel around the parked car. Still no one had gotten out. It looked like there was a heated conversation going on inside by the way the heads bobbed around. The courtesy light went on as the car door opened. Belvidere sped into the bushes on the side of the house.

Then the light went off and I heard the car door click shut. No one had gotten out. There was no further movement I could see. Maybe they were going to wait out the new visitor.

The air outside became heavier with humidity. It was only a matter of time before the threatened rain would start. The fog bank had climbed the mountain and would soon shed its tears on the parched landscape.

CHAPTER EIGHT

The Courage Of Commissions

Inside the Hyundai, Mildred and Albert were arguing.

"I'm not going inside with that girl there. She gives me the creeps the way she stares at me...and...and...she always tries to touch me in places where she shouldn't." Albert was sweating and jittery.

"Look, we have to get our share of the money in the gym bag. You were the one who told me it was filled with stacks of hundred dollar bills. Gabriel promised us a share for picking it up. I want to get it before he changes his mind."

"Yeah, but you know the things he does with that crazy girl. If we interrupt, we might piss him off and we'll never get anything."

The conversation went back and forth for some minutes, Albert getting more anxious by the second.

Mildred was quiet for a moment as she surveyed the clearly miserable man. "Okay, you may be right. Let's give them some time to play their nasty games. We can go for a pizza and come back in an hour or so. That should give them plenty of time, and he'll probably even be in a better mood. He usually is, after she beats the crap out of him." She shook her head, "...no accounting for taste."

Albert let out a long sigh. Something about Moroney made his skin crawl, and if he had to admit it, he was deathly afraid of her. There was something about her eyes...or maybe whatever was missing from her eyes. He shuddered, rubbed himself against the seat back like he had an itch he couldn't reach. When he was satisfied all thoughts of Moroney were gone, he reached over and took Mildred's hand. He was looking forward to a pizza with her.

The Hyundai maneuvered out of its parking space and left, just as the rain decided to start in earnest.

CHAPTER NINE

A Wet Water Dog

Belvidere staked herself out behind a giant bougainvillea. The base was a mass of stout trunks like a banyan with dozens of branches arching across the front wall to clutch the house in sprays of deep rose and a lighter peach. I watched as she wound herself through the colorful jungle to get close to a sidelight at the double entrance doors. It was the only way she could manage to look into the interior courtyard. Callista and I waited in the SUV. Another car came up the street and slowed down in front of the house. It seemed about to stop, then continued down into the shadows of mist and overhanging trees. I listened for the motor until it disappeared.

After threatening all day, the rain finally began. At first it was a gentle pitter-patter, but it quickly increased to a more serious drumbeat on the roof. A small whining and scratching sound alerted me to open the door. Belvidere. Outside. Wet. "Get into the back before you shake off—you're soaked."

"I know, it's my car. What did you think I was going to do—spray water all over the nice leather seats?" She didn't exactly speak the words as humans do, but the intent was clear. Over the years our kind has developed our own mode of communication, we're able to understand each other's body language, and canine sounds. I watched as she jumped over the back seat into the luggage area and pulled out a large towel with her teeth and rolled herself up in it. Then she lay on her back, paws in the air and wriggled most of the water off into the towel. For a water hunting breed, she doesn't care much for being wet. My sister can be grumpy when she wants.

When she finally flipped, her face was back to its usual tranquil self...hair a little damp, but that was expected.

"What did you see?"

"Two people were in the Hyundai—a man and woman. They were going to get out of the car until the Rolls arrived. Looked like they changed their mind and left.

"I couldn't see much inside the courtyard, the sidelights are leaded glass. Most of the designs are either frosted or beveled, but there were enough clear pieces so I could see the courtyard. A fountain in the center, a couple of loungers, table and chairs—cheap stuff if you ask me—couldn't make out anything in the rooms on the sides. Opposite the entrance a kitchen, dining table and chairs visible to the left, living room to the right. The place didn't look fancy—might be a rental?" Bel was drying her hair again with the towel as she spoke. Even her clothes were wet, quite unusual after a flip.

"I'd like to scope out the back of house—see if I can get a better idea what's in the side rooms. When the car parked in front, sloppy job, by the way, driver must be stoned, figured it was time to get out of there." She said.

Before I could respond, she had flipped again and was outside heading towards the back of the house.

The rain pelted down. Our world inside the Range Rover seemed unnaturally still beneath the drops drumbeating on the roof. Another car passed. I heard it park down the road on the other side. No one else came by. The rain, starting as a soft drizzle, had turned into a steady cascade so welcome in California where every drop is needed.

As I watched, the drops grew larger in size and increased in frequency until we were in the middle of a serious downpour. The wind blew water into the SUV.

Callista closed the windows to keep the interior dry, but soon the glass began to fog over. I put the air conditioner on and cracked the windows again. It was so torrential we could hardly see the house. All sound from outside was drowned out between the rain and the motor of the defroster. When I tried to see out the windows, my breath clouded the glass more than the defroster could keep up with.

Then a movement in the narrow space between the houses caught my eye. The developer had squashed the homes together so closely there wasn't room for more than trash cans if a normal human wanted to squeeze past. A dog would have felt claustrophobic if a run had been built for it. Maybe a Chihuahua could cope. I stopped thinking of dog runs and I was sure I saw movement again, this time further towards the back of the house. It was gone when I blinked. I rubbed my eyes. Nothing there. I turned to Callista. "Did you see anyone go in the alley between the houses?"

"No, but I wasn't really watching. I've trouble even seeing the house in this weather. It's probably just Belvidere. She wanted to see around the back of the house. I can't believe she went back out in this downpour, she hates to get wet."

I couldn't fault her, I might be a water dog, but I don't like being wet either. Hopefully, we haven't inherited a cat thing too.

"Sorry, I may just be seeing things." As soon as the words were out of my mouth, I saw a bright light flash and a rain-muffled sound like a firecracker. From my vantage point in the car, I guessed it was from the side of the courtyard, and what I saw might have been a reflection in the glass.

Before I even thought about it, I was out of the car and running to the house. I was about to flip when another shot rang out, and then a third. Was someone shooting at Belvidere? I shouted back to Callista to stay put inside the car in case we needed her.

The rain soaked my new Armani suit as I sprinted up the slippery walk to the double doors. I'd kick them down if I had to, no way was anyone taking pot shots at my sister. I was backing up for a kick when Belvidere streaked around the opposite corner from the alley. She looked sodden, but unharmed, and not frightened.

"What's going on in there?" I shouted. Maybe she had a better handle on the action.

"I don't know. I was worried about you and Callista. The shots were so loud I thought they might have come from in front of the house."

We looked at each other and said in unison, "The Courtyard." I looked in through the top of one of the sidelights and she peered in through the middle.

I couldn't see much, but it looked like a lounge chair was occupied. "What do you see?" I asked.

"A foot, and some liquid on the ground—dark like blood, and plenty of water. Do you think we should call the cops?"

"I do, but I want to see what happened first. Maybe someone needs immediate help."

"You are demented. What if there's a murderer in there?"

My sister is such a pragmatist, I thought as I backed up. With a running leap and a loud grunt, I crashed into the double doors.

Sometimes action just doesn't come out the way you might like. The door easily burst open at first touch and I flew onto the pavers of the courtyard. Face plant. Skidding inside, I was wet all down the front with more rain pelting at my back. Tore both knees out of the

Armani. Belvidere came over and licked my face. "You know you will always be my hero."

It's good to have a sister who loves you, I thought as I picked myself up. Hmmm, suede patches work on tweed or corduroy jacket elbows. Wonder if they'd work on Armani knees? I immediately dismissed the thought when I saw the two people in the lounge chairs, the incessant rain pelting down on them both.

One was sprawled with arms akimbo. A bare foot hung over the side, almost in the pool of blood forming beneath. The blood came from three obvious bullet holes, two in the man's exposed chest, the third in between his eyes...as if he wouldn't be dead enough from the first two shots. The rain streaked the blood down his face and into the black hair on his chest. He was wearing a Speedo he shouldn't have, and an open bathrobe over it. The Speedo was bright red, the blood looked much darker, more like the dark red in the floral Batik print of the man's bathrobe.

I sniffed, hoping for the acrid stink of gun shots in the air of the courtyard. Instead, I caught the wet scent of withering roses, damp earth, and the metallic tang of blood.

As if a corpse wasn't bad enough, the humming from the curled figure in the other chair completed the asylum scene. It was Moroney, baseball cap now off to expose her spiked hair, naked as a jaybird and crazy as a loon. Her eyes were wide open and jiggling, as if someone was shaking her and she was one of those old fashioned dolls where the eyes were round white disks covered with clear plastic and a black iris loose inside. The humming got louder and louder until it was almost a whine, like the sound of a motor that won't turn over.

She just sat there, oblivious to my arrival, shaking and humming as the water washed the aubergine rinse out of her hair and streaked it down her face to her neck, then lower to drip off her nipples.

Belvidere must have had the same idea I had. She was looking all around the courtyard, feeling behind Moroney and moving her to look under her. She sniffed Moroney's hands and her face before walking into the house. A few seconds later she appeared from one of the doorways in her human form. "I don't think she did this. I don't see a gun, and I sniffed her all over before the rain completely cleaned her off, and she has no trace of gunshot residue. She's high as a kite but I couldn't tell what she was on. All I got was a lot of garlic."

"Let's dump her in the car and then we can call the cops once we leave. Did you find any of her clothes? She was in jeans and a hoodie with a ball cap when she went inside." Belvidere came back from one of the side rooms with clothes. "I'll dress her while you look around. I'm surprised the neighbors haven't called the cops yet...and remember, don't touch anything!"

My sister is seldom flustered. She gets right to the point. "We have to call the police. This is an active crime scene, we shouldn't disturb anything but we need to leave. Now."

"I know. But I want to look around first. I can't leave Moroney here in this condition. We have to take her home. Her family will know how to take care of her."

"Okay, you're the boss. But this one is on you. I say we quickly make an anonymous call to the police, say we heard shots, and get the hell out of here."

I knew she was right, but my only thought was to protect my client.

The house didn't have much to offer. Not much food in the fridge, the kitchen looked unused. One bedroom had an unmade bed, some men's clothes in the closet. Not a snappy dresser but a good quality tweed jacket. A few items: watch, wallet and set of keys. The wallet gave me the man's name: Gabriel Saldanian according to his driver's license, the address this house, a few credit cards, several business cards with the address of the computer store and on the reverse was a teaser "If You Can't Find It Any Place Else, We Have It," then underneath in smaller script "For those of discerning tastes."

The other bedroom looked like it might have been the place where the video of Moroney was taken, but the video was made a while back and things change. The closet was more interesting. I found a box of flash drives, several Macs, a Snowball microphone, external hard drives, a digital camera, three spotlights, Softboxes and a gold reflector umbrella. All you need to set up a simple studio.

Back outside, Belvidere was struggling in the pouring rain with Moroney's limp wet feet and pull-on boots. An unhappy combination. "Don't even bother, I'll carry her to the car, just bring the boots with you." The body of the man hadn't gotten up and left, of course, so I went over and surveyed the scene carefully without touching anything.

He looked to be in his sixties, but dead doesn't do much for the complexion and he could have been younger. The top of his head was hairless and his comb-over had washed over an ear on one side. His lips were thick and probably looked pouty when he was alive, not sexy pouty, liver-lipped pouty. He had a big gut, more black hair on his chest and shoulders than he had on his head. I pushed at his shoulder with my knuckles and tried to see his back. My guess was he was the same guy Moroney enjoyed beating the crap out of in the pictures. I shuddered and gave up looking him over. There was nothing I really wanted to see anyway.

Belvidere looked at me carefully. I knew the look. She had something important to say and was sure I wasn't going to like it. "Our fee doesn't include saving Moroney from anything. I say we let her fend for herself and we call the police. Now."

I wasn't happy with the idea, even though I knew she was right. I felt an obligation to Mrs. Freedhoff and her family. "Let me think about it for a minute while I give the house another run through. This time I'll wear rubber gloves and turn everything over. Maybe the red gym bag is behind or under something."

As I walked around the kitchen, I started to slip and looked down. There were wet footprints leading out the back kitchen door into the alley. I know I didn't make them, I hadn't entered the kitchen before and the prints looked about a size eight men's cross-trainers when I held my foot next to them. I'm a size eleven Gucci. Nope, neither Belvidere nor I had made them.

No red gym bag. If I was a gambler, my money would be on the size eight cross-trainers having it. I'd also guess he was the shooter. A hundred thou is a good enough motive for murder, but the cops would never know about it unless I told them.

Still, I have the responsibility of confidentiality to my client. Mrs. Freedhoff wasn't exactly my idea of the kind of good citizen who might want to relinquish any red bag information. It would reveal things about her granddaughter she probably wanted to keep secret. I had no reason for being at the house without giving away the presence of Moroney and the whole blackmail scam. I couldn't give Mrs. Freedhoff back her money unless I found the red bag, but at least I'd have her granddaughter in hand.

Belvidere was waiting for me standing under the eaves with the rain pouring down in front of her. She was holding Moroney upright by one arm, not very comfortable looking, but it did the trick.

"I want to take her back to the mansion. Someone else can find the body. I don't want to explain how and why we were here if we don't have to."

If Gabriel was the blackmailer, the demands should stop and our job was done. Only time would tell if he had a partner, or wasn't to blame in the first place. Then we'd still have the problem to solve. With what we knew now, there was no way to find out who had the videos unless we went through all the files in the computer store. Gabriel could have sold hundreds, maybe even thousands, over the years since they were made. It would be a nightmare to connect the dots from his sales to someone who knew how to find Moroney, or even knew who she was.

I could see Belvidere wasn't happy with my decision. She looked at Moroney like a long dead fish ready to be tossed in the garbage, rather than put in the car and taken home. Somewhere in the back of my mind, I had a sneaking suspicion Mrs. Freedhoff would gladly pay the money if someone could relieve her of her pain-in-the-ass granddaughter, but then, that's just me.

As we left the courtyard, I looked back at Gabriel, sprawled in the rain, the blood almost completely washed off him. Something inside me wanted to cover the man up, protect him from the incessant beating of the water. But then I thought of the man who groomed a young Moroney to take pleasure in another's pain. I left him where he was. The devil had him now and wouldn't give a fig about the rain. If the believers were right about the tortures of eternal damnation, then it had started already on Gabriel's body, and the worst was yet to come.

We waited until we were sure the street was empty. Belvidere ran out and opened the back of the Range Rover, I ran through the rain and dumped Moroney inside. In her condition I could have thrown her in and she wouldn't have known the difference. Belvidere had found car keys next to Moroney's clothes; she'd follow me to the Freedhoff mansion in the Rolls.

Before we left, I looked around the outside of the house once more. The grey Hyundai was still nowhere in sight. I had written down the license plate. I'd find it another day. My priority was to get Moroney home.

Once in Orange County, I passed a café in Laguna Beach when I stopped at a light on the Pacific Coast Highway. I was amusing myself by looking at the people at the inside tables. Honking from behind tore my eyes off a sexy broad with dyed red hair puffed up with a bad perm. Felicity Etcheveria. I recognized the guy she was so intent upon, but couldn't put the name and face together. It would come to me later, I was sure, as I pulled away from the light and the irate driver behind me. Waving to him in an 'I'm sorry' palms up didn't assuage him. As his Crossfire roared by me in a no-passing zone he gave me the middle finger salute. In the rain. Asshole!

CHAPTER TEN

Return Of The Hyundai

The rain was letting up by the time the Hyundai was back in front of the Eichler house. Albert and Mildred had stopped fighting long enough to enjoy their pizza and a couple of beers. By the time Mildred parked in front of the house, they were amicable friends again. Until she saw the door to the courtyard was ajar.

"Look there, you dummy. Now his door is open. Gabriel never leaves anything open. What if he's been robbed? We might never get our money." She started to slam the car door as she got out, and thought better of it. What if robbers were still in the house? The big Rolls Moroney drove had gone. Mildred walked up to the front door and pushed it open. The sight in the courtyard took her breath away. She stifled the scream rising to her throat while she assessed the situation.

Backing out of the entryway, she slid the dead bolt out so the door wouldn't lock behind her. "Albert, close the car door and stay there in the shadow against the house until I tell you to come inside." She pointed to the Bougainvillea.

She crept back into the courtyard. Illuminated by the Malibu lights around the perimeter, Gabriel was slumped in the chaise longue, bedraggled hair draped over one ear, exposing his bald pate.

Why do men think a comb-over fools anyone? She pushed the inane thought away and stepped cautiously into the light. As she moved closer to the chaise, it was clear he was dead, and had been for a while. Bending, she touched his hand. Cold. Wet and heavy, very dead feeling, already stiffening.

The rest of the house was dark. The quiet was so dense, she thought she could have heard the breathing of any intruder. The silence of empty echoed loud in her ears as she tried to determine if they were alone, the murderer not hiding somewhere in the house. Pushing away the frightening feeling of being alone with a corpse, it was time for action.

Where the fuck was the red bag? She spared a moment of sadness for the end of the man who once inhabited the body splayed before her. She reached over and closed his eyes, somehow reluctant to have him stare at her, even though she knew he wouldn't ever see anything again.

Slipping out of the patio and leaving the door ajar, she shushed Albert before he could say anything, and dragged him around back through the alley. The kitchen door was open too. Once again, not like Gabriel.

They went in through the kitchen, quiet, but as soon as Albert saw Gabriel through the glass doors to the patio, before Mildred could stop him, he ran outside. When he saw the bullet holes, he began screaming.

"Shut up, you dumb fuck." Mildred snapped in a low voice. "Do you want to bring the neighbors...and the police? How will they know we didn't kill him?" She'd already decided that Moroney had finally slipped a gear and moved on to the final act. Mildred shrugged. She'd learned to like Gabriel, but still, she wouldn't blame the girl if she'd killed him.

Albert was silent, his eyes large and round, his arms clasped tight around his body as if for protection.

Mildred ran to shut and lock the courtyard door, then coaxed Albert inside the house. "We have to figure out what to do. There's no help for Gabriel now. He was stone cold. We have to find the money and get the hell out of here."

Albert nodded and began to shiver uncontrollably. "Can we go then? I don't like dead people. They make me feel squirmy inside."

"Get it together and help me look around. Forget Gabriel, think about money and the red bag."

Twenty minutes of searching did not turn up the red bag, but Mildred had another idea. "We have most of the store packed up, if we can keep Gabriel's death a secret for a day or two, we can clean out the store, stash everything in someplace safe, and sell the flash drives and the customer lists. The sale of inventory and lists alone should give us enough cash to get out of here...just like we planned."

"Okay, so let's just cover him up and leave before anyone finds us."

"Not good enough, Mildred hissed. We have to move him out of sight...and he could begin to smell."

"He won't smell anything, he's dead. He won't know what we're doing." Albert looked confused.

"No, stupid, he's going to rot, smell bad...the body... dummy."

Albert looked like he was going to throw up. He turned and gagged for a moment and then took a deep breath. "What do you want to do with him? How can we...stop him from...from....smelling?"

She was silent for a moment or two. Then inspiration came. "He's got one of those big coffin freezers in the kitchen. We can put him inside it. He'll be out of sight and it will keep the body...well...fresh."

"Yeah, but who will put him there? Not me!"

"Yes you will—if you want to get any money to move away from here—get a new start."

Albert stood in the patio as far away from the corpse as he could get while Mildred went into the kitchen. "Get in here, I need help emptying the freezer. Go find a garbage bag first...or something to put the frozen foods in...to make room."

When the freezer was emptied, Albert took the contents and stashed the food in the trunk of the Hyundai. It would give them something to eat for a few days while Mildred found a buyer so they could cash out.

"Get over here and help me."

Albert shuffled over to the chaise. His face crumpled into a grotesque expression of distaste as he looked at what remained of Gabriel.

"You take his legs, I'll get his arms. We have to get him to the kitchen." Mildred commanded. He obeyed.

The body was cold, wet, and becoming rigid. Albert gagged again as he touched Gabriel's bare feet. "I can't do this Millie. I don't like to touch dead things, my stomach don't feel so good."

"Quit whining, and don't be such a baby. Do you think I like this? Now get to work."

"But he's cold and stiff. He'll never fit in there."

"Yes he will, we'll make him fit. Don't think of Gabriel, think of loading a side of beef. Pick up his feet—now!"

Albert shuddered and did as he was told. They muscled the body into the kitchen and dropped it on the floor with a dull 'thunk' as Albert got as far away as the small space allowed. His eyes were wide like a scared rabbit about to flee.

Mildred surveyed the size difference between Gabriel and the interior of the freezer. "I think if we can bend him a little, push his knees towards his head, we can get him in on his side. I'll hold his head, you bend his legs and then we'll drop him in."

Albert found several kitchen towels to wrap his hands in so he didn't have to touch the cold flesh, and between the two of them, they managed to stuff the body in the freezer. Once the lid closed, Albert sat on the floor and sobbed. "That's the worst thing I've ever done. Never doing it again, neither." He kept rubbing his hands in the towels and shaking.

"Get up and quit complaining. I've already broke two fingernails off and you don't hear me whining, do you? I want to take one more look through the house. We're going to need some cash until I find a buyer." Albert hiccoughed and shook the entire drive. Mildred mumbled under her breath about being hooked up with fools.

Later, at the computer store, Albert finished packing, while Mildred checked Gabriel's records for a buyer. Cash would be needed, and fast. They hadn't found much of value at the house to sell, only several cameras a new looking gun in a box, and editing equipment along with a couple of pairs of cufflinks that might be gold. They had to move fast.

CHAPTER ELEVEN

Dumping Moroney

When I drove the SUV up to the Freedhoff mansion, the overhanging trees dripped an atonal dirge on the roof. Mist and rain shrouded both wings of the building—only the entrance visible. The impression of a ghostly mansion reminded me of the town of Brigadoon, appearing only at certain appointed times. I hoped Mrs. Freedhoff had a good heating system on this damp windy day, the kind of winter that takes Californians by surprise when it swoops in and blots out the ubiquitous sun for a few days or weeks.

Gupta was waiting outside the door when we drove under the porte cochère. He frowned when he saw Belvidere pull in behind us in the Rolls.

I got out of our Range Rover. Gupta's frown increased under his brilliant turquoise turban as soon as I opened the back of the Rover. Moroney's body had contracted into a fetal position, her hands in awkward rigidity, palms thrust backward, fingers clawed. Her humming had increased beyond the usual low, nerve-wracking drone, an unwelcome accompaniment to the entire drive down the 405 to Orange County. The damn traffic had slowed to almost a crawl because of the storm and a forty minute drive took more than an hour and a half. The best I could hope had been she wouldn't barf in the car. At least a little of my luck held out. She hadn't, just some drool.

Gupta leaned over, scooping her up into his arms and lifting her. She remained stiff. The humming got louder as he held her slightly away from his body, like a large, moldy, bad smelling hunk of cheese.

"Thank you, Mr. Pudel. I'll take care of her from here, and advise Madam you have brought Moroney home. I'm sure she will be suitably grateful." The expression on his face was nowhere near pleased. For the first time, I could read something in his eyes, a sorrow so distant from pleasure it was like looking into the void.

Just then, Belvidere walked up, jingling car keys at me. I came back to reality. "You've already met Gupta. I think he has the situation well in hand."

Gupta nodded as he reached out a few fingers and took the keys. "Thank you all." He nodded again and went into the house, leaving us alone under the porte cochère. The rain was so hard on the driveway it was bouncing at least six inches into the air, forming a miniature Las Vegas water feature. We got back into the SUV and drove away.

Once into the alley behind our house, I looked again at the cheerful colors Callista selected. She was right, even when the colors were misted and softened in the rain, it makes me smile when I come home. The house looks like an upscale gypsy carnival wagon on steroids. Some of our neighbors are outraged, they want everything California white or beige. There are others who love it. They stop and take selfies to post on Facebook.

I was glad to be home until I saw the SUV. Very out of place and disturbing was the black Escalade parked right in front of our crayon colored gate. Two large men took up the entire front seat. The back seat was obscured by dark tinted windows.

CHAPTER TWELVE

The Escalade

What was an Escalade doing in front of our house? It reminded me of stories of the Mexican Cartel drug lords. I was trying to figure out if there could be any connection but came up a blank. Must be something they wanted or they wouldn't be parked in front of our gate?

By the time we parked inside the garage and were through the back door, a determined finger was pushing our front intercom repeatedly. They had seen our car pull into the garage. Escape was not evident.

I answered through the intercom as usual. "Pudel & Compagnie, Problems Solved—at your service. How may I be of assistance?"

"Open the fucking door, creep, or I'll knock it down...that'll put an end to your problems all right!" A heavy New York accented voice echoed through the speaker. I looked at the screen of our security camera and, in black and white, saw an angry face with a broken nose, the bend and bulb at the end obviously the result of being punched too often. His ears were typical cauliflowers. A former boxer, he looked a bit too long in the tooth to still be in the ring.

"Who are you and what do you want?" I asked, thinking it a reasonable request.

The doorbell ringer obviously did not. He hunched his shoulders and started punching the door as if it was a punching bag. I stood back to the side, and as he was winding up for another punch, swung the door open fast. He kept going, stumbling into the house when the last punch didn't connect. As he tried to catch his balance, he came face to face with Callista.

My little sister is short, and so slim she could be taken for a twelve year old boy. Her curly carrot top and freckled nose add to the image of a modern day Huck Finn. She doesn't like the boyish image, so she tends to wear frowsy frocks, circa 1942, pink and red flowers on dark blue her favorite, lace at both collar and turn back cuffs. She usually tops the frocks with aprons, generally frilly—with ruffles. Sometimes more lace. Bobby sox and loafers. I think she overdoes the Little Orphan Annie look, but who am I to judge? It's her own style.

Callista is no match for anyone in a fight. Instead, she carries her preferred weaponry—two small 9mm double-tap Heizers—in her apron pockets. While she's a dud in hand to hand combat, she's lethal with the four inch guns. And who would expect Little Orphan Annie to be packing heat anyway? The big dude certainly wasn't when he looked down the barrel of the one in her hand. Her other hand was in her apron pocket and I'd bet it was clenched around another Heizer.

"Watch out girlie, you can hurt yourself with one of them." He said as he scrambled to right himself. Then he faced her. Flat eyes over a snub freckled nose tracked his every move. Her hand—steady as a rock. I knew what he was thinking by the look on his face. 'Maybe the kid does know what she's doing after all.' He backed up a step and said nothing.

His partner walked into the house quietly, his palms up in a motion of peace. "Whoa everyone. We don't want trouble. I'm sorry we got off to a bad start." He nodded to the door assaulter. "That's Punchy. As you found out, his name is descriptive. I offer apologies on his behalf. My name is Earl, and we're here at the request of our employer. He's asked us to come and talk to you, no rough stuff, just peaceful conversation. Punchy, well...I'm afraid he gets carried away some times." Earl shrugged his shoulders and tossed a venomous look in Punchy's direction.

Callista looked at him with her cold eyes, the gun never wavering from his partner. "This jerk did a real bad imitation of peaceful...if you ask me." Her eyes turned a little less cold, maybe more petulant. "What could be so important you have to try to break the door down to get my attention."

"We only want information, little lady. Not cause any problems. Please, put the gun away."

"I'll put it away when I'm good and ready. Now spill."

I looked over at Belvidere. She was quiet in the corner, trying not to laugh. Callista was putting on a good show. We both knew our sister too well. There was not a doubt Callista was enjoying herself to the max. Being in control of the situation, holding two big men at gunpoint—better than Christmas morning and a birthday party rolled into one.

"Look, our boss sent us to find out a few things. Like what you're doing for Mrs. Freedhoff? We heard she hired you to work on something and the boss wants to know what it is."

This was when I stepped in. "The matters we handle for our clients are confidential. If you're interested in our assignment, contact our client directly. Discretion is a major part of our services."

Punchy interjected, "Don't be using them fancy words, we want to know what the old lady hired you to do. Now tell us or I'll have to rough you up, and I don't want to spoil your pretty face."

"Listen buddy, my sister has a gun on you. This is private property. If, or when, she shoots you, I'll call the police and say it was a home invasion. So you calm down. Get it?"

Earl put his hand out, palm first towards his partner to hold him back before he interjected. "He got it." He turned and looked at the puncher. "Take it down a notch Punchy. Let me do the talking. All you ever do is make things worse. Keep your fat mouth shut." He turned back to me. "Our boss only wants to know one thing—are you looking for Carlos Etcheveria?"

"No."

Maybe it was too easy. It looked like he didn't think it was the right answer. "Are you sure? We heard you were hired to find Carlos."

"Then you heard wrong. I told you I wasn't. It's not what I was hired for, and my job with the Freedhoff family is completed. Now you can answer a question for me. Who do you work for?"

The two men looked at each other. Earl shrugged. "We work for Alfredo Cima."

Belvidere interjected. "Isn't he the crook indicted for fixing baseball games? Seems I read something about him in the papers. Wasn't he the guy selling players performance enhancement drugs? Then betting on their team?"

"He ain't no crook, girlie." Punchy interjected with a scowl.

Without lowering her gun, Callista picked up the conversation. "Yes, I remember, he was also supposed to be in with some quack doctor too. The investigation made the papers a couple of weeks ago."

"Okay, that's him. But he's innocent, he doesn't have anything to do with betting or drugs. He doesn't even smoke...he's a clean living guy." As Earl spoke, he put his palm up again for Punchy to shut up. I'd bet he's had a lot of practice. But the name clicked an image in my mind. Cima was the man in such heavy conversation with Felicity at the bistro. Things were beginning to be interesting.

"What's his interest in Carlos?" I asked. "Why does he care what we investigate?"

"Mr. Cima, he and his wife, Stella, were good friends with Carlos and Mrs. Etcheveria...used to go to dinner, clubbing, parties..like that. He likes Carlos a lot, they played golf, tennis, together. From what I know, the two of them, they go way back.

"He's been real upset since Carlos went missing. It would mean a lot to him to find out what happened to his friend."

He stopped, and looked around, like he was afraid he had said too much. Quiet for a moment, he tugged at his jacket before he continued. "They were real close, the two couples. Mr. Cima, he's been feeling very low since Carlos split without a word to him. He's been worried maybe someone hurt Carlos, and Mr. Cima, he doesn't like people messing with his friends."

I heard sincerity in his voice. Mrs. Freedhoff wasn't the only good friend of Carlos' feeling the loss. Carlos must be quite a guy.

"Well, I understand, but my assignment had nothing to do with finding Carlos. However, if he comes banging on my door after you leave, I'll give him a message to call Mr. Cima, or at least instant message him on facebook."

"Yeah, okay. A call, that would be nice, but what's all the facebook stuff? Something to do with handicapping? Carlos isn't a gambler himself as far as I know." He shook his head. "Sorry we disturbed you all." He motioned to his partner and without another word, they left.

Callista put her gun back in her apron pocket. "How strange. I wonder what the Carlos thing is all about?"

"I don't know. He was supposedly suspended for using enhancement drugs, however, according to Mrs. Freedhoff, his suspension was almost up. Maybe he just got tired of hanging around and went to New Zealand or someplace to fish while he waits out his time. Nothing in the rules would have stopped him from leaving the country. He wasn't under house arrest, or even charged with any crime, as far as I know.

Belvidere stepped out of the shadows. "This Carlos is becoming more interesting by the moment. Two very different people seem sincere about missing him. His wife—not so much."

"I saw Cima and Felicity sitting together at the bistro just an hour or so ago when I was stopped at a light. I recognized her, and had seen his face in the news, but couldn't remember his name until just now. Wonder what they were so intent on? Finding their dear Carlos, or is Felicity just another reason why Cima might want to get rid of him?"

"Has anyone reported him missing?" Belvidere asked.

"I'll check with the police and find out what I can." Callista said. Her gentleman friend, Sol, is a detective with the Orange County Sheriff's Office—and also a flipper.

Talk about a strange lash-up. Sol is six-six to her four feet eleven inches, and dark enough to have just walked off the boat from deepest, darkest Africa. He is also a Rottweiler cross when he flips. Sol looks so tough even Belvidere is afraid of him. But Callista has him wrapped around her tiny paw. He adores her, would do anything to please her.

Solomon Jefferson—veteran homicide detective, was a dangerous son-of-a-gun if you were on the wrong side of the law, but once he walked into our house, and put away his badge and gun, it was another story. Think of a pussy cat, a giant gentle one who lives to cuddle. That's our Sol around Callista. Does she love him? I think so. But I think she also likes the fact she can boss him around. My sweet little sister has a Napoleon complex and won't admit it.

She was on her cell asking for him. "Hi Sol, did I catch you at a bad time?" I could hear his deep voice on the other end of the line but couldn't make out any words. "I have a little favor to ask you." More rumbling. "Yes...perfect. I'll expect you as soon as you're free....oh, you think you can be here in a half hour? Great, I was just about to make dinner and you'll join us." The rumble on the other end had a lilt of joy to it.

Callista clicked off. Her eyes were bright, as always when she spoke to Sol. "He says he has some free time, something about waiting for a warrant. Anyway, he'll be over in a little while. I have a lovely stew in the refrigerator I made yesterday— always better when they sit for a day." She put her finger to her chin and I was reminded again of Little Orphan Annie. "I also have a baguette in the freezer and some salad. Better get started. Who'll help set the table?"

Belvidere followed her into the kitchen shaking her head. "I don't know what's up with those two, but if you want an odd couple, they're it. I can't imagine what people think when they go out on dates. He always looks like he's about to eat her."

"Mom always told us, there's no accounting for taste in love. The heart wants what the heart wants."

"But could you imagine them having a litter? How could it even be possible? She's so tiny and he's...he's...gigantic!"

"Don't let it worry you, they'll work it out."

She sighed and walked away. "Call me when dinner's ready. I'm going to powder my nose after I set the table."

I was worried. I knew I should tell Sol about Gabriel, but it would mean admitting we not only took Moroney away, we had disturbed a crime scene—something I didn't want to tell anyone, especially Sol. As problem solvers, we didn't have to worry about losing a license, but there could be other problems for us, like jail time. Not a great place for a tall, fair skinned blond haired man, who might turn into big white poodle if cornered.

CHAPTER THIRTEEN

Dinner With Sol

In less than twenty minutes, a siren blared down our street and, accompanied by a screech of tires, stopped in front of our house. I wasn't worried the neighbors might think it's a bust, they're so used to strange goings on at our place they don't pay attention anymore. The doorbell rang. When I opened the door, lights from the street were obscured by the body filling the doorway. Sol had arrived. The only things visible in the porch shadows were the whites of his eyes, his teeth displayed in a broad smile, and a bright pink cake box decorated with gold and pink ribbons and three pink roses.

"How are you, Antonio?" My hand was engulfed in a grip both strong and soft at the same time, a hand familiar with power and how to control it—muscles relaxed and pillowing my hand rather than squeezing. I found it oddly comforting. Every time I met Sol, I understood another reason why Callista liked him so much.

"So, where's my girl? I brought a little sweet for my Sugar." His face cracked into an even bigger smile.

"In the kitchen getting dinner ready. Come on in, Sol. Can I get you a drink?"

"Just a soft drink or some juice would be great. I'm still on duty, we got a nasty one we're working on." Since Sol was in homicide, I understood he meant a murder. Like most cops, he didn't like to talk about work. Getting away from the job was always a relief.

A red-headed blur flew in from the kitchen and jumped at Sol. He caught her in mid leap with one arm, hugging her as he swung her around like a child. The joy on both faces was something to behold. And I was totally impressed he hadn't dropped the cake box he still held steady in his other hand.

"Dinner is ready to put on the table. I'll bet you're hungry...got a nice stew with salad...your favorite."

"Honey pie, you're my favorite." He snuggled his face against her neck.

"Put me down, my teddy bear. I've got to get everything off the stove before the stew burns."

I could see he was reluctant to let go of her, but he gently placed her on the floor and before she scampered off she took the cake box from him. "Yummm, dessert, thank you my thoughtful man."

Dinner was delicious. Callista cooks as a hobby. She's a true foodie haunting ethnic markets and recording her favorite cooking shows. She's been our resident chef since she was in her teens. Mother gave over the kitchen to her when she discovered Callista was a far better cook than she was. Belvidere, to my knowledge, has no idea how to even turn on the stove. But then, she has other assets.

After dinner, Sol called the station to see if his warrant had arrived. The judge was out of town and wouldn't be back until the next morning. Sol's evening was free. Now officially off duty, he settled down on the couch in the living room, a balloon of Cognac almost hidden in his hand. Callista cuddled up against him. Sol looked like a very happy man.

Belvidere began the conversation. "Antonio has found a problem to solve, a new client with a lot of odd questions."

"And aren't there always?" Sol was used to our business. He helped our parents out from time to time and was always interested in some of our more bizarre problems.

I took over. "Yes, but this might involve the Sheriff's Department. I wanted to fill you in...and see if you have some ideas. I've been hired by Mrs. Freedhoff in a matter concerning one of her granddaughters."

Sol rolled his eyes and made a face. "No wonder there are odd questions. The old gal is okay—I've met her several times and always found her to be a straight shooter, tough, but all right. Those girls— from another planet." This time when he rolled his eyes, his mouth puckered like he tasted something bitter. "The older one, Felicity, is an ice princess and a drunk. She's married to Carlos Etcheveria, the ball player who was suspended for drugs—the enhancement kind. I hear he's a regular guy though...likes the ladies...a player, but no more than the next jock."

"I've heard the same, but did you know he's missing?"

"Yes, our missing persons department had a report and looked into it. No sign of foul play, no struggle, no blood, no body...nothing. He was still on suspension, but there was no evidence to point to any crime. There were no missed appointments or a job where he didn't show up, so they had nothing to go on. No one knew where he was, but he liked to fish and he liked the ladies. With nothing more suspicious than he just wasn't around; missing persons figured he went off with some groupie to wait out his suspension. He and his wife were still living together, but the scuttle is they go their separate ways."

"All that is true. But, his suspension is almost over, and he's still not back. Mrs. Freedhoff indicated they were very close. She was pretty torn up when he went off without a goodbye. As for his wife, she didn't seem to care much about him. However, I thought she was nervous about something. All she did was grill me about her grandmother, and if she hired me to find Carlos. Which she didn't."

Examining my balloon of Cognac, I couldn't suppress a snicker. "Felicity seemed quite taken by Bel. Until my darling sister told her not to smoke in our office. Then she took off in a huff."

Sol was beginning to look interested. I continued. "The strange thing is—earlier today, we had a visit from two of Alfred Cima's boys. Their boss wanted to know if I was looking for Carlos. I figured Carlos owed Cima money and they were out to collect. Wrong. One of the boys told me Cima and Carlos were close buddies and Cima was worried about him. The Cimas and the Etcheverias were close friends apparently, went out for dinner, took vacations together. Cima hasn't been able to contact Carlos for the last week or so—no answer on his cell phone, no call back or texts. It was unusual for Carlos. Anyway, Cima sent them to see what I found out. I told them I wasn't looking for Carlos and didn't know anything and they left."

"I'm amazed they were so docile. His boys have a reputation for not being grateful when they don't get the information they want."

I couldn't help laughing. "They didn't have much choice. Your girlfriend had her gun in their face the whole time."

Sol looked down and poked Callista with a thick finger. "Did you do that?"

"....uhmmm, yeah."

"How many times have I told you not to pull out your guns unless you intend to shoot?" Sol often took her to the police firing range for practice. She's a crack shot, better than either Belvidere or me.

"I did intend to shoot the bastard. First, the big goon was trying to break down our door and then he looked like he was going to slug Antonio as soon as it opened. That was not going to happen on my watch." The last words were said with an invisible foot stomp. My sister is very protective of her family. Sol just held her closer with a smug look on his face. He's very proud of his little lady.

Belvidere and I left the two of them to their own devices and went into the office to tidy up some paperwork. Two hours later, she went to get a glass of water.

Back in the office, she shushed me and motioned to follow her. A very large black and brown Rottweiler cross, was snoring loudly on the family room sofa; a tiny orange puffball of fur sound asleep across his neck. It looked like he was wearing a fur collar. Trying not to laugh out loud, we snuck back out of the room.

As we left, Belvidere whispered. "Why didn't you tell him about the body at the Eichler place?"

"I thought about it, but I couldn't figure out a way to do it without getting our client involved. Have any ideas?"

"Not a one. I guess the police will find Gabriel; someone must miss him—eventually."

"I forgot to tell you before, but when I went back into the house to check again for the red bag, I found some wet footprints leading from the back door into the kitchen. They were in a place where I hadn't walked. They were too large for Moroney, and you were wearing high heels. Someone else must have entered while we were watching. You remember, the rain started after we began the stakeout."

She mulled that over for a while. "Must have been the dark shadow you saw in the alley. I don't know how I missed him, unless he got in while I was on the other side of the house." She thought for a moment. "After I looked in the kitchen, it surprised me the door had been left open. Then I figured with the narrow alley, probably no one would think to come in that way unless they were familiar with the house. I left the kitchen door as it was and went around to the opposite side. I was there when I saw the flash and heard the shots. By the time I ran to the courtyard entrance, you were at the door. I didn't see anyone. If you think whoever shot Gabriel snuck into the house, then they must have left the same way they came in—through the kitchen to the alley."

All night, I dreamt of chasing a ghostly figure wearing size eight men's cross-trainers, a black hoodie, and carrying a red gym bag. My dream kept looping to the figure running down a long alley in the rain. I must have been woofing in my sleep when I awoke to Callista shaking me.

CHAPTER FOURTEEN

An Interloper In Daisy Dukes

It took a moment for me to push the sleep out of my mind. When I finally cleared my brain, I heard a commotion below.

Belvidere sounded angry as she yelled up the stairs. "There's a Goth monstrosity at the door demanding to see you...says she's a real good friend of yours, and does it with a nasty sounding innuendo."

My sister was in her don't-give-a-shit-who-hears mode. She can be abrupt, but seldom so rude. I hoped it wasn't who I suspected had come to call.

I looked at the clock. Nine AM. I never sleep so late.

Then I remembered what happened the day before. Not a pleasant memory to wake up to. I was glad to have shut down for so long.

Dragging on a pair of jeans and a tee shirt, I ran down the stairs in my slippers. When I rounded the corner landing, I saw a pair of heavy black combat boots with studs, long slender legs above, too much leg for the pair of Daisy Dukes cut-off jeans. The butt cheeks of the owner were visible below the ripped denim.

It could only be Moroney. About the last person on my list of who I wanted to see. No wonder Belvidere was rude. Moroney brought that out in people...along with other things.

When I reached the hall, I saw why Belvidere was so pissed off. Over the ripped shorts, a foot or more of bare midriff was displayed, an elastic bandeau top with just the barest curve of breasts peeking out the bottom. In the middle of each curve, large nipple rings with decorative beads clearly visible. Damn things dangled below the end of the top.

How could anyone go out like that? But Moroney wasn't anyone. The broad got off on shock and affront, so why was I surprised?

She turned and gave me an up and down eye-fuck, taking note of my buffed six-pack under the tight tee shirt. Her x-ray eyes felt hot on my abdomen.

Nodding approval, her gaze rested on my crotch for several beats too long. My intuitive reaction was to bunch my shoulders forward

and cover the jewels with my hands. But I wouldn't give her the satisfaction.

Instead, I stood facing her, a smile on my face that was hard to hold.
"Everything meet with your satisfaction?" I spread my arms out to
frame the display. "What in hell do you want?" I can be rude too.

When she finally looked at my face, her smile was predatory as she
slowly licked her lips.

Sorry, Moroney, I thought. The hair on my arms stood up on end. I
knew that wasn't the reaction she was aiming for. The old expression
from when I was a teenager raced to my mind—'I wouldn't touch her
with someone else's dick'.

She assumed a coy stance, entwining her wrists in front of her
waist, just enough to bunch her breasts together and set the nipple
rings jingling. Next, I expected her to pout and twirl a strand of her
hair. The hair wasn't long enough, but damned if she didn't try a pout.
With all the dark eye make-up it came out grotesque.

"Thanks for getting me out of...there...yesterday. I don't remember
much. Gupta said you brought me home. I came to say 'thanks'. I appreciated it."

Moroney tried to look sincere—it wasn't working. "But now there's
a teeny-weenie problem. I can't find my gun. It was a present...for my
protection. I like to go...places..." She trailed off for a moment, as if
she lost track, or maybe just caressing a nasty memory of one of those
places. Visions of crack houses, opium dens and S & M parlors flashed
through my mind. I suppressed an involuntary shudder.

She continued. "Anyway, I had it with me when I left home yesterday, now I can't find it. I thought...maybe you or your sister picked it
up at the...house?"

I hadn't seen a gun anywhere when I checked the place for the gym
bag. When I turned to Belvidere, she shook her head. She hadn't seen
one either. The question shrieking through my mind in flashing neon
lights was, had the bitch shot Gabriel?

"What kind of a gun was it?"

"A little one I could carry in my handbag...or my pocket. I think it's
called a Derringer."

"Did you shoot Gabriel?"

"No! I did not! I did like to hit him...he liked it too, but I would
never shoot him. He was my Dom...introduced me to the life...taught
me...things...I...I loved him." For the first time since I met her, she al-

most looked sincere. Almost.

I understood what she meant, that is, everything but the love part. They were carrying on their nasty little games together for years. Could the rules have changed? She got carried away—wanted more?

"Now I have no one to play with...maybe you and me?" She lunged toward me, a feral smile crossing her face. I backpedaled and she did a little dance to regain her balance. Her eyes darkened into slits and she moved towards me—fast—like a panther on its prey.

Her hands clawed at my nipples. She got a grip before I grabbed her wrists to hold them away. At that moment I felt her skin: cool, clammy, and slightly sticky—the way you would expect a long dead corpse to feel.

Then, her unmistakable odor assaulted my nose: a sick combination of vaginal effluence, old perfume. The ooze of last nights' booze and drugs mixed with it to leach out through her flesh.

My nose wrinkled in distaste and I pushed her away harder than I intended. She stumbled against the banister.

When she raised her face to me, her eyes glittered. "So...you do like to play." A harsh, high-pitched giggle was followed by her infernal humming.

"It's time for you to leave. Go home, and don't ever come back. My sole obligation is to my client—your grandmother. I'm done with you."

Belvidere stepped behind her and opened the door just as Callista scampered from the kitchen snapping at the intruder's ankles and yapping, her version of "Get the hell out of my house."

Moroney took the hint and left. The cheeks of her ass below her shorts jiggled in defiance as she stomped down the walkway.

Once the door closed, Belvidere leaned against it. "That woman is one of the most awful people I've had the bad luck to meet. She could be attractive, I mean the physical attributes are there, but she looks rotten...even smells rotten. How does someone get like that?"

"I have no idea, but I'm going upstairs to wash any trace of her off and put on some clean clothes. Anyone up for coffee when I come down?"

"I'll make a new pot. I have croissants in the freezer and some raspberry jam I made last week." Callista piped in. She had flipped when the door closed and I smiled as I looked at the rolled up jeans, crisp red and white checked shirt and sneakers. She almost looked like

Raggedy Andy; the only thing missing was a pair of red suspenders. Her pert nose and freckles were so familiar and endearing I felt better already.

"Yumm! Be right back."

CHAPTER FIFTEEN

A Non-Felicitous Visit

The coffee was hot and strong, just the way I like it. Callista always makes it especially for me. I admitted to myself that I'm spoiled while I ate a warmed croissant dripping with butter and homemade raspberry jam...also just the way I like it.

Our kitchen is in back of the ballroom—cum—office, in the family living quarters of our house. The place is much larger than it looks from the street. Originally a triple garage and storage space, now converted into a great room, it serves as kitchen, living, and dining area.

Belvidere and I put our paws down and banned Callista's decorating skills. This is for family and everything has to be livable. No antiques, nothing fragile. Club chairs with hassocks, sofa and loveseat, all in soft cognac Spanish leather. Rustic coffee table, end tables, media center, refectory table and chairs all custom made in Mexican hacienda style dark wood. Plenty of lighting, high wooden beamed ceiling and stone fireplace opposite the kitchen. Homey, comfortable. Just the way we like it. That is, except for Callista.

She thinks everything is too big and too new and tries to sneak in a little Art Deco or Art Nouveau when she thinks we won't notice. We catch her, and out it goes.

True, Callista's feet don't reach the floor when she sits on most of the furniture, but Pomeranians can jump high enough to curl up on the soft leather to be petted. As a human, the love seat is hers to stretch out on with her tablet and watch what she wants on Netflix. Compromise in life is everything.

This part of the house smells of old wood fires, cookies baking, and roasts sizzling in garlic; of soft leather and basil plants in the greenhouse window behind the kitchen sink. Homey.

I sat at the counter dividing the kitchen from the rest of the room inhaling fresh coffee and warm croissants to clear out the last of Moroney's stink.

Just as I thought life was going to be livable, the office doorbell rang. Belvidere gave me a foul look and I went to answer it. Felicity was standing outside peeking in one of the side lights. Great...just what we needed...more Freedhoffs.

I opened the door. "What do you want this time? Our job is over, we've done what your grandmother wanted." As soon as the door was open, I could see she was drunk. The smell of alcohol was a miasma surrounding her. Yucky, still not as bad as her sister.

She had been leaning on the door, and, without support, slipped down the door jam. I caught her under the arms and propped her back up. I was amazed at how she had managed to get here when Gupta showed up. He took over the propping.

"So sorry Mr. Pudel, but she was insistent about seeing you. I tried to get her back into the house, but she ran into the garage with the keys in her hand and I couldn't let her drive in this condition."

"Okay Gupta, you did the right thing. Let's get some coffee into her. If she throws up, you get to clean it up. Got it? Taking care of drunks is not one of the problems we solve." I knew I was cranky, but I was on Freedhoff overload.

"Yes Mr. Pudel. I understand." This time he forgot the hand twirl.

Together we manhandled her into the living quarters and I pulled over a wooden dining chair to prop her in. If she hurled it would be easier to clean than the leather sofas and we could get the smell out. If I could have justified it, I'd have sat her in the bathroom on the tile floor where I could use disinfectant. The two Freedhoff granddaughters were high and very unpleasant maintenance.

Felicity was dressed in one of those Grecian draped numbers she favored, easy to part the bottom drape and easier to show a lot of cleavage. Without a sound, Gupta bent down and pulled her skirt over her exposed thighs and closed the gap across her breasts. He did it with such deft surety it was obvious he had a lot of practice. His flourish was almost reminiscent of his hand twirl. I suppressed a smile as I wondered if the two movements were connected.

After we got her to take a few sips of coffee, her head flopped over and she began to snore. I was about to suggest we take her out to the limo and he could bring her back home, when he began to speak.

"She misses her husband. She and Mr. Carlos went their own ways, but she knew he was always there if she needed him. He was still family, really all she had other than Mrs. Freedhoff, and no one knows how long she'll be around. Moroney is more of a problem than any help.

All the attention is always on her and her latest catastrophe." He shook his head and looked suitably sad.

"Do you have any idea why she was so intent on talking to me?" I figured I might as well ask since he was in a talking mood.

"I think she wanted to know if you heard anything about Mr. Carlos. Mr. Cima stopped by last night and said his men had talked to you. She and Mr. Cima are good friends. They spend a lot of time together since Mrs. Cima disappeared around the same time Mr. Carlos did."

"Mrs. Freedhoff told me the police closed the case on Carlos when they heard Mrs. Cima was gone. Carlos' Alfa Romeo was never found, so the assumption was they got in his car and left."

"Yes, but Mrs. Etcheveria doesn't believe that is what happened."

"I agree with her. Wouldn't it be strange? I mean, why would Carlos leave then? His suspension was almost over and he was giving up a contract with several high paying years remaining."

Felicity moaned. A dribble of spittle made its way from the corner of her mouth towards her chin. Gupta leaned over her and gently wiped it away with a crisp white handkerchief from his breast pocket.

"It seems to me that Cima is the one with the strongest motive to get rid of Carlos, if he was having an affair with his wife." I said.

"I don't know sir. I just know more people are worried about his disappearance than might have caused it. Mr. Cima doesn't seem to be as concerned about his wife as he is about Mr. Carlos."

Felicity started loud snoring. I looked at Gupta, "I don't think she has anything she wants to say to me at the moment. I suggest you take her home and put her to bed."

He nodded, scooped her up, and left.

CHAPTER SIXTEEN

More Information

As I watched the Rolls round the corner, I thought about the Freedhoff family. All the advantages anyone could dream of having. But rather than using them in a positive way, the granddaughters chose a path of self-destruction. The whole thing made no sense. I was glad we would soon have nothing more to do with the family.

With Gabriel dead, I assumed the financial demands would stop. There was no way of knowing how many copies of the video of Moroney had been sold, or to whom. For that matter, I had no idea how many different videos were around. She had been with Gabriel for years and there could be a flood of different ones floating around in the pervert marketplace.

With a little luck, no one would think to connect the adult Moroney to the feral child beating Gabriel with such joy. But in retrospect, while the Freedhoffs were long in fortune, they seemed to be short on luck.

I planned on meeting with Mrs. Freedhoff. It wasn't going to be pleasant to reveal what we learned, tell her about Gabriel's death and what he meant her granddaughter. Then I was going to explain where we found Moroney. I hoped then to learn her wishes in terms of finding the red bag with the money. In my opinion, the problem was solved as much as it could ever be. Gabriel was most likely the blackmailer we were hired to find. Nevertheless, no guarantees could be given. Considering Moroney's penchants, similar issues were certain to crop up in the future.

Still, Gabriel's murder bothered me. Callista checked the newspapers, television reports and the internet—still no mention of a murder in Thousand Oaks. Maybe the body hadn't been found yet. It usually takes few days for a corpse to ripen enough to alert the neighbors. The rain could have delayed the decomposition or disguised the smell. The idea of what shape Gabriel might be in after several days in rain and sun was not something I wanted to dwell upon.

I kept dragging my paws every time my sisters wanted me to tell

Sol about what we had found. My reluctance was now an elephant thigh bone of contention at home.

When I thought back to the scene, the holes in the body made by the gunshots were much larger than would have been made with a Derringer, and with the condition Moroney was in, I was pretty sure she wasn't the killer. My money was on the size eight cross-trainers.

And where in hell did the money go? I wracked my brain about who might know and kept coming back to the woman and man with the red gym bag. Had the guy come back when we weren't looking, snuck into the house, killed Gabriel—snatched the bag? Could he have been the shadow I saw in the alley? It seemed the only logical answer.

I took Belvidere aside. "I'd like to take another look at Gabriel's house. I keep having the feeling that we're missing something. Let's go there and flip. We can snoop around and be less obvious."

She looked at me with anger and reluctance.

"I'll make a deal with you. As soon as we get back, if the police haven't discovered the body yet, I'll call it in."

"Okay, then I'm up for it." Belvidere was always up for it.

Callista had been silently listening. "Can I come too? I'll stay in the car, think of me as getaway driver." She puffed her chest out. My sisters certainly had stronger constitutions than I did. Just the thought of poking around a crime scene with a several day old corpse made my stomach lurch, but they were both eager.

Before we could get out the door, Callista's cell phone rang. It was Sol. I could tell by the ring tone—'Who Let The Dogs Out?' "Hi big boy, what's up." She was always smiled when he called.

"Put me on speaker sweetie, I want Antonio to hear this too."

"Okay, here I go."

His voice came over loud and clear. "Just heard some scuttlebutt I thought might be of interest. I was talking to my pal in missing persons and it seemed they dropped the Carlos investigation when they heard Cima's wife was also missing.

"Seems the two of them were real cozy. First thought was Cima might have had a contract out on Carlos for something, I haven't gotten the word on what it was, but I'm asking around. There's an ongoing Federal investigation into Cima's activities, suspicions concerning involvement with enhancement drugs." He stopped for a minute and I heard him yell at someone before he came back on line.

"A couple of the guys heard rumors about Carlos making a deal with the Feds to testify against the doctor who was pushing enhancement drugs to his patients. If Cima was involved, that could be motive. But once they heard about Mrs. Cima and Carlos, they figured either Cima got rid of them both and we have no leads on finding the bodies, or most likely, they're sunning themselves on a beach in the Canary Islands. Either way, nothing to investigate. No one's ever been able to pin anything on Cima in the past."

"Interesting. Maybe that explains why Cima and Felicity Etcheveria are so buddy-buddy. I saw them talking close; head to head at a bistro on the way home yesterday."

"Yeah, well maybe misery loves company, or maybe there is no misery, just a love of the company?"

CHAPTER SEVENTEEN

Search And Search Again

The lovebirds said goodbye. Once again, I felt bad about holding out on Sol, but if I told him, we couldn't go back and poke around. I wasn't going to break my promise to tell him as soon as we were back from Thousand Oaks.

After Callista clicked off, she gave me a dirty look. I knew she was thinking the same thing I was.

"If you want to tell Sol, as soon as we leave the place, you can call him. Just leave out the part that we were there before. Say we had a lead on Gabriel from the matter we were working on and when we went there to speak to him, the door was unlocked. Okay?" It was the best I could offer her.

She didn't look too happy about lying to Sol either, but she nodded assent, turned her back on me and stomped out to the car.

Once again we took the 405 north to catch the 101 to Ventura County. Once again we were in traffic. I've lived in California all my life and I can hardly remember a time when the 405 wasn't under construction of some kind. I sighed as I worked the Range Rover into the HOV lane. At least the rain had stopped. Once again we were graced with California sunshine. Even the weather didn't make me feel any better.

I parked the big SUV four houses away, and around the curve—a discrete distance to avoid prying eyes. Everything was quiet. Because of the general design of the homes, if someone wanted fresh air, they were probably in their open courtyard rather than outside on the street.

Belvidere and I flipped. We were surprised at the lack of activity at the house. No police tape, the front doors closed. I didn't want to push to see if they were open after my crash through them. Someone might see two dogs going into the courtyard and call the police, or worse, Animal Control.

Instead, we trotted down the narrow alleyway to the back. Even in the bright daylight the alleyway was obscured by overhanging trees and garbage cans. The kitchen door was still unlocked, but closed as I had left it. There was no noise from inside. We stood quiet for a few moments. Belvidere sniffed around. She shook her head. No one around at present. But then she nudged me. She had picked up the faint scents of two other people. Someone had been there ahead of us.

I opened the door. Before going inside, I barked a few times. No response, no one coming to chase a noisy dog away. I poked my head in further. Empty as a cathouse on Christmas Day.

I nudged the door further open with my nose and barked again before we went in. Everything looked like it had when we left—with one glaring exception.

Gabriel was no longer on the chaise. His blood beneath had been washed away without a trace. By the rain or human hands. I had no way to tell.

All the courtyard furniture was neatly arranged. The house was tidy as we searched from room to room. No sign of the body. Someone had done a good clean-up.

Had the killer come back to get rid of the body? Was it a mob hit? Had a 'cleaner' been sent in? At least we knew what the unfamiliar scents meant.

We sniffed around, looked under everything, opened cabinets and drawers. No sign of Gabriel. It looked like he might have gone on vacation, except his suitcase was still in the bedroom closet.

On a last run through, Belvidere saw a large coffin size freezer in the laundry room. All the appliances were white and she hadn't noticed it before. She pawed it open, looked inside, let out a screeching loud bark and jumped back. The top dropped with a dull thud. .

When I ran in to see what the noise was about. Belvidere was sitting like a statue staring fixedly at the freezer. "Go have a look for yourself." She said in a flat monotone.

When I pried the top up to look inside, there was Gabriel, folded here and there to fit, staring up at me with open, frosted over eyes. It gave me the creeps and certainly had freaked Belvidere out.

Gabriel lay silent as a stone saint in his tomb as we looked down at him. He wasn't going to mind. For that matter, he wouldn't mind anything anymore.

Who the hell put him in there? The cast of characters spun through my head like a carnival wheel of chance, but I had no idea on what face it would stop. Step right up, place your bet and win the little lady a prize. Could it have been Moroney? If so, she'd have needed help to muscle a body the size of Gabriel into such a tight space...and what if he had been in rigor?

It usually takes between twenty-four to thirty-six hours for rigor to dissipate, and it was about forty-eight hours since he'd been shot. He was as stiff as a side of beef. How long might it take for a body to freeze? The rain had been warm, and that might have accelerated the relaxing of the rigor to make it easier to stuff him in the freezer. Anyway, it was a problem for the forensics team who would eventually work on him to figure out.

Whoever put him in the freezer was a pretty cool customer himself. Freezing Gabriel's body would not only mask the time of death, but make it difficult to even determine what day he was killed.

I nodded to Belvidere. It was time to take one more tour of the place and get out as soon as possible. We each took one side of the house and did a thorough search.

It didn't take long for her to find something. She came over to where I was poking my head between a mattress and box spring and nudged my tail. She was holding a small gun in her mouth.

Moroney's Derringer. It had fallen down into the workings of a La-Z-Boy recliner in the living room. Ten minutes more of poking around yielded nothing else of interest. The gun was enough of a find for our trouble. We left.

Back at the car we flipped and told Callista what we'd discovered. I took the gun from Belvidere and, with rubber gloves, put it in a plastic baggie in case it might be needed as evidence. Both of us had sniffed it carefully. It wasn't the murder weapon. It didn't appear to have been fired recently. The only scent we picked up was from a Cabela's gun cleaning kit.

"Now can we tell Sol?" Callista was agitated about holding out on him.

"How about this: we went to the house, rang the bell and no one answered. We can also go to the computer shop again and ask for him. If they say he didn't come in today and seem worried or suspicious, we can tell him that too."

I knew it was thin, but I couldn't think of another way to alert Sol to check the house out without dragging our client into it—or for that matter getting all of us arrested for withholding evidence, perverting justice, evidence tampering, aiding and abetting a homicide, hiding the scene of a crime. I could have gone on, but I had already passed life imprisonment when I stopped counting.

Since no one had a better idea, I turned the car toward the store.

When we arrived, Jonathan was playing outside. He had an empty carton he was using as a fort and was busy shooting everyone who walked by. There weren't many imaginary corpses littering the sidewalk. Pedestrian traffic was light.

Callista flipped to go play with her friend for a few minutes while Belvidere and I tried the door at the store. A tall woman answered. She looked suspiciously like the one who drove the Hyundai to Gabriel's place. I tried to get close enough to sniff her but she held me well outside the door. "Whadda' ya want?" Not exactly a charm school welcome for a place of business.

"We're looking for Gabriel Salanian. I understand he's the owner of this establishment." I said.

"Yeah, he is. He also hasn't been around in a couple of days." She opened the door a little more and I could see a guy stuffing things in moving boxes. The guy resembled the one who'd been carrying the red bag. I looked around, didn't see anything red in view. There was a stack of taped boxes piled up against the back wall. Appeared as if they were getting ready to split with the inventory. Did they know Gabriel wouldn't be coming back?

I thanked her for her time and was about to leave when she yelled, "Hey you. Who are you? What should I tell him when he comes back?" Nice save lady, I thought, good to cover your butt in the event I'm from the police or some other agency interested in either kiddy smut dealers or guys with bullet holes in their chest.

"Just tell him Tony was looking for him. I got some footage he might like. He'll know who I am."

"Funny, you don't look familiar. How can he get in touch with you?"

"He knows." That was as far as I was going to go. We turned and left. Just before she shut the door, I thought I caught a whiff of perfume like the scent Belvidere found at Gabriel's house. But it wasn't conclusive of anything. The woman worked for him, her scent could be all over his house.

Then I wondered if Gabriel had left a customer list? Creeps will pay almost anything to satisfy their cravings. Such a list would be useful to not only continue the business but also for blackmail. Or, if someone was a smart negotiator, Gabriel's competition might pay big money for it, if they hadn't killed him for it.

What worried me was the thought that anyone on the list or whoever might buy it, would have the means to pry more money out of Mrs. Freedhoff.

Maybe the case wasn't over yet? I felt uncomfortable, not the nice feeling closure usually brings. Instead, the unpleasant feeling there might be problems yet to solve lingered on.

Callista was curled up in Jonathan's lap while he rubbed her ears. The million dollar smile on his face was worth the entire trip.

"Mr. Antonio," Jonathan asked, "if you ever need someone to take care of Callista while you're gone, please think of me. I promise to take good care of her, not let her run in traffic or anything, remember to feed her, fill her water bowl, and take her out for potty on time."

"I'm sure you would Jonathan. I trust you and I'll keep it in mind. In the meantime, if you can get me the license plate number of the truck that picks up all the boxes being packed in there, it will be worth fifty dollars."

"Wow! That would be great! I still have your card with your telephone and e-mail so I'll get it to you as soon as I know it."

"Okay, but be careful and don't let anyone know what you are doing, I don't want you to get caught or get hurt. I don't know if those people are dangerous."

"Don't worry about me. My parents have taught me to be careful, and the people inside the computer place have seen me playing here for months. They don't even notice me anymore."

Once again I was impressed by the boys acumen and good sense. "Thanks Jonathan. Your father and mother should be proud of you for being a big help...and such a smart boy."

Jonathan gave Callista one more hug and snuggle before she hopped into the open car door. He looked sad and waved to us as we left. Callista put her paw on the rear window again—her own farewell.

"Are you feeling generous today? Fifty bucks is a lot of money for a license plate number from a kid." Belvidere said.

"I'd have liked to make it more. The boy is polite and smart. It's obvious he comes from a respectable family trying to get through some hard times. I'd like to help them but I don't want the money to look like a handout or be an insult to them."

"Maybe after this case is over, we might find work for his father." Callista said.

"I'm for that." Belvidere and I both said in unison.

CHAPTER EIGHTEEN

Melissa

Callista has her Sol. Belvidere has...I haven't a clue. The woman is so secretive, I hardly know what she likes to eat for breakfast. But I shouldn't talk. I have a girlfriend I haven't introduced to the girls yet.

Usually, I'm not into long relationships. I get plenty of estrogen at home and it has shortened my patience for it when I'm out and about. But Melissa is different. She's managed to keep me interested and on my toes for at least five times my all-time record. As I edged my Beemer up the drive towards Dana Point and Melissa's home in an eight digit neighborhood, I couldn't help thinking about our relationship.

I met her at the gym. Something about her sleek body, her soft, wavy blonde hair streaked with grey, black and buff highlights, and her long sensuous legs called out to me the first time I laid eyes on her. I started a conversation about free weights while sipping cold water infused with cucumbers and lemon juice. As soon as I looked into her amber eyes, I knew she was trouble. She looked back at me intently, checking out my white hair, dark brown eyes and buff torso.

It was lust at first sight. Words weren't spoken, there was no need. She leaned towards me, discretely sniffing my neck, then flicked her tongue across my ear. We were in the gym. Anything more intimate would be noticed. She turned and leaned her butt into my groin moving slowly side to side. My inner dog kicked in. I got the message and she immediately got mine. Without a word, she walked away, tossing her towel around her neck. I followed her to the parking lot, and slid my Beemer behind her Jaguar as she waved at me to follow.

Driving through an opulent neighborhood, I hardly saw anything other than the tail lights when she put on her brakes to turn into a driveway. Parking behind the Jag, and trailing her into the house, never for one second did I think about the possibility of a jealous husband, a murderous lover, or a serial killer lurking behind her amber eyes. I was a stud overcome by the scent of a bitch in heat and nothing else mattered.

We barely made it into her bedroom, leaving a trail of gym clothes from the front door to the bed. Cupping her breasts as I held her tight in front of me, backside to my crotch, I suddenly felt a change—her breasts flattened, something long and fluffy impeded my tumescent entry. She twisted towards me, nipped me on the neck, before turning back to brush me again with her rump.

Damn if she hadn't flipped! An Afghan hound! Hot dog! That was my last conscious thought as I flipped too. The rest of the evening—joyous sex. Locked together, we bit, humped, and nipped each other, and when we were uncomfortable, we flipped and made love as humans. What a night! I'd never thought such fabulous sex was possible. When we needed a break, we went outside and ran along the nearby bluffs, howled at the moon, barked at strangers, chased kids on skateboards and laughed our way back to her bed.

Melissa might be a distant relative, at least have some Pudel DNA in her lineage, but she was the only woman I ever met who I could be my real self with. I was smitten.

The next morning, over coffee and a little more sex, I finally took note of her house. It was decorated entirely in the style of a Barbie nest. Pink. Lots of pink. Hot pink leather sofas. Plastic flowers. Photos in pink glitter frames of Melissa growing up. All Barbie poses. There were even a few Kens in evidence, water skiing together and waving at the camera in unison. Another photo in a cute pink convertible with a different dark haired Ken type, an arm slung around her shoulders. A photo of Mom and Dad smiling with a pretty little blonde girl in between.

Holy shit! If I thought Callista was bad in the decorating department, this was beyond bad, like a rabid pre-pubescent drag queen interior decorator with a color fixation on...pink? And then I woke to reality. What had I been thinking? An Afghan hound? The dumbest dog around. Beautiful, yes. Brains? The size of a pea. But damn if the sex wasn't great.

That was almost a year and a half ago. I still haven't admitted to myself I'm afraid to have my sisters meet Melissa. She's a sweet woman, beautiful, sexy, great in bed and wonderful to run with. Without a doubt, I've never been in better condition.

As a sight hound, she's so fleet she outruns me with no effort. I've tried to keep up, but no way can my poodle body come close to her speed. At night, on our runs, she hunts rabbits and squirrels. Gophers are a cinch. She likes the neighborhood foxes and often runs and plays with them. Some have become friends and join in our chases.

But in the morning, over coffee, it's a trial. One day I counted one hundred and forty two "you knows" in the course of two cups. Another morning, there were twelve "uhmmms" in less than two minutes. I timed it on my stopwatch. Long ago I gave up counting the "likes," sprinkled like pepper, into every utterance. The woman is unable to have a conversation about anything more stimulating than television sitcoms or the Disney channel. She has never asked what I do for a living and I've never volunteered.

One morning on the way out the door, I had the insane idea to ask. "Melissa, do you have a job? Work?"

"Oh no, I don't have to...like...you know...work?"

"Actually, I don't know. Why is that? How do you pay for all this?" I motioned around the house, the well kept grounds, the sparkling swimming pool outside. The hideous décor.

"I don't...like... pay for anything, you know? Mommy and Daddy, took care of all that stuff...like...a long time ago, you know? A nice man at the bank, Fred, I think...like, puts money, every month like, in my account. For things I might want to buy, uhhh...like...clothes and stuff. I have one of those plastic thingies, like when I need cash money or uhhh...pay for things? All the bills, you know...like...go to him."

"I see. Okay. I'll call you." I remember fleeing, the choice was to either run, or strangle her for murdering the English language. Forever after, when we got together, I filled my head with a mantra: "Mental note to self, do not speak to this lovely woman or ask her questions. She will answer and you do not want to hear. See her only in dog form. Booty calls are most excellent. Sex—yes. Sit—yes. Down—yes. Stay—OK. Speak? Definitely not!"

Belvidere and Callista gave up asking about my girlfriend. Instead, I often get sly looks when I beg off to go somewhere. They know what I'm up to. They just don't know with whom.

And now, here I am, still driving to Melissa's. I've learned to do the same thing to her idea of décor as I do to Callista's—ignore it. There is no other way—looking leads to insanity. What could I possibly have done in a prior life to deserve such women around me? And I love them all.

Melissa and I were snuggled on her sofa watching "Star Trek Into

Darkness" for the fifth or sixth time. I'd lost count. It was better than "Beverly Hills Chihuahua," her other favorite. I sighed and dreamed of a good old fashioned mystery. "True Detective" wasn't on HBO, even the re-runs were gone for the moment. Thinking of a nice long romp in the meadow kept me going. Then my phone vibrated. Belvidere. "What's up? ...something important?"

"Gupta just called. He says there's been a murder at the Freedhoff home."

"Is Mrs. Freedhoff all right."

"No, not her. She's not the victim. He said it was one of their employees. He's asked if you could come to the mansion right away. Mrs. Freedhoff is in a bad state and calling for you."

"Okay, I'm on my way."

Melissa stared at me with those big soft eyes. "Does my big poodle-boy have to go?"

"Yes. Sorry; something came up with one of my clients. I'll call when I get a chance."

"Don't worry, I'll be here waiting for you." She patted the sofa cushion next to her and I imagined a long feathery tail slapping the pink leather.

I didn't want to leave. That woman gets under my fur.

CHAPTER NINETEEN

Back At The Mansion

The Freedhoff household was a disaster area. Gupta was trying to organize the chaos in vain.

Moroney stood in a corner of the domed entrance foyer, her breasts openly visible, humming, and running her tongue around her lips. Her lascivious looks in the direction of the uniform sheriffs, plain clothes detectives, emergency medical team members, crime scene investigators and photographers, weren't giving her any joy.

Some younger sheriffs looked either interested or frightened while the older ones knew her kind on sight and shook their heads. Experience had taught them trouble comes in all kinds of wrappings.

Gupta nodded to Belvidere and took her arm while he beckoned to me. "Please, come this way. Madam is waiting for you." Callista had come as her alter ego Pomeranian. He looked down at her prancing around next to his feet. "Please bring your little dog too. Madam is very fond of animals, especially dogs, but we can't keep any around here since the granddaughters have come to live. Animals either disappear or seem to meet with unfortunate accidents." He shook his head. I noted today's turban was bright orange. Not a fortuitous color considering the reason for our visit. Probably white for mourning might have been better.

Belvidere and I looked at each other. We both bent down at the same time to pick up Callista. "I'll take her." Belvidere said, as she stuffed the orange fur ball inside her leather jacket. No way was our sister going to disappear.

Mrs. Freedhoff was in her bedroom. It was almost as large as our family room...maybe the garage too. The bed was a twin, covered in lace and pillows, a white mink throw folded neatly at the foot. The walls were pale green with a white crenulated cornice, white molding framed subtle darker green foliated designs on the walls. Sage green silk drapes billowed into gold and green tasseled tiebacks fastened on the window frames before pooling onto the floor. Gauzy curtains muted outside lights trying to intrude on the somber interior.

Mrs. Freedhoff lay on a chaise longue of the same muted green as the walls. She looked much better than I anticipated, considering the murder and disruption in her household.

A frail looking hand reached out to me. When I took it, the grip was still strong.

"I'm so glad you could come. I'm very sorry to take you away from whatever you were doing, but it seems the only people left in this world who I trust are you and Gupta." She sighed. I imagined it was difficult to outlive everyone you were close to.

"Carlos was one of those I knew I could depend on, but now he's gone too."

"I'm so sorry for your loss." I squeezed her hand slightly. "Let me introduce you to my sister and partner, Belvidere."

Belvidere stepped forward and clasped the frail hand in both of hers. "It's a pleasure to finally meet you, Mrs. Freedhoff. My brother is one of your biggest fans. I'm sorry for the circumstances, but nevertheless, glad to finally make your acquaintance."

Sharp eyes covered my sister from head to toe. The older woman nodded her head twice and a slight smile found its way to the surface. "It's a pleasure to meet you too. And heavens, you're almost as tall as your brother, and equally stunning. What a handsome family you have." With that, Callista let out a sharp yap and stuck her nose out of Belvidere's jacket. Bright eyes surveyed the room, her ears pricked up and one paw pushed into sight. Belvidere unzipped her jacket and held Callista in her arm.

"My, my, what have you there? I do love dogs so. Please, may I hold her?" Callista wagged her tail and perked her ears. It was all right with her. Belvidere placed the orange ball of fur on the older woman's lap. Callista graced her with a tiny tongue flick on her hand. Dog acceptance. Then she curled up and pretended to go to sleep. I knew she was listening to everything while she checked out the scents and sights available to her in the room. She lay unmoving as the frail hand caressed her fur.

"What can we do to help you, Mrs. Freedhoff?" Belvidere likes to get down to business right away.

"There has been a murder here, as you know. Bobby, the chauffeur. He was shot in his living quarters over the garage."

"Are there any leads? Did he have any enemies?" I asked. "Did anyone see who it was?

"Not that I know of. Sadly, that is my answer to all those questions. Now I realize how little I really knew about someone living under our roof. He was in prison for some petty drug charge, possession of a little marijuana, I believe. Foolish law, the whole thing should be legalized. I hired him when he got out of jail several months ago and he's worked out well. He liked to tinker with cars, and kept the Rolls in excellent running condition. I don't know why anyone would want to kill him—I understand he hardly ever left the property.

She picked up Callista and rubbed her face in the soft ruff around my sister's neck for a moment before continuing. "He and Moroney were often together, and I preferred not to be totally acquainted with whatever it is they did. I knew she spent an inordinate amount of time in his quarters while I paid him to take care of the cars."

She gripped her white handkerchief and twisted it. "He was rather a nice young man, quite polite and kind to me all the time. I am very sorry to have this happen to him."

"I saw the police when I came in. They seem to have the matter in hand. What do you have in mind that we might do for you?"

"I'm no expert in dealing with police and the girls are useless I had hoped you might represent the family. Kind of a liaison, if you will."

"Don't you think such dealings might be better handled by your attorney?"

"No! He's an old fuddy-duddy who deals with dead things, you know, estates, corporations, and trusts. He wouldn't know a thing about police and investigations."

"We will be happy to assist you in any way we can, but only with the understanding we are neither attorneys nor detectives." Belvidere to the rescue.

The older woman looked relieved. "I fully understand your limitations. But I also appreciate your acumen. I much prefer the latter in this matter. Thank you my dear. It takes a load off my shoulders to know you will be looking out for our interests, whatever they may be. Now, if you will excuse me, this has been very tiring for an old lady. I need a little rest."

Callista jumped off Mrs. Freedhoff's lap. In a flash, she was out the door, running down the hall and around the corner before we could catch her. After what Gupta said about Moroney, I didn't want Callista alone in the house. I nodded once to Belvidere and she sprinted off in search of our tiny orange devil-dog.

Gupta led me down the hallway. "Do you want to see the chauffeur's quarters? I think the crime scene investigators are finished. Since you now represent the family, I imagine you should be allowed in."

Luckily, the detective in charge was Murphy, someone I knew and also a friend of Sol's. I looked around for Callista's big man, but didn't see him. I walked over to speak with Murphy.

"We've been hired by Mrs. Freedhoff as a liaison between the family and the police. She's over eighty, and the granddaughters...well..."

"Say no more Antonio, I know the rep those broads have and it's a relief to have you and Belvidere to talk to instead of them." He shook his head as Moroney caught his eye. She was still smirking in a corner, half hidden by the large bouquet on the entrance hall table. The sound of her humming must have been enhanced by the acoustics of the dome because it sounded like she was right next to us. Unpleasant thought. I wondered, could she hear us as clearly?

"Let's move, Murphy." I nodded to the hummer in the corner. "I'd like to see the crime scene if you'd take me."

"Sure. It's over here." I caught a brief glimpse of Moroney turning, her head, as if something caught her eye, then slinking out of her corner.

I followed Murphy towards the main part of the house. We walked down the hallway to the left of the entrance and up a narrow flight of stairs. "Over there is a separate apartment where Gupta lives." He pointed towards the opposite end of the hall. "Those are the quarters for the chauffeur at the end over the garage, and here, at the middle, are the groundskeeper and his family. His wife and oldest daughter do the cooking. The youngest daughter goes to school, but I think all the women do the inside cleaning." He opened the door to a tidy apartment where two women sat on a sofa holding hands. One was quietly weeping.

"The oldest daughter over there found the body." Murphy nodded to the weeping woman. "She knocked on Bobby's door to see if she could use his cell phone...had forgotten to charge hers. The door opened when she knocked, and there he was, sprawled on the floor— shot twice, once in the chest, once in the neck. She'd never seen a dead body before. Still tore up as you see.

"By the time the Doc saw him, he thought none of the shots had been fatal but the kid bled out. Bad luck, I say. We'll know more after they get him on the table."

"Do you have a time of death?" It was already eleven o'clock at night.

"Best guess is about eight o'clock. She found him around eight-thirty...nine. She's so upset she's not sure about much, but between her and the statements from the rest of the family that's about it."

"Didn't anyone hear the shots?"

"No. They were all in the kitchen on the other side of the house, cooking and eating. This place is built with walls so thick they could have probably been in their own quarters down the hall and never heard a thing. But the staff—Gupta, and the groundskeeper's family, were all together having their dinner and then cleaning up."

"What about Felicity and Moroney?"

"Felicity is away. She left this afternoon and said she was going to be gone for a couple of days. She had nothing to do with Bobby. He never drove her. She generally preferred to drive herself or have Gupta take her...said Bobby's driving made her nervous."

"...and Moroney?"

"She said she was in her room with her headphones on Skyping with a friend in New York."

"Did you check?"

"We looked at her computer and there was a trail like that, but we'll take it to the station and have our tech guy check it out...and contact the alleged friend."

"Why wasn't Bobby eating with the rest of the staff?"

"He told Gupta he had a hot date—taking her for a big dinner and didn't want to spoil his appetite."

I looked around the room. Not much to see. A baseball trophy from high school, a family picture of a smiling man and frowning woman with two boys. I looked in the closet, a baseball letter jacket, two off-the-rack black suits, a dozen or so tee shirts neatly folded on a shelf next to three pairs of jeans. Seven clean white dress shirts on hangers and three black pre-made ties hanging on closet coat hooks.

The shoes at the bottom were a pair of worn Adidas running shoes, brown scuffed deck shoes and a pair of cheap, black, well shined lace-up dress shoes. The drawers didn't yield anything more interesting.

The body had already been taken. I was delighted to have missed it. But there was something I wanted to know. "What did he have on his feet when he was killed?"

"Interesting question. A pair of flip-flops. Looked rubber to me."

"Thank you. Did you find the gun that killed him?"

"No. I have a team checking the grounds but so far, nothing."

We left the room, closing the door behind us. As we made our way down the hall to the entrance, a loud yodeling screech pierced the air. Callista! A sound I'd know anywhere.

CHAPTER TWENTY

Small Dogs—Big Bites

I pounded down the stairs, flew across the hall into the entrance foyer, and was trying to decide which way to go when Belvidere streaked past me towards the opposite stairs leading up to the right wing bedrooms. Sol was right behind her. So he was here after all. I hadn't seen him and wondered if he'd been assigned because it was such a high profile case.

Another screech followed by loud cursing and banging led us to the third room off the hall on the right. The door was closed, but the sound of frantic paws scratching against the wood let me know who was in there. Sol tried the knob. The door was locked. "Step back, I'm coming in!" His voice was loud and deep with a hint of panic as he kicked the door down.

Callista jumped into his arms as if propelled from a cannon. Moroney hissed as she backed up against the window on the opposite wall. The hissing was replaced by a loud deep thrumming sound in between garbled phrases. "She bit me! That fucking dog bit me." More hissing. Her eyes slitted as she pointed at Callista cradled in Sol's arms. "That's a bad dog...rabid...put her down...right away...someone shoot her, now...she's rabid, rabid, rabid!" With each repetition her voice rose higher and louder, turning into an unintelligible squawk.

Before I could stop her, Belvidere was across the room. She lifted Moroney by the throat with one hand, the girl's feet dangling above the floor. Belvidere gave her the sharp terrier-kill shake. Moroney's limbs flailed out like a rag doll.

I put my hand on my sister's arm and gently pushed it down until Moroney's feet touched the floor. What I saw in Moroney's bulging eyes told me she was in some dark place only she could inhabit...and she it there.

The hair on my arms stood at attention and it was hard to breathe. I tried to calm myself by putting horrific thoughts as far out of my mind as possible. This wasn't the time to imagine what fate might have been waiting for Callista.

Belvidere leaned in close to Moroney's face. This time she hissed, "If you ever touch my dog again, the next time I won't put you down inside the house, I'll throw you out the damned window." Before she released her grip, she gave another shake and shoved her hard against a large dresser. "Get it?" Belvidere could hiss too, and she was even scarier.

Moroney nodded her head but her face was sullen and angry. She got it, but wasn't the least bit happy about it.

The two uniformed sheriffs who followed us into the room had averted their eyes at Belvidere's dash. Their distaste for Moroney was patently obvious, standing as far away from her as the room allowed.

Sol motioned Belvidere to look around while he instructed the two sheriffs to keep their eyes on a still humming and hissing Moroney.

Sol fixed Moroney with his own version of a slitted stare as she rubbed her throat. Her shrill mantra of "kill the dog" over and over between hisses and hums continued as he walked up close to her.

His voice was calm, flat and even. But the underlying menace in his words were palpable as he looked her straight in the eyes. "Don't worry about a thing. I'll take care of the dog. I promise she won't hurt you."

Callista was safely tucked under one arm as he turned and walked out of the room, deliberately trampling on the shattered door.

I followed him after one look back at Moroney. A string of saliva trickled down her chin, her eyes had dilated to all black. I don't do crazy very well. I left Belvidere and the two uniforms to deal with Moroney.

"Shoot her, she's a rabid dog. Shoot her, shoot, shoot her right now." Moroney's shrieking followed us down the hall.

I could see Callista quivering in Sol's arms. He was stroking her and cooing, "It's okay baby, I got you now. That rabid bitch isn't going to hurt you...ever!"

Belvidere found us a few minutes later and motioned for privacy. When we stood together outside the house, Belvidere handed Sol a switchblade wrapped in the blue scarf she'd been wearing. "Thought you might like this. I found it, blade open, stashed under the bedding on the side where Moroney was standing. I picked it up in my scarf and held it through the fabric to close the blade before slipping it in my pocket. The damn thing looks sharper than a box cutter. I don't even want to think about what the she-monster was doing with it, or what plans she had for Callista."

With that, she poked her sister roughly. "Damn it, how many times have I told you not to run away from either Antonio or me when you're flipped? You do understand that woman is a sociopath and was probably about to open you up to see what was inside, just for a little evening amusement." She poked Callista again, this time harder. "Don't you?"

Callista nodded, her ears flattened back against her head. She knew it had been a close call. Sol held her up to his face. "You are my little darling...and...don't scare me like that again either." On the last part, his voice went from soft and sweet Sol to a booming basso. Callista got the message.

"I don't think there's anything more we can do here. Sol, are you going to be working this case with Murphy now?"

"Yes, he's asked me to take the lead. He's got a full load already. Since this is high profile with the Freedhoff involvement, I told him I'd help out. I also thought you all might have some insight I could use." The look he gave me was harder than an Easter Island monolith. The time had come for me to come clean.

I looked away for a moment.

"Antonio, something you want to tell me?" Sol's voice is usually deep, soft, caressing. This time he sounded like a cheese grater on granite.

I hate it when the police are so smart. "Yes, there is. Come sit in the car with us for a few minutes."

CHAPTER TWENTY-ONE

The Journey Of The Red Bag

The story I told Sol was only slightly censored. I did tell him we had been working on a blackmail case for Mrs. Freedhoff. I described the red bag, how we followed it to the computer store, and then to the Eichler house, but hadn't seen the bag.

I told him about the flash drives, the porn I took from the guy I'd followed, and that we had someone watching for the license number of any car or truck taking the porn out of the store.

When I finished, Belvidere was silent for a long beat. One eyebrow quirked up. I still hadn't told him about Gabriel's murder. She looked at me like I'd be her next victim, but instead, she put her hand on my arm to stop me saying more, and looked at Sol. "I found something else in Moroney's room you might be interested in."

Sol and I turned to her, eager to hear what she knew. I nodded. My sister had taken the heat off me.

"When you all left, Moroney was screaming, shaking, and having what I thought was a seizure. The two Sheriffs were tending to her while I took the opportunity to look inside her closet—like I was looking for the bathroom to bring her water. There was a red gym bag, zipped closed, but I managed to slide it open. It was still filled with money. Should I say something to Mrs. Freedhoff, or just leave it for you to find, Sol? I wasn't sure what to do with it. Isn't the whole house a crime scene? You can search the entire premises without a warrant?"

"Yes, you're right. Great info Belvidere, thanks. I'll get the bag out of there right away. It might be the motive for killing Bobby...maybe Moroney found it in his room and killed him for it. With that bitch, anything is possible."

I was hoping all this nice information would cover up my leaving out a few tiny tidbits, nothing too big, only the fact Moroney had been at the Eichler house, or a dead man was stuffed in the freezer. Just little things. Sol could find them out himself. Fingers crossed.

Somewhere in the back of my mind, if I were a betting man, I'd place a bundle on odds the bullets that killed Gabriel came from the same gun as the bullets that killed Bobby. Good thing I don't bet. The one thing I was pretty sure of was that Moroney hadn't killed Bobby because I still had her gun. Still, she could always get another, or maybe even had another one stashed. She was that kind of woman.

My rationalization for lying was about as airtight as a trout fishing net. Then I remembered the Pudel Family motto "Act first and apologize later." It didn't make me feel much better as I sat in the passenger seat and let Belvidere drive us home.

CHAPTER TWENTY-TWO

Strange Findings

The next morning I awoke to Callista punching me on the shoulder. I hadn't gone to sleep until almost four in the morning and the one eye opened told me it was only seven thirty. Even coffee and croissants weren't going to make up for this, I thought as I pushed her gently out of the way and headed for the bathroom.

As soon as the toilet flushed she was pounding on the door. "Sol is on the phone and says he needs to speak with you...got some interesting new development."

"Tell him I'll call him back as soon as I brush my teeth." I needed a few minutes to clear my head, not enough sleep and too many events were crowding together in my mind.

Combed, dressed and teeth cleaned, I sat at our counter in front of a steaming cup of coffee with my Smartphone on speaker so we could all hear what Sol had to say.

His voice boomed into the room, "...before the crime scene team left, one of them found a gun in Bobby's room...was tucked up in a corner of his closet where a side board hadn't been fitted correctly and there was a small hidey hole. Lucky for us, this tech is a little ADD and likes crawling up into tiny spaces...just in case. This isn't the first time she's made a good find, bless her little cotton socks."

We could hear the grin in his voice and the pride in his team. "After ballistics checked it out, it had been recently fired, but not into Bobby. Autopsy retrieved the bullets that killed him, and they're checking now to see if they match anything in the system. Maybe it will give us a lead to someplace where we might find the killer, but so far, no match." He paused for a few seconds. Belvidere and I exchanged glances. We knew Sol's style, whatever he had to say next wasn't going to be as straightforward. We were right.

"Remember that address you gave me in Thousand Oaks? Where you said you went to check out the owner of the computer shop—the porn depot? Well, I contacted the Ventura County police and asked them to send a unit to the house. All the doors were open when they got there, so they went inside, like they smelled smoke or some other bullshit. No one around, but one of the guys opened the freezer, wanted ice for a soda he'd just bought, and guess what he found?"

No way was I going to take that bait. "I've no idea, what did he find?" Even to myself, I sounded guilty as hell. I'm a lousy liar—there's no way around it.

"Uh-huh. I see. Well, he found the owner, Gabriel, in the freezer—frozen stiff as a mackerel and folded as neatly as a fancy dinner napkin. They took him out, not easy as he was rock solid. The body's down in Autopsy now...defrosting. You don't know anything about this, do you?"

The one thing I have a policy against is flat out lying to the law, especially if it's Sol. I make the distinction between flat out lying and leaving something out. I mentally crossed my fingers and hoped Sol would put this in the omission column. "Okay, I knew he was in the freezer. When we went to scope out the place, the door was open and no one answered when we called out, so we flipped and looked around. Didn't see anything until we checked the freezer. I didn't want to say anything that might get our client involved."

"Yeah, thanks, Antonio." I heard the anger in his voice. "When did you find him? Since he's a frozen stiff, the time of death isn't going to be easy to assess."

"We found him yesterday, around mid-day we went inside. He looked like he had been in there for a while, if that's any help."

Belvidere came into my line of vision, rolling her eyes and making cut motions across her throat. She wanted me to hang up the phone before I blew the conversation. I nodded. "Sol, I've got to cut this short, have a client waiting." If he knew I had only just woken up, he would catch the lie, but it was the best I could come up with.

When I ended the call, Belvidere and Callista were facing me, hands on hips, both giving me long, dirty looks. "What?" I responded. I knew they were angry at me for not telling Sol the whole story, but I still felt a responsibility to our client. Later, when Gabriel thawed out, autopsy could find the bullets and I was sure the first thing they would do was compare them to those that had killed Bobby. Case closed, I could apologize to Sol and that would be that...I hoped.

But I've found nothing in life is ever so easy. How did the red gym bag find its way into Moroney's closet? It just didn't make sense. The bag must have gone into the Eichler house with Gabriel, but no one seems to have seen it come out. It wasn't there when we searched the house before taking Moroney home.

Who was the shadowed figure I thought I saw in the alley? Had they taken the bag? Could the figure have been Bobby? If so, how would he have come to be at Gabriel's, and why would he have shot him? Questions were still to be answered.

Then the phone rang again. The number on the screen was unfamiliar and a very young sounding voice asked politely, "May I please speak to Mr. Antonio Pudel?" It was Jonathan, my own Baker Street Irregular.

"This is Antonio. Do I have the pleasure of speaking to Jonathan?"

"How did you know it was me?"

"I'm very astute. What's up?"

"How is Callista?"

That girl has more fans than a Chinese souvenir shop, no matter what form she's in. "She's fine, waiting to have fun with you again. Have you got something for me?"

"Yes. I was playing behind the computer store when a black pickup parked by their door. They filled the truck bed with boxes. It was a Ford F-150, maybe only two or three years old. Anyway, I have the license plate number for you." Then he recited the letters and numbers for a California plate.

"You are one smart kid. Are you sure no one saw you writing down the plate number? I don't want to have you in any trouble."

"No problem. I memorized the plate...didn't write anything down until I was inside our house."

My heart lurched a bit when I heard the word 'house.' He could only have been referring to the taped together conglomeration of boxes I had seen pushed to one side at the other end of the alley. When this mess was over, I was going to try and do something for his family. No one should have to live like that in this day and age. It broke my heart.

What I said was, "Jonathan, you are a star problem solver. I can't wait to tell your father how proud I am of you." I could almost hear his chest puff out on the other end. "I'll be over to see you in the next day or two and give you your consulting problem solver's fee."

"Thank you, Antonio...glad I could help."

Okay, now I had to mend my fences with Sol. He knew I'd held out on him, so it was time to give back a little info. I called him and was patched to his cell. "So, Antonio, got your memory back...have anything interesting for me?" He knew what I was up to.

"I told you I'd find out for you where the porn inventory from the computer store was going? Well I have it on good authority it was loaded into a black pick-up truck, Ford F-150, two...maybe three years old." Then I read him the license number. "If you can track them down, you'll probably find the porn. From what I could see, there wasn't much else of value in the store that would be worth stealing."

"Thanks for the tip. I'll put out a BOLO on the car. Anything else you'd like to add?"

"Not for the moment. Good luck finding the truck." Mental fingers were crossed again. My bad.

CHAPTER TWENTY-THREE

Out Of Work

When I hung up the phone, my sisters were staring at me. "What?" It seemed like that was going to be my only response to them for a while. I knew they were both mad I was still holding out on Sol. But he had now found the body and I could relax. Or so I thought.

"Is that it?" Callista asked. "Are we officially finished with the case now?"

"What else would you have me do? The blackmailer is dead. Mrs. Freedhoff will get her money back once it's released from evidence. We can't get back any compromising pictures of Moroney unless there is a way to find out how many copies were made or who bought them. In my opinion, yes, we are out of work, and it's time for another case to come in the door. What have you got in mind?"

Belvidere's brows were furrowed. Not a good sign. "Actually, I'd like to know what happened to Carlos. Everyone is concerned about him, but no one is looking. It seems to me he's the elephant in the room."

"I agree. Especially if we could get paid for finding him." Callista likes to see the money come in since she does the books. She also likes to spend it as fast as it arrives.

"You'd think Mrs. Freedhoff would be more interested in finding out where Carlos is than worrying about her awful granddaughter." Belvidere wrinkled her nose as if there were bad smells in the room.

"You ladies can do what you want, but I'm taking the night off. It's been a stressful week and I need to catch up on...my beauty sleep."

Truth was, I really wanted to go to Melissa's for a little exercise...any kind she might be interested in.

Belvidere shrugged. Callista looked thoughtful. I knew what she was thinking. Sol would be tied up for the next few days trying to unravel the two murders. Since the homicides might be related, Ventura County was happy for any help from the Orange County Sherriff's Department on what they were calling 'the case of the stiff stiff'.

"Hey, I know, let's you and I go for some hot wings and beer."

Callista loves hot wings and beer.

So does Belvidere. She perked up at the idea. "Sounds good to me, I'll get the car keys."

I watched as the little redhead in retro floral chic and the Amazon in black leather and spandex headed out together. Ah, my family, I thought.

An hour later, Melissa and I were running off the left over tension from the case, and I was in joyful anticipation of a little after-running sex games. I think of the runs as foreplay, like a warm up to great acrobatic sex. Once in a while, we stop our runs, find a quiet place and let the games begin. No one seems to pay much attention to dogs mating if we get caught. I was looking around for just such a place, peeing on the occasional rock, nosing in the bushes. Melissa came up, poked her long nose into the bush I was sniffing. "What 'cha doing?"

"Looking for a place to play a little private game with you."

"Okay, let's find a place with some moss. I like moss, you know?"

"All right, moss it is. How about over there?" As soon as I turned to talk to her again, Melissa was off and running in and out of the bushes around the park. Dammed sight hounds. They see something move and off they go. Whatever she was chasing was fast, all I could make out was a dark blur.

Then I knew what happened. Busted! The dark blur was followed by a yapping fur-ball obviously having trouble keeping up. Melissa passed her with a graceful leap, clearing the scampering orange devil by about three feet. Impressive, I thought, in spite of being miffed my sisters had followed me.

After a few minutes, a thoroughly winded Belvidere gave up the chase. She flipped into a panting human form. "Okay, you win."

"Hey, you're a poodle too...you know? Just like Antonio. Hey Antonio, look, I been...like... chasing another poodle...you know?" Melissa had flipped to human.

I slowly trotted up to the two women and flipped. "Yes, Melissa, I know. That poodle is my sister. Belvidere, meet Melissa. Melissa—Belvidere."

"Pleased to meet'cha." Melissa liked to chew gum. She popped it on the 'cha.' I could never figure out what she did with the gum when she flipped. I've never seen an Afghan hound chew gum.

Always a lady, Belvidere extended her hand. "The pleasure is mine."

Yapping in the distance caught our attention.

"Damn Callista! Doesn't that girl ever stay at home?" I asked; already knowing the answer.

"I thought I gave her the slip, she's not very fast, but she is determined...and I had promised her dinner out." Belvidere shrugged her shoulders.

Melissa watched as the fluffy ball of fur with perk ears came into sight. "She's awful cute. Do you think she'd let me pick her up and cuddle with her...like...you know, just a little snuggle?"

I held back a grimace. "I don't think I'd try. She looks sweet, but she can be aggressive...you know...like...all small dogs." Damn, now I'm doing it too.

Callista flipped as she came closer. "So big brother, is this lovely lady who you've been hiding from us?"

Melissa punched me in the shoulder. My shoulder had been getting a lot of punching lately. "You're a bad boy...you know. You shouldn't have hid your sisters from me. Especially one so, you know...like...cute and little." She bent over and gave Callista a hug.

Belvidere and I looked at each other in wide eyed shock. Callista hugged Melissa back and smiled. We'd expected at least a stiff back, worse case a punch in the nose.

Grabbing Callista by the arm, Belvidere pulled her away. "Come on sis, let's leave them to their date, we don't want to be fifth wheels."

"Don't worry, you'd only be...like...ummm the third and fourth wheels, you know?" Melissa added proudly.

Even Callista rolled her eyes at that. "Yes, you're right. But we have to go. Sorry to interrupt...have a good evening."

Belvidere added, "I promised Callista hot wings and beer. If I don't take her now, she'll be snapping at my ankles later."

My sisters flipped and the small Pomeranian and the large black poodle strolled away together. I imagined that once out of earshot, the Pom would say to the poodle, "like...yummm... hot wings and beer?"

"I'm good for that...you know?" The poodle would reply. They would never be hurtful to anyone, but, left on their own...well, anything was possible.

As we watched them leave, Melissa squeezed my arm, "They sure are nice gals, your sisters, ...you know?"

"Yes, they are...and I do know." I looked at her tracking them across the park with her eyes. Did I detect a little longing? Was it a wistful expression I saw? Sex was no longer on my mind, my sisters had taken care of that. I decided to see if my guess was right. You'd think I'd be better at figuring out what women want, but to me they are as clear as trying to prove string theory. I figured I'd give it a try. "Want to go with them for hot wings?"

Her expression brightened immediately. Bingo! I got it right. "Oh yes! I love hot wings...they're my favorite...great idea...let's catch 'em." She flipped, and with her usual joyous abandon, sped barking across the park towards the girls. I was puffing like a locomotive by the time I caught up.

CHAPTER TWENTY-FOUR

The Surprise

Since sex seemed to have loped its way out of my mind with my sisters' interruption, after hot wings and beer, I excused myself, too much work to take care of. I'd call Melissa later on in the week as soon as I had time.

"No problemo. One of the cable channels is running a, you know, a "Happy Days" marathon and...ummm...like I've wanted to see some of the shows I missed. I love those old shows, especially the Fonz, you know?" Melissa is always understanding...one of her endearing qualities to keep me coming back. I can't remember ever hearing a negative word from her. But then, I mostly try to avoid hearing any words from her.

Belvidere and Callista looked at each other. Callista nodded. Belvidere spoke. "We were going to see if the new Jennifer Aniston movie was playing. Want to go with us?"

Melissa appeared thrilled at the idea. I'd never heard her mention friends and maybe she didn't have any. "Sure, that's...like...yeah, sure. Count me in. You know...I really like her, something about her hair and the shape of her face is...like...familiar." I left them to their movie, still contemplating the image of Jennifer Aniston superimposed over an Afghan Hound. Surprisingly, it worked.

On the way home, I felt guilty. I'd lied to Melissa to get away. I'd been lying to my sisters about the woman I'd been seeing for the past year...and then lying to Sol. It was time to change my ways. Maybe we could have dinner at the house, Sol and Melissa invited? Make amends. Invite someone for Belvidere. But who? Or what? That woman is so secretive she makes me look like the local gossip rag. I have no idea of Belvidere's interests or love life. Sometimes I think it's better that way.

She and Callista hang out a lot. They do like hot wings and beer for dinner...not one of my favorite menus, but who am I to judge? They didn't seem to mind hanging out with Melissa. Was this a good thing, or would I now have three women to deal with? I shrugged. What was the big deal? I'd been negotiating between the three of them for the last year and a half anyway. Could it be easier if they all entertained each other? Hmmm....

When I parked the Beemer in the garage, something felt out of sync. I looked up and down the street for anything unusual. No black Escalades with gangsters lurking around as far as I could see. But I was still uneasy. You know the feeling, that twinge in the pit of your gut, the hair on the back of your neck behaving oddly.

Shaking it off, I pulled into the garage, closed it, turned off the alarm and walked into the house. Everything looked like it usually did, but there was an unfamiliar scent in the air—faint, but different. Even in human form, my senses are heightened. Something was definitely off.

The hair on the back of my neck stood on end again. I flipped. Sniffed some more. My sense of smell is even more acute in dog form. I sighed, if a dog can sigh. I smelled Moroney. That underlying vaginal scent was unmistakable. But how could she get into the house? We have an alarm system and never leave without arming it. I had just turned it off on the way in, or at least I thought I had. Sometimes it's hard to remember doing those little things—the ones so common they become automatic and unmemorable.

I walked over to the key pad and the alarm was still working, the green light flashing ready to be armed. Strange. I checked the office, my concern was she might have hacked the computers. Maybe the safe where we kept files, documents and flash drives was her target? Nope. All in order, the safe closed, computers as usual. What could she possibly be after? Hard to imagine we could have anything she might want.

There was an uncomfortable sound coming from our living quarters, a strange low buzzing. I trotted up the stairs and down the hall. The door to my bedroom was ajar. I pushed it open with my nose. Moroney. In my lair! The covers were pulled up to her chin, her clothes tossed on a bench at the foot of my bed. Naked?

All my fur stood on end and I barked as loud as I could, which is very loud, then growled deep in my throat. Just in case she wasn't getting the message, I snarled and made sure my teeth were visible in warning I would bite. But a big white poodle isn't very frightening.

Moroney looked at me and gave a tight, white lipped smile. "Come here doggie, look at the nice treat I have for you." She held out her hand. A large piece of filet mignon hung from her fingers, the smell of almonds not disguised by the pungent odor of a well aged piece of meat. A random thought passed through my mind. I wondered how long it would take cyanide to kill a dog my size if it ate the tempting steak? The bitch was motioning and speaking with a sweetie-sick coaxing voice. Her eyes glittered and I sensed she wanted the enjoyment of watching the dog die.

Instead of giving her the pleasure, I backed up and padded away, still growling and showing my teeth. Her voice followed me down the hall, calling, enticing. I could hear her as I flipped.

Then I called, "Bruno, Bruno!" as if I were calling to my dog. "Good boy, that's a good boy. What have you found that has you growling so?"

Walking down the hall to my room, I purposefully made noise, letting her to know I was coming. I wanted to see what her next act was.

When I opened the door, I saw she had gotten rid of the filet. I hoped she'd rub her face by mistake and inhale the cyanide from her hands. Serve her right if it made her sick...killed her. Then I saw a baggie with the meat inside, and a moist antibacterial towel crunched up next to it. Damn. She knew what she was doing. That brought up other questions for another time.

I stared at her. The bitch was still—under my sheets—in my bed. In my lair! Unsupportable. My inner wolf ancestor wanted justice for the intrusion.

She smiled what she probably thought was a sexy smile, put an arm behind her head and stretched enough so I could see one naked breast above the sheet. Thankfully, the nipple ring was gone.

"What the fuck do you think you're doing here?" I bellowed, hoping it was not the response she expected.

"I thought we could play some games." Her voice changed to baby-doll seductive "I'm real good at games. Maybe I could teach you some of the ones I like to play." She squirmed under the sheet, thrusting breasts and pelvis forward in invitation while she slowly licked her lips with her pointed little feline tongue.

"The only game we're playing is getting Moroney the fuck up, out of my bed and into her clothes, before I call the cops to have you arrested for breaking and entering." I was still yelling and could feel my face turning red with anger. Client's granddaughter or not, she had invaded my private space and she would pay. Dogs are very territorial. I was well and truly pissed.

She tried a pout. On her it looked stupid. I walked towards her with hand raised. It was taking all my self-control not to flip and rip out her throat. I had to keep control because in that split second I was more a descendent of the wolf than of man.

When I realized my hand was raised to her, I managed to stop both the flip and the urge to grab her by the scruff of the neck and throw her out of the house.

Using all my self control, I lowered my hand. "Put your clothes on—NOW—and get the fuck out of here!" I pointed in the direction of the door.

No way would I lay a hand on her. First of all, my parents had ingrained in me a fierce desire to protect women, not abuse them; and then there was the very real danger of her screaming rape. I realized I could leave no marks on her. She'd lie in a heartbeat if she got a chance. I put nothing evil past the woman. Visions of jail and lawsuits danced through my head.

Instead of gathering her things up, she turned to me, showing sharp, feral teeth as she crouched against the headboard. "See, I knew you'd like to play." She said, her face in an imitation of gloating.

My stomach lurched. Just as my control began to slip, I heard our garage door creak. Belvidere and Callista back from the movie already? Saved...I hoped.

"Belvidere!" I shouted so loud it almost came out as a howl. My sister and I have been rescuing each other all our lives, and I hoped this would be another such time. My panic must have been evident. Her high heeled boots pounded down the hall. "She broke in..." was all I could say as I pointed.

While I didn't want to be accused of hitting a woman, Belvidere had no such compunction. "What the fuck does that bitch think she's doing here?" Snarling like her dog self, she grabbed Moroney by an ear and jerking her to her feet, tossed her out of the bed.

Shit! That must have hurt.

"Don't you ever come near us you monster! Didn't you get the message the last time I saw you?" Bel was furious.

Moroney didn't seem to feel pain. Giving Bel a look of utter malice, she wrenched herself free and gathered her clothes. Not even bothering to dress herself, she stomped down the hall buck naked, and out the front door, holding her clothes and shoes in front.

As she got to the middle of our front walk, she turned and gave us a radiant smile. "Hope this tells your neighbors how nicely you treat all your clients." She turned her back to us, squatted in the middle of the walk and peed—a long pee—the puddle spreading slowly across the brick walk into the grass on the sides.

Lucky for us, we've known our neighbors for years. Most are senior citizens in bed by eight. They are so used to strange comings and goings no one raises an eyebrow anymore.

Callista had come outside in time to catch the dénouement. She took my hand and led me inside. "Hey, Antonio. Stop it. I can feel you shaking. Don't worry, she's gone. Tonight was your lucky night. By the time we had our hot wings and beer, the movie we wanted to see was almost over so we called it a night. We'll catch the film with Melissa another time.

"It's a good thing we got home early. Belvidere protected you and," she patted her apron pockets, "I'll shoot the crazy bitch if she ever shows her face around here again! In fact, I'm going to call Sol and see what it takes to get a restraining order." She let go of my hand and stomped to the phone.

"Whoa! Don't bother Sol. I won't be getting any restraining orders or doing anything else about her. I think she got the message. But it would be great if you'd help me change the linens on my bed, and while we're at it, let's turn the mattress, and change the bed pad."

"Sure, we can even burn the sheets and pad after we take them off, if you want?"

"Nah, that's not necessary. I'll wash them with bleach, that'll get rid of her cooties."

Belvidere was in the corner watching, smirking at our conversation. My taste in linens runs to Ralph Lauren while Callista favors the Horchow Collection. Belvidere sleeps on a cot with a sleeping bag on top. No matter how hard we tried to make her more comfortable, it's what she wanted. Ready to pack up and go with a minute's notice.

We laughed as Callista described how we might make a tribal ritual of the sheet-burning.

Before turning in for the night, we checked the house to find out how she managed to get in and not set off the alarm. Callista was the one who figured it out. A small doggie door father had put in when we were puppies hadn't been used in years. Father had nailed two boards across the inside of the door a while back, and we forgot about it. Callista found the wood shattered on the floor. Moroney had kicked the boards off and crawled inside. It must have been a tight squeeze for her. I found a piece of ripped fabric and a smear of blood.

"That one is smarter than she looks." Belvidere said. "She must have understood, since we had a doggie door, if she stayed below dog height, she wouldn't set off the alarm."

Right again. Whenever we updated our alarm system, we always provided the alarm was not activated by a dog entering or leaving the house. If we were in the house and needed the alarm to go off, Belvidere or I could stand on our hind legs and pass a sensor, if flipping wasn't convenient. Callista had a remote panic button on her collar along with the GPS. It had been so long since we used the feature I had forgotten all about it. Moroney was cunning, she weaseled her way in and slithered on her stomach like a snake to my room. Couldn't have been easy going up the stairs. The next morning, first stop will be Home Depot to buy a new door.

We photographed the broken boards, the small door, and the bloody fabric. I put the fabric in a baggie, just in case Moroney wanted to file an assault charge against Belvidere or a rape charge against me...would be hard to prove since I hadn't touched her...still.

When I finally got into bed, thinking about the events, I was glad I didn't stay with Melissa. Who knows what might have happened if my sisters had found Moroney in the house. There might have been a very different ending to the story— probably not what Moroney intended. While my sisters are not violent by nature, they are dogs, and as such are both territorial and protective. The pack mentality we are all hardwired with does not bode well for intruders. Both of them, when threatened, have more killer instinct than I do.

CHAPTER TWENTY-FIVE

Disclosure —Skateboarder

When I came down for coffee the next morning, Sol was sitting at the counter with Callista gazing up into his face. I shook my head. They were a really odd couple.

"Heard about your little adventure last night. Good thing it was Belvidere who roughed the bitch up instead of you—don't need a mess in court. I'll check her out when I get back to the station, but, if I re-member right, she's got quite a rap sheet...been a busy girl." He laughed for a moment. "I'll bet Bel scared the shit out of her." He shook his head and laughed again.

"Got some news. We found the black pick-up truck last night. The guy was unloading cartons into a garage. Damn fool was a runner. Why they think they can get away escapes me. Anyway, the house is rented to some dame named Mildred. He's her 'boy-toy' she said. At least she's a good twenty, maybe twenty-five years older than him." He stopped, patted Callista's wrist and took a sip of coffee. "Umm, my girl makes good coffee!

"They're both going to be questioned this morning...thought you might want to come to the station and listen in with me during the in-terrogation. Might find out some things to help in your case too."

"I'd really appreciate that. I'm all yours...and thanks!" As we left, I followed in the Beemer.

As soon as the door opened, it smelled like all police stations around the world, no matter how new or old, except maybe the old ones smell worse. Fear sweat, old coffee, unwashed bodies, Vicks, laundry detergent, gun oil and detectives' cologne all mixed with floor wax and antibacterial cleanser.

Sol was waiting for me by the coffee machine. He had a cup and some information for me. "Turns out the woman worked for Gabriel in the computer store for quite a few years. She knew Moroney, called her the Warped Witch and knew she got off beating Gabriel, who also, by the way, enjoyed the beatings. He started off as her Dom. Taught her everything she knew about the S & M life. The bastard groomed her from the time she was about eight years old. He paid her mother to use the child, if you can believe that one."

Shaking his head, he looked into his empty cup. "I can't believe one of the Freedhoff's got money from a pervert by pimping out her own daughter. Guess it really does take all kinds."

We took chairs behind a large window made of one-way glass. There was a television screen off to one side of the room. A video camera up in a corner was focused on a small table, two chairs on one side, one on the other.

A very young looking man in khaki slacks and a light blue button down shirt, open at the neck, sat down on the side with two chairs. He was joined by a uniformed officer, and after a few beats, two other officers entered with a medium sized man held between them. I saw he was handcuffed as they steered him to the chair on the opposite side and motioned for him to sit. When he was seated, they attached his handcuffs to a chain. He had enough slack to put his hands on the table, but wasn't able to move them as much as half-way across. I understood it was for the safety of the team questioning the suspect, but this suspect didn't look to me like he was about to give anyone any trouble.

Sol nodded to the room. "The little mousey guy is Albert. Doesn't look like much. The khaki pants is Blaine. He's one of our new detectives, studied criminal psychology and is our best interviewer.

Blaine spoke. "Hello Albert. Sorry to meet you under these circumstances. My name is Blaine, this is Officer Browning. Please tell us your whole name for the record."

"Albert Flax." He said, keeping his eyes lowered.

"We're here to speak with you about the events of the last few days, to get your side of the story. There is a lot of forensic evidence, but, rather than piecing the events together from only the evidence, which is subject to the interpretation of the CSIs, I prefer to have your side of the story—what you saw, what you did, what happened, and why. That way, I can present your mental state and thoughts along with the evidence. This is often an important part of the defense's case if the matter comes to trial. Do you understand, Albert? Please answer yes or no."

"Yes, I understand." Sol was right. Mouselike timid too.

"Okay, that's good. Next, I want you to know that this interview is being recorded. Do you understand that?"

"Yes."

"Fine. Then let's get started. Have you been read your rights? And, by whom?"

"Yes, I've been read my rights, and by Officer Browning." He nodded to the officer.

"Thank you for that information. Now let's begin. Do you know a woman named Mildred White?"

"Yes."

"When and how did you meet her?"

"I met her at Biff's Bar & Grill about four, maybe five, years ago. We been seeing each other since then, more or less regular."

"What did you come to learn about Mildred and her job?"

"She worked at this computer store, for a guy named Gabriel. At first I thought it was really computers, repairs, supplies and things. Then she told me it was a front for this Gabriel's real business, like he was heavy into porn, but the real weird stuff, you know, kids, whips. I never could see how she could stand that kinda' stuff, give me the creeps, but she said she didn't have nothing to do with it, just ran the office, went to the bank, paid bills...like that."

"How long had that type of business been going on, to your knowledge?"

"Oh, she was working for this Gabriel when I met her, She said she'd been working for him for a few years before that. He paid her well—okay to work for, didn't give her no trouble or nothing. She always seemed okay with working there. Never said anything to me about any problems...other than she didn't like the crap he sold."

"Did there come a time when Gabriel asked you to work for him?"

"Yeah. I was between jobs, the last place I worked, a car wash. Their lease was up and the landlord jacked the rent so they closed. Wasn't easy to find something else, so when Mildred said Gabriel was looking for a little help, I was ready."

"What exactly did you do for Gabriel?"

"Mostly I delivered or picked up stuff. I think he wasn't keen about using the mail for his business. I made pick-ups and deliveries all over Southern California, from San Diego all the way to Santa Maria. He paid my meals, gas, and maintenance for my truck, and gave me good money too. I like driving, put the radio on, hit the highway, see some new places...like that...thought it was a good job."

"Were there any other things you did for him?"

"Moved furniture around in his house, ran errands like pick up the laundry or take out Chinese or pizza. Little things that needed repairs, change light bulbs, fix broken things. I'm good with my hands and my pa taught me how to fix stuff to make it last."

Blaine turned around to look at Sol, then excused himself, leaving Albert alone with the officer. In a minute he was in the room with us. "So, what do you think so far?" He asked Sol.

"Frankly, the guy looks like he's missing a few cards from his deck, and was just a go-fer for Gabriel. I'd like to know how he got involved with Bobby. It seems like a stretch."

"I think he's telling the truth. He seems pretty comfortable, he's not sweating or showing any signs of nerves beyond normal during a police interview. I don't get the feeling he's hiding anything."

"Agreed. Why don't you bring him around to the last few days and see what comes out."

"You got it." Blaine headed back into the interview room. Before he sat down, he faced Albert. "Is there anything we can get you? Would you like something to eat...a soda or water?"

"Yeah, water would be great. All this talking makes my mouth dry."

Blaine nodded to the officer and smiled. "Don't worry Officer, I'll be fine here alone with Albert."

Albert looked up, startled. His expression was surprise someone could think him dangerous. Interesting.

After Albert had some water, Blaine began again. "So Albert, from what you've said, you and Mildred had a comfortable lifestyle, easy jobs—an employer who treated you correctly. I gather that situation changed not too long ago. Is that correct?"

"Yes. Gabriel was worried 'cause some of his clients were arrested Mildred said. He was afraid the Feds would be after him if the clients ratted him out for, like, selling dirty stuff. He wanted to close the store and move...maybe even another state. He said we'd come too and not to worry, but Mildred, you know, women, they always worry."

Blaine continued. "And then what happened?"

"He came in all happy 'bout a week...ten days ago. Told Mildred he had a plan and we was all going to have enough money to move to Texas...that was what he said...Texas. We talked about it, Mildred and me, Texas was okay with us." He shrugged his shoulders and weakly smiled. Albert was not uncomfortable with a change of scenery.

"The next day when I come into work, he has me start packing up all kinds of stuff in the shop...like files of photographs, 8mm and 16mm films, BETA, 1 inch, ¾ inch tapes, any kind like that. Didn't look like much at first, but when it had to be put away, I was working at it for at least a week."

"Was that all he wanted? Just packing?"

"No. A couple a days ago, he asks me if I still have my skateboard. When I broke my arm Mildred made me give it up...but I snuck out and used it sometimes when she went to visit her sister."

He gave a little cunning smile, and for the first time, I understood this was a simple little man who took pleasure from gliding along on his skateboard. Suddenly he became a person, not just a perp or a possible murder suspect. In my gut, I thought he might be only a casualty of circumstance. I didn't see Albert as a calculating psychopath.

"When I told Gabriel I still had the skateboard, he said he had an errand he needed me to do for him, and if it turned out good, there would be a lot of money in it for me and Mildred to make our move...set us up in Texas with him. I knew that would make her happy, my Millie...she likes money a lot.

"Anyways, all I had to do was go to this bicycle rack in front of a coffee shop not too far from the computer store. Kind'a ritzy area, but someone was going to leave a red gym bag out by the rack, and all I had to do was zip by on my board and bring it back to the store. Oh, I had to make sure no one was staking it out and no one followed me. To be sure, I walked around the area a couple of times, changed my hat and jacket when I done it. Didn't see anyone around, dog walkers, a nice big white poodle waiting for some broad—had to be a woman, the dog was real pretty and clean."

Sol elbowed me with a grin on his face. I knew I'd never hear the end of that one.

"When I was sure no one was watching, I built up a little speed, grabbed the bag, and was off back to the office. A little orange dog and the white poodle chased me for a while, both of them damn dogs barking like crazy. When they left me alone I went right to the store. Didn't want to get caught or nothin'—handed Gabriel the bag. He opened it and was real pleased looking.

"A few minutes later he left out the back door with the bag and said we should meet him at his house in Thousand Oaks later in the day to get our share. In the meantime, he wanted us to keep packing and lock up at closing time like always."

Blaine stopped him there. "All right Albert, you've done very well so far. Let's take a break and I'll be back. The officer will take you for a bathroom stop and bring you a sandwich and a soda. You can rest a few minutes and then we'll continue."

Albert nodded, and I thought the look on his face was a bit sad, as if he was actually enjoying his time in the limelight and was sorry it was interrupted.

I thought we were coming back to hear Albert some more, but Sol and Blaine had other ideas. Blaine was waiting for us in the hall. "My opinion—we're doing well so far. What do you think?"

Both Sol and I were in agreement. Sol reinforced my thoughts. "Albert seemed calm, inclined to talk without much prompting. Your attitude and method work well with him. You've already built a strong rapport with him. I think Albert will be anxiously waiting for you to come back so he can continue the conversation. This is a man who doesn't often get the chance to be the center of attention."

Blaine smiled and slapped Sol on the shoulder. "I've got to keep you away from my interviews, otherwise you'll take over and I'll be out of work." Then he stepped back and took a long look at Sol. "Nah, maybe not. No matter what your attitude, I think you'd scare the piss out of most of them the minute you walked in the door."

Sol managed to look crestfallen for a second. "What? Little me?"

I headed to the lunchroom, but Blaine touched my arm. "Hey, where are you going?"

"Lunch?"

"All right, if you want to miss the interview with Mildred."

"Sorry, I didn't know."

Sol interjected. "We want to hear her side now so we can use any discrepancies when we go back to Albert. The longer the time passes, the more chance they have to get together and corroborate each other. We can only hold them for twenty-four hours without charging them—we have to move fast."

CHAPTER TWENTY-SIX

Disclosure—Mildred

Watching Mildred through the two-way glass, she appeared as comfortable in the barren room as her boy-toy, not at all ill at ease as I had suspected she might be. While Sol discussed the line of questioning he wanted the interviewer to take, I studied Mildred. I recognized her from the computer store, now I had the time to assess her in detail.

Her clothes were tasteful—a nice mix between sexy and conservative—like the ladies selling men's cologne at Bloomingdales. I always liked to shop there, look at the women walking in and out from the malls, the salesladies with their sly smiles as they looked their customers up and down, appraising their clothing to know what price points to push. As an Armani lover, sporting a Tag Heuer watch, I always came out at the top end of their 'big spender' charts. Since there was nothing to appraise in the interview room, she pushed back her cuticles and adjusted the cross-over vee décolletage of her basic black wrap Diane von Fürstenberg dress. I couldn't help wondering how she managed to hook up with the likes of Gabriel in the first place. She wasn't quite classy enough to work at a private girls school, but she'd be perfect as the voice of control over bunnies at the Hefner mansion.

Blaine stepped into the room, introduced himself, and began with the standard questions: name, address, and if she had been advised of her rights. Standard answers.

Then he got down to business. "Mildred...is it all right if I call you Mildred?"

"Certainly, whatever you like Officer Blaine."

"Fine. Then let's get started."

For the next hour, he took her through the time frame Albert had described, and, for the most part, they told a similar story. She corroborated everything Albert said, but there were enough other small details and differences it became obvious they had not rehearsed their stories in advance.

Suddenly Blaine stopped the rhythm of question and answer. He paused a beat, then looked Mildred straight in the eye. "Mildred, I want you to tell me the truth. Did you kill Gabriel?"

She looked shocked, taken aback. "Me? Kill him? You gotta' be kidding. Gabriel was my meal ticket. No way would I have killed him." She shook her head in affirmation of her statement.

"Did Albert kill him?"

Her answer was terse. "No, not Gabriel." As soon as the words left her mouth, she clamped shut. As if she had already said too much.

After this, the easy rapport of question and answer stopped. All her responses became monosyllabic.

Blaine came out of the room to speak with Sol. "What do you think so far?"

"They seem to be both telling the truth. I wouldn't waste any more time on this line of questioning but I'd like to know what shut her down. Maybe start on Gabriel and what happened when they went in his house. Then you can bring Albert around to the same time frame."

"Okay. Got it. I agree they're telling the same story, each in their own way, but I agree, something happened to make her clam up. I'm going to study the video when we finish. Let's see where we go on the next part."

When he walked back into the interview room, Mildred looked like she was glad to see him again, her tension was gone and she was back to enjoying both the attention and the conversation. I wondered too what disconcerted her.

Blaine started right in. "Mildred, I'd like you to tell me about Gabriel's personal habits, his clients, and the people he knew and spent time with. You worked with him for a long time and must have seen plenty of people come and go over the years. This will give us information to find out who killed your boss."

She nodded her head. "I'll give you a list of his clients. We kept track of them all, their tastes, and...you know...the things they liked to watch." She squirmed a bit in her chair. The face she pulled clearly expressed her feelings for the kind of materials Gabriel dealt in.

"What do you mean, 'their tastes'?"

"He had categories of porn and the clients he serviced were listed in each of the categories they liked."

"Can you remember some of the categories?"

"Yeah, sure. Like S & M was divided into adults and children, then by gender and by age. He cross-referenced it by dom or submissive. Lots of the clients were in several categories. We even had snuff films sent in from Argentina or the Ukraine, kiddie porn with all ages, boys and girls, even some infants."

The list was going on longer than I could have imagined.

She gave an involuntary shiver and continued. "Gabriel was good with computers, he had a data base with everything cross-referenced and a code for all the various 'tastes'. I called it sick and disgusting perversions myself." She followed with a very loud sniff.

"Why did you stay with him for so long if you found his business so unpleasant?"

"Because he paid well and Gabriel himself wasn't a bad guy to work for. We all have our little idiosyncrasies. His were maybe not so little and more disagreeable than most, but I've done things in my past I'm not proud of. I've learned not to judge." She sighed and wiped away a tear.

"Moving back to the people he associated with, who did he spend more time with?"

"There was this kid, Moroney. She was his favorite and they were together for years. Her mother, Sophie, was an addict, the kind who'd do anything for her next fix. She was the daughter of this very rich old lady—Freedhoff family. More money than the Queen of England according to the papers.

"The old lady disinherited Sophie, so the only way she could stay high was to pimp out her daughters. The oldest daughter, her name begins with an F, I think, a fancy name, she wouldn't have any part of it. Kept running away, once even took a hammer to her mom. Threatened she'd kill the bitch if she ever tried to sell her again. I guess Sophie believed her, 'cause next she brought in this Moroney, the younger daughter. Kid was only about eight or nine years old when Gabriel began grooming her. I remember she was a pretty little thing but something wasn't quite right about her." She stopped for a moment. "Can I get a soda or a drink of water?"

"Sure, let me get you some." Blaine poked his head in to us on his way to the vending machine. "Anything you want to know?"

"You're doing just fine." Sol said. I nodded agreement.

When Blaine returned, he picked up where he left off. "How would you characterize what happened? With Moroney?"

"I think Sophie knew the kid already had a screw loose and liked hurting things, so she figured, no harm, no foul. Dropped Moroney off at either the shop or Gabriel's house a couple a days a week after school. Gabriel, he had a private room at the back of the shop, cameras, lights and all...just like he had at his house."

At that she put her lips together and blew out as she shook her head...like she was expelling sick thoughts from her memory. "That's all I know, other than it went on for years between them. I'd hear stuff from the back room, like they were beating each other up and liking it. Got so I'd stay in the front of the store with the radio turned up loud. They wanted to play their little games, I let them play in peace...no judgment from me."

"When did things change?"

"A few days before Gabriel asked Albert to pick up that bag for him. Maybe a week or so ago. Gabriel started getting nervous, talked about moving someplace else. Albert and I were supposed to go with him. We started packing the place up."

I nudged Sol, "Can you speak to Blaine, ask him to start on how they found Gabriel's body."

Sol tapped on the glass and Blaine came out. When he went back inside, he began with the question I wanted to hear the answer to. "How did you and Albert come to find Gabriel's body?"

"When Albert gave Gabriel the red bag with all the money, Gabriel told us to meet him at his house after we closed the shop. He wanted to give us our cut there. When we got to his house, just as we parked, Moroney pulled up in that big fancy Rolls Royce of her grandmother's. I thought she was going to rear end us...probably stoned on something. We didn't want to mess with her.

Anyway, Gabriel probably wouldn't pay us if she was around. We decided to go to for a pizza, then come back later when they'd finished their games, and collect our money."

"Did you see anyone else around, other than Moroney?"

"There was a big SUV, black, I'm not sure, maybe it was a Range Rover, but it was down the hill from where we were. A truck went by and another car, I think, maybe two cars. I'm not sure, wasn't paying much attention. I was a little pissed Moroney showed up and we had to delay getting our money. If we had the cash, we were planning a nicer dinner than pizza—you know?"

"Then what happened?"

"We went for pizza. By the time we got back to the house, the rain had stopped, the Rolls was gone and I don't remember seeing the SUV either. We knocked at the front door and it swung open. Gabriel, he has those lights on his courtyard that go on after dark, and I saw him lying on his lounge chair. It was real creepy. Gabriel wasn't moving and we were making enough noise so he'd notice. Albert thinks Gabriel's asleep and wants to take him inside. I tell Albert to stay out of the house, I'll go in and look around and see about Gabriel. I can tell he's dead by just looking at him." She sighed and adjusted her dress.

"Then what did you do?" Blaine asked.

"My first concern is the red bag. I make Albert go around the back of the house, look in all the windows, try the back door, make sure no one else is around. I don't tell him, but I want to make sure whoever killed Gabriel is gone.

"He comes back, says the kitchen door is unlocked but he couldn't see anyone. That's when we go inside. Albert and I look everyplace, closets, drawers, under the bed, then to the garage...nothing...except for a gun, a small handgun I remembered Gabriel buying a few years back. It's still in the original box with the small cleaning kit it came with. That Gabriel, he'd buy things on a whim. I gave it to Albert, figured he could probably sell it to someone and make a few bucks.

"After we looked everywhere, we decided whoever killed Gabriel took the bag. Now we're not only out of work, we didn't get the promised cash.

"But we couldn't figure it out. Who would have killed him? No one ever seemed to have a beef with him. Gabriel was quiet, kind of a Caspar Milquetoast type. It always surprised me he'd play those rough pain-games with Moroney. Then I remembered Moroney's mother—that bitch would have killed her best friend for a buck. Like mother like daughter as they say. Maybe Moroney got tired of the beating games and was going for the real thing...and a pay-off to boot!

"Then Albert comes in waving something. It's Moroney's drivers license. He tells me he found it on the floor behind a chair. She must have dropped it when she came to visit, or maybe she was coming to pick it up and stayed for the fun? Who can tell with that humming freak?"

She ran her fingers through her hair to push it off her face. Her make-up had run. She's older than I thought, fifty at least, maybe more. Her hands were on the table and I noticed a tremor. She lost her job and the bundle of cash she was counting on. At her age, not easy to find another position paying so well. It's why she's been so co-operative, anything to avoid adding jail time to the mix of disasters.

"Albert and I needed time to think things over, plan our next move. Gabriel is already dead, so I get the idea to hide the body, keep him on ice, so to speak. Without a smell, the neighbors won't be suspicious if he's not around. Then I remember the freezer. Albert didn't want to touch the body...he's scared of dead things...but I made him take out all the frozen food and then help me carry Gabriel to the kitchen. We had a hell of a time fitting Gabriel inside, nothing wanted to bend right. I was crying, Albert's squeamish and afraid someone would come in and find us. I tell you, getting Gabriel into that freezer is something I never in this lifetime want to repeat."

There's a shaking mountain next to me. Sol is laughing like a mad-man, tears running down his cheeks. "What is wrong with you? What is so damn funny?"

"When we took Albert in, he had a gun on him, and it was the same caliber as the bullets we found in Bobby. At the mention of Bobby, he insists it was an accident, they fought over the gun, but then he added, in these words, 'But I didn't have nothing to do with icing Gabriel. '" Sol started laughing again.

"We just heard how he and Mildred managed to stuff Gabriel into the freezer." He started laughing again. His words were muffled be-hind his hand.   "So, while he may not have killed Gabriel, he actually did ice him."

"Sol, quit it! Please." He was laughing so hard I was afraid he was going to flip and start barking.

"Okay, okay. He took a deep breath to collect himself.

Blaine walked out of the interview room, leaving Mildred to con-template her future options, but before he could join us, Sol looked me in the eye. "Funny she mentioned a Range Rover in front of the house. Anything you want to tell me about that? You and me, we can have a nice chat a little later."

As I watched the rest of the interview, my hands dripped cold sweat.

CHAPTER TWENTY-SEVEN

Chasing The Bag

Albert had his head resting on the table. His body language was like a man who had been up for a week with no sleep. As soon as Blaine walked in, Albert perked right up, immediately directing a big smile in Blaine's direction.

Blaine began right away. "Let's move on and talk about Gabriel's death. How did you come to know about that?"

"Once Gabriel decided to move his operation, he put Millie and me to work packing up the films, tapes and photos. He kept promising us both good jobs and enough money to make the move. We felt good about it and didn't mind...that is, until the day I picked up the red bag for him. I didn't unzip it or nothin', but it was heavy like. Felt like it had stacks of paper inside. I figured it was money, but I trusted Gabriel when he told me not to open the bag to look. After all, he'd always been square with us." Albert looked down at cuffs binding his hands together. Then he bent his head down and I realized he was wiping tears away before he began.

"Millie and me, we got to the house in the late afternoon, but there were other cars there and we decided Gabriel, he wouldn't want us to barge in. Especially since the crazy rich girl's car was there, the Rolls Royce, you know? And some big black foreign looking SUV not far away. That weirdo, she give me the creeps, always trying to touch me. I told Mildred I wasn't going to see Gabriel until the loony left. Millie was pissed and argued with me at first, but finally we went for a pizza...give him some time...then come back and catch him alone."

He stopped for a moment and gulped. I thought it looked like it was hard for him to begin and wondered if he was trying to dream up a lie, but his response was unexpected.

Albert turned large sad eyes towards Blaine. "It's been on my mind since we went back there after we ate. I can't help it, but I keep thinking if we hadn't gone for the pizza, Gabriel, he might still be alive. Maybe we could have stopped something, could have scared someone away. I don't know, maybe, maybe we'd all be dead...or maybe not."

Tears rolled down his cheeks. I believed he was moved by Gabriel's death...or I had underestimated the man? Was he a world-class actor? Somehow, the latter image didn't fit.

"When we get back to the house, see, the front door to the patio wasn't locked. Mildred gets out of the car first and pushed the door open, went into the courtyard for a minute while she made me stand outside. Then we went around the house and in through the kitchen. That door was open too."

"Okay. Then what did you do and see?"

"Gabriel, he has those lights on timers, so even though it was dark outside, I could see real good in the patio, even with the rain. There's Gabriel lying in one of his lounge chairs in his bath robe, water running off his face and all. I didn't think he was sleeping. Thought he might'a had a heart attack or something.

"Then I saw the blood. I didn't want to touch him, I'm kinda' afraid of dead things...don't like them. But I touched him anyway and he was real cold. Then I started screaming."

He took a deep breath, like he hadn't been breathing for the last five minutes. Even with the breath, he was ghostly pale. I thought for a moment he was going to faint. Then he started breathing again and color began to creep back into his face. No way was this guy lying. I didn't care how good an actor might be, this was the truth.

"I put his hair back over his bald spot...the way he always did, and Millie, she came over and looked at him, pulled his bathrobe across his chest and tied it closed. Then we went in the house to get out of the rain and try and figure out what to do next. My vote was to find the red bag and split, but Millie, she wanted to look around and see if there was anything worth taking."

As he went on, Albert confirmed what we already knew, including a description of the nightmare trying to fit the body into the freezer. "Gabriel, he was already getting stiff, we could hardly bend him to fit. He was heavy to begin with, but dead, jeez, I never thought I'd be able to lift him.

"I wrenched my f-n' back and Millie, she broke a couple a fingernails and swore like a trooper. I didn't know she even knew such words." Albert seemed genuinely surprised. "When we got his legs bent, his head stuck out at the top so we had to turn him on his side a little and twist his shoulders around. I don't like touching dead things to begin with, and he was not only dead and cold, but slippery and wet from the rain."

He stopped and rubbed his head again. "I had to puke three times, all the way to and from the toilet Millie yelled at me 'cause she had to hold the body to keep it from slipping. By the time we were finished, she was real pissed at me."

He wrung his hands a few more times and took several more deep breaths.

Blaine prompted him. "That must have been very difficult to do. I can't imagine how hard it was for you. But once you got him in the freezer, what did you do?"

"I thought Millie would never speak to me again, but when we finally got the lid closed, she hugged me, even gave me a big kiss. Then she explained to me that if no one knew Gabriel was dead, we would have time to clean out the computer store and put the porn in a safe place until she could find a buyer for it. There were a few things in the house I could sell to keep us for a little while.

"She figured we'd get a decent price for the lot of the porn. Then that, plus the money in the red bag, if we could track it down, would set us up someplace to start a legitimate business of our own."

The rest of the story was more or less the same as Mildred had related. Sol was pleased.

"The Ventura guys found her broken nails in the freezer. Now we won't have the trouble of trying to find out who they belonged to." One less detail to follow up, but I knew they would check the DNA to make sure anyway.

After the sessions with Albert and Mildred, we all concurred on one thing. We were convinced they hadn't killed Gabriel. We could be wrong, but their stories both rang true. They corroborated each other, but with enough different details to not sound like a lie they had practiced together.

"But if they didn't kill Gabriel, then who did?"

"All in good time my dear Watson." Sol likes to tease me, but I wanted to get to the bottom of this mess and make sure the Freedhoff family was forever out of our lives.

I was hoping for more answers when my cell rang.

Belvidere. "Cima is here at the house in person. He's left his goons outside and wants to speak with you privately. Says he'll wait. Callista is not pleased. I think you should come home."

I clicked off and told Sol I had to go.

He nodded. Sol knows my family always comes first.

CHAPTER TWENTY-EIGHT

A Missed Wife

Driving around the house into the garage, I saw a familiar Escalade parked in its now usual place in front of our gate. Two shadows sat in front. At least Cima had the courtesy to stash his muscle outside when he came to call.

As soon as I went inside, Belvidere grabbed me. "I don't know what this guy Cima wants, but he was adamant. No way would he leave before speaking with you."

"Where is he now?"

"He's in the office. I didn't want to leave him alone in there with all our files, so Callista is with him. They've been pretty quiet for the most part, but once in a while I hear some voices."

When I went into the office, the scene was not exactly what I expected. My little sister and Cima were sitting at an antique game table, playing Scrabble and laughing.

As soon as they saw me, Cima got up and came over to shake my hand. "Antonio, I presume?"

I nodded. After meeting his henchmen, I was surprised by the man who was their boss. Cima was medium height, pleasant looking with a slightly Latin cast to his features. He was well dressed in a conservative, but casual, tweed jacket, gabardine slacks, button down shirt and knitted tie. If I had seen him on the street, I might have taken him for a college professor rather than a shady character. It made me wonder if his reputation was earned or just blown up by the media.

"I'm so glad you're finally home." He said. "I don't know how much longer I could survive the shellacking your sister has been giving me. She just turned 'phone' into 'xylophone' for triple points."

Callista looked suitably pleased. My little sister is a total shark at Scrabble. I pitied Cima, my limit for being trapped into playing with her is ten minutes. The man must at least have patience.

"A pleasure to meet you, Mr. Cima, and I'm sorry to have left you in the clutches of my sister." He had a good firm handshake while he looked me straight in the eye. Good body language. I was beginning to reassess my opinion of the man. Perhaps the reputation was a façade.

"Not a problem. We have been having a very pleasant afternoon of word jousting—and please call me Freddo. I'm here because I want you to come with me to meet someone. We won't be long, but I think I can provide you with an important piece of a puzzle. I've checked you out—you have an excellent reputation for discretion. You'll understand why prudence is necessary when we get to our destination."

This was becoming more interesting by the minute. If the man wanted to harm me, he could already have sent his muscle to do the job, so I had no feeling of danger. I just wasn't sure how he figured in the Freedhoff blackmail or the death of either Gabriel or Bobby. Still, I didn't want to miss out on any possible information or clues. I nodded acquiescence.

He placed his Scrabble tiles face down on the edge of the board and turned to Callista. "You can come along too if you'd like. And if you promise to be a good girl and not peek at my tiles, I'll come by another time and we can finish our game."

"I like both of those suggestions. And I promise not to peek." She moved the small table over to a corner of the office and placed an embroidered Spanish shawl over it with a flourish. "There you are. That will keep the maid from moving anything when she dusts. And I'll hold you to your promise to finish the game." She flashed him a giant Callista-bright smile. "Let's go."

As we walked out the door, Belvidere joined us. She muttered in my ear, "There is no way I'm letting you two go anyplace without me, no matter how harmless this guy seems."

The ride was short in distance but interminable in time. It hadn't occurred to me before, but two people could actually talk for over a half hour about Scrabble words.

My darling sister started the torture with a simple question: "What is the best word you ever used playing Scrabble?"

Cima took her up in a heartbeat. "I've done a little reading on the subject, and came up with 'quizzify'—to quiz or question. I made over four hundred points across two triple word squares with the Z on a double letter. I thought my opponent was going to cold-cock me when we tallied it up." The excitement was clear on his face.

I needed rescue. Now! Trapped in a car with two Scrabble freaks was not my idea of fun.

Callista's enthusiasm was unbound as she continued. "That's awesome. I thought I was stylin' with 'quixotry' once where I made over three hundred and seventy. With the seven letter bonus, Q and S were on triple spaces and Z was on a double."

"If you read some of the blogs on-line, they have great tips for high count words. That's where I learned words like 'quetzals', 'muzjiks', and 'syzygy'. Another good one is 'za' the slang for pizza."

This went on and on. I didn't want to know about the derivation of 'oxyphenbutazone' or 'zax', and began to pray for a quick and painless death.

Belvidere's head was on my shoulder. Smart woman, she'd gone to sleep. I wanted to join her, but I was interested in where we were going.

After an hour, we stopped in front of a tall, solid looking, stone and adobe wall, interrupted by serious looking gates. Cima announced we had arrived. Not a moment too soon for me. I was on the verge of flipping and barking or biting both Cima and Callista, in which order, I hadn't yet decided. Just one more winning Scrabble word discussion would have put me over the top.

I knew we were somewhere up in the Cleveland National Forest, but that was it. We had wound through so many canyons I had lost track. If we had to walk home, we'd be screwed, unless Belvidere had brought her survival kit with her. I had a vision of Callista stuffed in Bel's back pack while they left me to my own devices. I'm about as useful in the mountains as a humming bird in midtown Manhattan, maybe even worse. Okay, I know poodles are hunting dogs, but we just bring back things hunters kill, especially birds, ducks are good, geese, maybe even a rabbit or two. Tracking? No way.

While many might refer to the compound I saw behind the gates as a country retreat, to me it looked more like a fortress. A rustic Mexican hacienda style edifice peeked over the top of the high wall surrounding the property. Earl reached out and punched in a code. Wrought iron and wooden gates, that might have once been at the end of a castle moat, slid silently aside.

Once inside, a courtyard with a sparkling fountain, a lap pool, many multicolored pots of flowers, palms, and luxuriant greenery gave the impression we were in a tropical garden instead of semi-arid desert.

Several cages held brilliant hued parrots, who apparently took umbrage at our arrival. Once out of the car, we were assaulted by squawks sounding remarkably like "dumb fuck" and "what'cha want asshole?" I wondered who trained the birds. The thought slipped away as two women walked out of the house to greet us.

One was Felicity Etcheveria in form-fitting jeans, a green and blue plaid shirt, and Ropers. She was accompanied by a shorter blonde, at least thirty pounds overweight, wearing a loose floral shift patterned with brilliant parrots like the ones sounding off in the courtyard, a 1940's page boy hairstyle and a welcoming smile. A miasma of aromas followed her out of the house—pot roast simmering in garlic, and chocolate chip cookies were predominant. I have a good nose for food. Callista trained me well. The cook had added a healthy pinch of basil to the roast...my personal favorite.

Cima walked over to the blonde, gave her a hug and a kiss, a peck on the cheek for Felicity. "Antonio, I think you have met Felicity, and this is my wife, Stella."

She was not at all what I expected. When she came outside, I thought she was the housekeeper. "Stella, it's a pleasure to meet you."

"You too, Antonio—and ladies. Freddo has told me you have a problem solving business. I find it a fascinating idea."

As she was introduced to my sisters, she laughed. "Please forgive the parrots. Punchy taught them to talk, and his choice of greetings are questionable...but typically Punchy."

She tossed a theatrical frown at Punchy and his usual aggressive glower melted into a slightly embarrassed and awkward smile. The tension evaporated.

Stella was the consummate hostess, making everyone feel at home and comfortable. She was certainly not the femme fatale I had imagined whisking Carlos away for titillating sex games. No way. Stella looked like the type who was much happier in her big kitchen making comfort food like pork ribs in sauerkraut, and lasagna.

I imagined her like an older version of Callista bustling around the kitchen and filled with joy to be doing so. The aroma of the pot roast cooking was making it hard to not lick my chops.

Callista was already looking at her like a long lost friend. I wasn't sure if it was Stella's smile, the 1940's parrot print shift or the promise of chocolate chip cookies. Whatever, the two of them chatted like soul mates.

I turned to Cima. "I don't understand. I thought your wife was missing with Carlos?"

"That's what we wanted everyone to think. Come in and sit down. Have a bite to eat and a drink while I fill in some of the missing pieces for you."

Callista was already in deep conversation with Stella so I left them to it and followed Cima into the house.

Belvidere wandered between the two discussions while at the same time snooping around the property on the sly.

The house was built in the style of the old Spanish *fincas* with large open center courtyard to allow room for horses and carriages, or a regiment of knights, depending on the century. Certainly a far cry from the postmodern Eichler version of the design where we found Gabriel.

These rooms were open and airy, rough textured adobe walls, high wooden beamed ceilings graced with medieval looking wrought iron chandeliers, oversized streamlined Italian furniture.

How could anyone be evil if they lived in a place like this? The decor maintained a relaxed elegance, while still comfortable and cozy. I sank into a dirt colored, distressed leather couch and felt like I would be happy to stay forever. Facing the couch was a fieldstone fireplace with a sixty inch television above.

Cima sat on a club chair and put his feet up on a hassock covered in the same distressed leather as all the furniture in the room. The only colors were from mounds of pillows in bright tone and designs that I would bet were Peruvian. Callista was nowhere in sight, but I could still hear the chirp of her voice in the distance chatting with a more modulated Stella.

"I wanted you to meet my wife, Antonio. Then I could explain the whole story to you. See, Stella and I, we've been friends with Carlos for a long time, since he was a kid.

"His mother died and his father was a deadbeat. The kid ended up living with his grandmother. She did the best for him, but she was old and it was hard for her. He was a good kid dealt a bad hand. Stella and I, we never had kids. It wasn't an issue—just never happened."

Stella came in holding a tray filled with appetizers. I put several on a paper napkin and waited for Freddo to continue.

"I volunteered as a 'big brother' when we gave up hope for a family, I always liked kids so it was a pleasure for me.

"That's when I met Carlos. He was about twelve, just at the age when he could go either way, good or bad. I helped him find his way into the baseball game, encouraged him, and helped his grandmother financially when she needed it. Stella loved Carlos too. He and his grandmother often spent weekends and holidays with us, and he became like our son in many ways. When he married Felicity, we hoped he could start his own family, but it just didn't work out that way." He shrugged and looked away for a moment.

"And me, I got a bad reputation after I bought half ownership of a casino. Before that I was in real estate development. My partner in the casino wasn't a stand-up guy—did some bad things I didn't know about when I funded him. A lot of his shit rolled downhill onto me. I bought him out, but the damage had been done. Anyway, that's water under the bridge."

I wondered where this was going. Cima didn't have to impress me with his clean record. Why the confession and whitewash? My confusion must have showed.

"The thing is, our Carlos is the reason you're here."

He was finally getting down to the reason for our trip. "I told your boys, Mrs. Freedhoff didn't hire me to find Carlos...so I've not been trying...not my problem."

"Yeah, Punchy told me. Okay. So there wouldn't be any conflict of interest if I hired you to find him? Right?"

"I'd have to think about it. On the face of it, that's correct. But now you tell me, what is everyone's interest in Carlos? And why is your wife making believe she and Carlos went off together?"

"The police have had it in for me ever since the casino fiasco with my partner. I hear from some of my friends at the station the buzz is I've killed Carlos—for two reasons, the first being he's agreed to rat out Dr. Landsworth for providing him with enhancement drugs. A business with its office in one of my buildings and in which I have a substantial financial interest. However, nothing could be further from the truth.

"I am not now and never had any connection with illegal narcotics of any kind, neither recreational nor enhancement. Just not my thing. Sure, you can make a bundle in the drug trade, but the downside isn't worth it. You have to make deals with the cartels, get involved with all the lowlifes on the street...no way!

"The thing is, nothing Landsworth sells is illegal. Sure, it's supposed to enhance performance, but with vitamins and a few natural ingredients that sound like they may be illegal enhancements. But they are not. I actually encouraged Carlos to speak to the DEA. His willingness to meet with them was why his suspension from baseball was only a few months. After the truth and all the testing was made public, they acknowledged he hadn't done anything wrong."

Then he laughed. I looked quizzical until he continued. "I'll admit it. The whole thing was kind of a scam, but a legal one." He laughed again and leaned over to take a couple of snacks. "The free publicity Carlos, Landsworth and I got for the vitamin business was worth a fortune. My idea, and I'm pretty proud of it.

"But when Carlos went missing, my plan backfired. Because the funding for the vitamin business came from me and Landsworth, Carlos too as a silent partner, everyone assumed we were angry at Carlos for working with the DEA. We became the main suspects in his disappearance, but without a body, there could be no murder charges.

"Neither Landsworth nor I have any idea where Carlos is now, and we're both worried. He wouldn't have run off with some chippie. He'd have let someone know where he was. This isn't like him at all. Sure, he's a player and likes the ladies, but a disappearing act is way out of character for him."

The more I listened to Cima, the more my head spun. Convoluted was too mild a word, maybe Byzantine was better.

Lucky for me, Callista came in the room. She had been eavesdropping for a few minutes before interrupting. "Stella says we'll eat in ten minutes so you guys better wind things up."

Freddo nodded to her before continuing. "The only way we could keep the cops off my back about Carlos was to invent a story that he and Stella took off together. I'm supposed to be okay with their leaving because now I'm having an affair with Felicity. We keep the story alive by going out together in public and putting on a little show from time to time. You know, holding hands, a little public smooching. Meanwhile, we're all calling in our markers everywhere we can to see if we can find out where Carlos is. So far, no luck."

He turned and threw a kiss at Stella in the kitchen. I could see the love in both their eyes.

She came over, gave him a hug, and picked up the conversation. "This is becoming wearing on all of us. I feel like a prisoner in this house. There are things I'd like to do outside the walls. I might be a homebody at heart, but too much is too much."

Cima nodded agreement. "Look, I'm a businessman. I made a bundle in real estate. When the market went nuts, I sold at the right time. Stella and I, we have more money than we'll ever spend in this life- time.

"We have no kids. We love Carlos, but he's made his own fortune. Antonio, I'm being straight with you, I've got no horse in this race. Except I'm worried about Carlos. Stella is crying every night about where he could be." His hands were fisted in his lap like he had to control himself. He looked like he had lost his best friend and whether he was controlling anger or sorrow, I couldn't tell.

And just like that, I believed him.

CHAPTER TWENTY-NINE

Another New Client

We sat down for dinner at the Cima's. There was no way we were going to dislodge Callista before she had a chance to sample Stella's cooking...one foodie to another. The way her eyes closed in ecstasy when she ate the chocolate chip cookies told me my little sister was almost on the verge of the big-O!

Belvidere was having a hard time not laughing at Callista's reactions but I threw her a dirty look and she behaved. Belvidere also managed to clean her plate, go for seconds, then thirds. But who's counting?

As we left, Cima took my hand in both of his. "So, Antonio, you'll help me solve this problem? Unless I can find Carlos, Stella is stuck here in hiding and I'm being watched by the local cops. Any time now some agency is going to turn this over to the FBI as either a murder or a kidnapping. This is no way to live...and I miss my friend."

"I'll see what I can find out. Maybe nose around a little. If I think I can help, I'll get back to you. If there's nothing I can do, I'll tell you that too."

"Fair enough. I look forward to hearing from you. Let me know your fees and what you need as a retainer and I'll transfer whatever you want to your account."

The ride back home was uneventful. Punchy lost the attitude and he and Callista chatted together all the way. They were both NCIS fans and were hot and heavy into a discussion of Tony's love life as we pulled in front of our house. Not great, but it beat Scrabble talk.

I shook Belvidere, who had been once again sleeping on my shoulder, and we went inside. No nasty surprises this time. Two by fours were nailed over the dog flap and a new door was soon to be delivered.

Belvidere and I sat in the family room and mulled over our day at the Cima's while Callista entered Stella's recipes for pot roast and chocolate chip cookies into her foodie database.

"Do we have anything with Carlos's scent on it?" Belvidere asked.

"No, but I'm sure we can get something from either the Cimas or Freedhoffs. I'll go tomorrow and ask Felicity or Mrs. Freedhoff. Do you have an idea you want to share?"

"I've got a buddy I work out with at the gym...he's part bloodhound...owes me a couple of favors. I'll ask him if he's got some free time to sniff around...see what he can find."

"What do you have in mind and where?"

"Didn't you say the last time Carlos was seen was at dinner with Mrs. Freedhoff?"

"Yes. What's your point?"

"Has anyone figured out where he went afterwards?"

"I don't know. We might ask Sol what the file at Missing Persons has to say."

"I'd like you to talk to Gupta too. I think he knows more than he's saying. He's very protective of the family, but if you ask him when Mrs. Freedhoff is present, she might be able to make him say things he wouldn't otherwise reveal."

"Good idea. I'll call and make an appointment to stop by tomorrow. It will also give me a chance to ask her if she has a problem with us working with Cima. I wouldn't think so, but then I'll have an excuse to ask about Carlos' last night at the mansion. And at the same time, ask if she has something with Carlos' scent. You can contact your friend."

Callista finished with her computer. After sitting in on the discussion for the last hour I saw she was frowning. "Hey kiddo, what's up with you? You look like there's something on your mind. Spill."

"I've been listening to you both and agree with your plans, but I still think we're missing something. If we want to find Carlos, don't you think we need to look into that quack doctor, Dr. Landsworth...the guy who got him suspended? No matter what Cima says, he might have a real grudge against Carlos for turning states evidence. If anyone might want to get rid of him, it seems to me Landsworth would be the one."

"According to Cima," I said, "it was all part of a plan to get publicity for Landsworth's new vitamin line. Supposedly, there was never anything illegal in Landsworth's regimen for Carlos. Still, let's check him out to make sure."

"So far, we don't know anything about Landsworth. Certainly not enough to cross him off our suspect list." She put her index finger to her cheek to think for a moment. "It also will verify what Cima's told us."

As usual, my little sister goes to the heart of the matter. She was right, we shouldn't just take Cima's word for it. Someone had to take a look at Landsworth. "Okay, what do you suggest?"

"I was thinking Belvidere might be in the market for some diet pills and could pay a visit to the good doc with her little dog." She looked over at Belvidere who seemed suitably peeved at the idea of needing diet pills. "So, what do you think, big sister?" Callista couldn't keep the mocking tone out of her voice.

When Belvidere didn't answer, Callista continued. "We could put you in one of Mom's old muumuus and stuff you a little around the waist...maybe stick a few weights in your shoes?"

"My weight is just fine, thank you, I don't need any pills...and for your information, muscle is much heavier than fat." It's hard to understand Belvidere when she speaks through clenched teeth.

"Hey, we need some excuse to get in there. I sure wouldn't be able to pass for needing human growth hormones or weight loss pills...well maybe I could say I was a gymnast and was in the market for steroids? I'm willing, but then how will we get you in to look through his files, and would you know what to look for?"

"Okay, you've made your point. I get it. I'm just a big fat dummy."

My competent and reserved sister is quite often lacking in humor. Like all of us, she has buttons that shouldn't be pushed. This was one of those times. Callista was dangerously close to a big red one that screamed "don't touch."

I decided to intercede before Bel's fur was further ruffled. "Ladies, I have an idea. Why doesn't Bel say she's in training for a television show where they do Ninja and strength feats. You know, those shows that dump contestants in the water if they can't get through the next obstacle. Then she can go as herself and her story is still believable." Bel looked mollified, her scowl lifted. She nodded her head in agreement.

Callista, however, couldn't contain a smirk. Even I was tempted to smack her, not hard mind you, just a mild 'thwack' to bring her to heel.

The next morning, Belvidere showed up for breakfast in a navy blue track suit with white stripes at the sides and matching running shoes.

Callista was wearing a black leather collar with dangerous looking metal spikes all around. Her peace offering to Belvidere. The Ninja ploy might have worked, but Bel was not thrilled to carry a poufy little canine around with her. Even if the beast happened to be her little sister in dog.

The collar had been a disguise for Callista a few years back. Dad had shaved her down almost to her bare skin and put the collar on so she could go undercover as a Chihuahua. He was working a problem for a Mexican banker. But I digress.

They took the Range Rover and were off early in the morning to Dr. Landsworth's office in the San Fernando Valley.

Belvidere had made an appointment to talk about building up her strength for the TV appearance. Hopefully, Callista would have the time to look at some of his files. If she couldn't get any information, then she might be able to unlock a window so she could get back in at a later date if a more thorough search might be needed.

As I was opening the garage door, my cell rang. Sol.

"Just got a call from the CSIs. They matched the bullets in Gabriel to the gun hidden in Bobby's closet. Only Bobby's fingerprints on it. Looks like he shot Gabriel and must have stolen the red bag Belvidere found in Moroney's room."

I didn't say anything, but the news also solved both the mystery of the shadow in the alley at the Eichler house and the cross-trainer footprints in the kitchen.

"There are still a lot of knots to be unraveled, but we're working on them." All I heard was dead air for a moment before he clicked off.

CHAPTER THIRTY

Croissants, Turbans, And Sweat

By ten AM, Mrs. Freedhoff and I were eating warm croissants and sipping coffee while enjoying the sun shining on the Pacific. The sea-gulls were back overhead swooping down in search of breakfast when I began.

"I wanted to update you on several things. The Sheriff's Office has a suspect in custody for Bobby's murder. It appears to have happened in a fight over the blackmail money. They are not clear how Bobby was involved. The shooting might have been an accident, or part of the commission of a crime—a felony murder. When they know more, I'll keep you informed.

"But what is more to the point, the gun used to kill Gabriel, 'your friend' was found in Bobby's closet. The Sheriffs are working to put all these pieces together."

"Good, I knew you'd be the right person to help me out."

"But there is something else. Mr. Cima would like to hire me to find Carlos. I told him I'd speak to you about it first and see if you consider it a conflict of interest?"

"I thought Mr. Cima was being looked at as a possible suspect in Carlos' disappearance?"

"The police do consider him a person of interest, but after speaking to the man and hearing his end of the story, I'm convinced he genuine-ly wants to find Carlos as much as you do. If you would like, I could arrange a meeting between the two of you, whatever would make you comfortable."

"I might like to meet with him in the future, but for the moment, what's of more interest to me is how he convinced you."

Then I filled her in on the events of our meeting the day before. When I finished, she drew back into the chaise longue until only her face showed, her hands under the fluffy throw, and her color as pale as her surroundings. I watched her think for several moments until she re-emerged from her coverings. "You are sure he has only good inten-tions towards Carlos?"

"Yes. I am. Especially since he assured me he was the one who convinced Carlos to testify against Dr. Landsworth. Cima had nothing to do with the illegal drug business. When you meet Stella Cima, you'll see how silly the idea is that she and Carlos were having an affair. She thinks of Carlos like her son, and is worried sick about him."

"I trust your instincts, Antonio. I agree you should take the case for Cima. When you have more information, I would appreciate meeting with him and his wife. Just not quite yet." She was still and silent again, but this time she didn't withdraw into her throw while she stared at the gulls and the ocean. I wondered what she was thinking, but didn't ask. By now I understood if she wanted me to know what she thought, she'd tell me.

After a moment, she looked me in the eye. "How can I help?"

"I'd like to know who the last person was to see Carlos before he disappeared. You told me you both had dinner together. Was there anyone else in the house? Who saw him leave?"

"Gupta, you let him out, didn't you?"

"Yes, Madam, I did." He gave his little hand twirl.

"Was there anyone else around?" I asked.

He looked uncomfortable. He stiffened and I smelled his body odor change from comfortable to fear sweat.

"I'd rather not say."

"Gupta, you must tell Mr. Pudel what you saw. Who was here? Mrs. Etcheveria was gone for the weekend, wasn't she?"

"Yes. She was not around."

"Well then, speak up. Where was Bobby, the other staff? Who was there?"

"Bobby wasn't around when Mr. Carlos left. I had seen him go up to his room with Miss Moroney. But Bobby didn't come back down-stairs again."

"Spit it out Gupta! Where was Moroney when Carlos left?"

"She was in the hallway. Standing far enough back in the shadows to be almost hidden. But I saw her. When Mr. Carlos left, she fol-lowed him outside."

"That was easy, wasn't it? What happened next?" Gupta had with-held this information from her and she was angry.

"I don't know exactly, Madam. I saw Miss Moroney run over to Carlos. She jumped up and wrapped her legs around his waist—threw her arms around his neck. It took me by surprise and...I'm sorry, but I watched...didn't close the door all the way. Mr. Carlos yelled at her. He sounded angry, I couldn't make out the words. Then he pushed her off. Miss Moroney fell to the ground, he jumped into his car and spun gravel out the driveway. I closed the door so she wouldn't know I had been watching. She had to ring the bell to come back inside. When she came into the house she was making that loud humming noise of hers."

Sweat ran down his face, soaking the edges of his turban. The fear smell was strong. He was very afraid of Moroney. But he continued. "I don't think Miss Moroney knew I'd seen what happened. She just stomped into the house and up to her room. I locked up and went to bed.

"In the morning, when I came to get breakfast organized, I saw Mr. Carlos' room had been slept in. He must have come in late. It was not out of the ordinary for him. His running clothes were missing, so I figured he went for his morning run. Nothing stopped him from his usual workout."

I nodded at Mrs. Freedhoff. "So Carlos still lived here?"

"Most of the time. When he didn't stay overnight at one of his lady friends, or travel with the team."

"Was his presence a problem for Felicity?"

"Not at all. She had her own life and they had become friends more than lovers. It seemed to work for them both and...it was none of my business."

Gupta still looked uncomfortable. I smelled we didn't have the whole story from him yet.

"Where was Miss Moroney the next morning?"

"By the time I saw her, she was with Bobby. They came downstairs together in the afternoon, laughing. I have no idea how long they had been together." He looked over at Mrs. Freedhoff, afraid she'd be angry with him. She only nodded for him to continue, but I saw the tightening around her mouth.

"When I checked the rooms on my morning rounds, Miss Moroney was gone, but had slept in her bed. At least it was disturbed. I noticed her clock was on the bedside table. I did find it strange her alarm was set for four-fifty AM. Five AM was the usual time Mr. Carlos left the house to begin his workout. I'd never known her to get up so early before. Later, when she came down with Bobby, her clothes and shoes had dirt on them."

"Did Bobby have running shoes on too?" I asked.

"He had a fancy pair of cross-trainers he was proud of. They looked just like new to me. Paid a lot for them with his first pay check as I remember, he showed them off to all of us staff."

"Do you remember what size he wore?"

"No, but we can check, I haven't disposed of the things in his closet the sheriff didn't take. I think they are still there."

I wanted to confirm Bobby was the mystery man with the size eight cross-trainers. Sol had already figured he was the one who murdered Gabriel and had the gun to prove it now.

When we looked in his closet later, the shoes left behind were size eight, and there were the cross-trainers sitting neatly next to his dress shoes. The cross trainers had been worn, but there was no mud. "Has anyone been in here since the police left?" I asked.

"Once the tape was down, the room was cleaned and straightened up. The blood stains wouldn't come out. The carpets have been ripped up and new ordered."

"I don't remember these shoes being here when the police were searching."

"They weren't. When the maid cleaned Miss Moroney's room they were under the bed. I took then from her to put them back in Bobby's closet. When I had the all clear, they'd be disposed of with the rest of his belongings. Is there a problem?"

"No. Just interesting." I didn't want to say anything about the footprints I had seen at Gabriel's. I picked up the shoes and looked at the soles. There was no trace of mud, the sole configuration looked like the pattern I'd seen at Gabriel's, but there was no way I could prove it now

"Has the garbage been picked up yet?" I asked, hoping we might find some other clues to give some insight as to why Bobby went to Gabriel's home.

"Yes. It was picked up yesterday."

As I left the mansion and drove home, I began to put the pieces together.

Since Bobby was the one who killed Gabriel, the two of them could hash out his motive in hell.

But I had my own suspicions. Bobby was infatuated with Moroney and it was clear they were screwing each other..or whatever she wanted to do. When he followed her and saw the 'games' she played with Gabriel, Bobby might have misunderstood what was going on and tried to protect her. I shook my head. Sad. Misguided. But it fit. How was the poor love-smitten kid to know what nasty tricks they had been up to for years?

I'd call Sol and let him know what I found out. He already had the ballistics report on the gun taken from Bobby's closet and it matched with the bullets in Gabriel. Now there was no doubt in my mind, I could tie Bobby to the Eichler house—one problem solved.

But my meeting raised another problem. Did Moroney have something to do with Carlos' disappearance? How deep was the bitch involved in this whole mess? My nerves were on high alert when I thought of how I'd insisted on protecting her to the detriment of my sisters, forget about the trouble I was in. It was beginning to look like I'd made a seriously bad call on that one.

Later that afternoon I returned to the mansion. Mrs. Freedhoff was surprised to see me, and even more so when I handed her a small cell phone. "What on earth are you giving this to me for?" She asked.

"I want you to keep it charged and with you at all times. If it rings, it will only be me or my sister. Pick it up, please. Be assured we won't call unless it's important. My cell number is entered in there along with Belvidere's, our home, and the office. Here, I'll show you how to use speed dial."

She was a quick study and I was satisfied she knew how to use it.

"But why do I need this? You still haven't answered my question."

"Let's just say I might not want to have anyone eavesdropping on our conversations; or perhaps you might have an emergency. Things could become complicated now." She nodded, quietly took the phone and concealed it on her lap under the fur throw.

CHAPTER THIRTY-ONE

Time To Fess Up

As soon as I walked out of the mansion, I knew my moment of truth had arrived—time to tell Sol about finding Moroney at Gabriel's. Prepared to take my punishment and grovel for forgiveness, I called Sol and asked for a meeting. Preferably where we would be alone.

I was not looking forward to the conversation, but it had to be done. Callista didn't like holding out on him. At every chance, she hit me with: "What should we do about telling Sol?" She and Belvidere were upset about withholding information.

Sol knew I was holding something back. He'd been cool since I suggested someone check Gabriel's house. He'd sent me barbs, and I'd pointedly ignored them. We planned to meet at my office late in the afternoon. My goal was to make sure he was clear—this was all on me.

My sisters were having dinner in the San Fernando Valley with friends after snooping around Landworth's office. Sol and I would have the office to ourselves.

Sol arrived with a face like a thundercloud. My nerve began to fail, but I had to go through with it, even though I couldn't stop feeling like I was in the Principal's office confessing to one of many pranks. I had not been an easy teenager.

I began with what I hoped might be taken as a peace offering. "I've just come back from the Freedhoff mansion and have information for you, as well as something I've been holding out. I need to come clean, Sol, and apologize."

"Damn you, Antonio. I knew something was wrong. You and your sisters have been jumpy these last few days and your behavior was way off."

"Yeah, I know. They are both angry at me for not telling you everything. I was trying to protect our client then. Now I know I can't any longer." Then I related the conversation with Gupta, adding my speculation Moroney might have been involved in some way with Carlos' disappearance.

I told him everything—following the Hyundai to Gabriel's, Moroney going inside, the shots from the patio, the footsteps in the kitchen and taking a comatose Moroney back to the mansion. The more I spoke, the madder he got, but he sat silent and stewing. The only sound he made was an occasional sharp intake of breath.

When I told him we went back to the house, continuing our search for the red bag, he made a sound like steam hissing from a kettle. Then I told him we found Gabriel in the freezer, and Belvidere uncovered Moroney's gun down behind a recliner. I stopped for a moment and he exploded.

"You son of a bitch, I knew you were holding out on me. As soon as the guys found the stiff in the freezer, I could smell you were hiding something...but I thought you were smarter than...than all...this!" He spread his hands out as if grabbing an armful of disgustingly dirty laundry, and the expression on his face confirmed my thoughts.

"I know I should have told you, but I was sure Moroney hadn't done it. She was so stoned she was catatonic when we came into the patio, only seconds, maybe a minute and a half at the most, after the shots were fired. She was crouched in a lawn chair making her humming sounds. When she saw us, she started shaking like she was on a vibrating machine. I tried to get her up, but she was rigid and couldn't move." Sol's hissing had changed to deep sounds, like low growls.

I figured I better get it all out and not prolong the agony. "We checked her, Belvidere sniffed her and she had no gun residue on her hands. The girl was naked and when Bel dressed her, she said it was like trying to put clothes on a manikin, nothing would bend." I took a deep breath, hoping it wasn't going to be my last.

"I'm sorry, Sol. My sisters both kept telling me to give you all the details, but I kept ignoring them, or pushing them off. My thoughts were only about trying to protect the Freedhoff family. I don't know how I can apologize, but please understand, they had nothing to do with this. I am so sorry."

He cut me off. "Shut up. You'll have plenty of time to figure out how to apologize to the Judge. I'm taking you in and booking you for withholding evidence, perverting justice, evidence tampering, aiding and abetting a homicide, both leaving and hiding the scene of a crime, accessory to murder. I plan on going on with as many counts as I can throw at you—preferably enough for several life sentences."

I was speechless, then frozen as an icicle. He took his handcuffs out and turned me around. He was so fast, I didn't resist until I heard the click when they closed. "Aw come on Sol, you don't need to do this." And then we both flipped. Handcuffs don't mean much to a large dog and they slipped off as I backed away. I was still barking at Sol as I sprinted out of the house.

The huge Rottweiler-poodle mix chased me outside, showing his teeth and snarling. Once in the driveway, I stopped, mesmerized by the string of drool winding down out of the corner of his mouth. Then he lunged at me. We started off snapping and barking, jumping back and forth as if in mock attack, the way puppies do at play. But this was no play. I tried to get it into my head that my friend was serious and I was in real trouble. Maybe even facing a problem I couldn't solve.

Mouth open, his canines glinting, he launched himself at my flank, tearing off a patch of fur with some skin attached. I hopped backward in shock as blood flowered against my white fur. I showed my teeth and growled in warning. His message had been delivered and I got it loud and clear. I had trained for combat, human tactics useful when combined with the skill of a dog. None the less, an oversized poodle is no match for the brute strength of a rottie.

I could probably outrun him. Pondering my dilemma for a second too long, I felt powerful jaws close around my throat. It was the beginning of the kill. Next, he'd lift me off my paws and shake me until my neck broke.

There was only one way to end this with both of us alive. Sol was right. I had been wrong—all my fault.

Pulling away from him as far as I could, I twisted my hindquarters to roll over on my back. Only complete submission could save us. I offered him my unprotected belly—acquiescence to total dominance. The acknowledgement of the alpha male. More important to me, we were both still in one piece.

He stood with his front paws on my soft midsection and released my throat. Acceptance of victory. Turning his muzzle to the sky, he let out a yodeling howl. Just in case the rest of the world needed to know who the victor was. My fur stood on end at the sound.

As I felt his paws lift off my chest, I thought of my family. What of the effect my death might have had on Callista? The love of her life killing her brother in combat? It was unthinkable—too Shakespearian and too close a call.

We flipped back to human. "Sol, you win. I'll go with you. Do you really need the cuffs?"

His face was stern as he picked up the steel rings and opened them again to put on me. "You have the right to remain silent, anything you say can and will be used against you in a court of law. You have the right to retain counsel of your choosing, if you can't afford an attorney one can be..."

Sol was reading me the fucking Miranda Warnings! I couldn't believe it. He continued reciting them as he pushed me in the back of his car and drove away. Sitting with my hands cuffed behind my back was painful. This was going to be a lot more serious than I had thought. I figured he'd yell then forgive me. Being a problem solver meant I had no law or private investigator's license to lose, but it didn't prevent me from serving time. I kept thinking of our family motto, but it didn't appear that any plea for forgiveness was going to work.

Many hours later, I had been booked on tampering with evidence, with the caveat more charges might be added in the future. My once cream colored Armani suit was dingy beige, my hair greasy and lank, and I felt like shit while I sat in the holding cell awaiting someone to discover I was missing, and pay my bail. I could dream, couldn't I?

After giving up hope anyone would come for me, at least until the morning, I stretched out and tried to catch up on my rest. I figured a blond man might need to be in top form if put in with the general prison population. Surprisingly, I was still in my own clothes, even though my wallet, cell phone and everything in my pockets were taken and locked away.

If Sol was trying to teach me a lesson, it was working. I promised myself I would never in this lifetime hold out on him again.

My biggest fear was flipping. When I wanted to control a flip, I could do so most of the time. But there was always the possibility I might flip from stress or fear. Since I am a dog by nature, the fight or flight adrenaline rush could turn me into a poodle in a heartbeat. A white poodle in a prison yard was something I couldn't even contemplate. Would I be skinned for my fur, cut open to see what made me tick, eaten, or taken under someone's wing as a pampered pet? And what would happen when I flipped back? I was a freak show in the wrong place.

After finally falling asleep, I felt someone shaking me. The angry eyes of Sol looked down at me. "OK Antonio, your bail has been paid and you're free to go after you come with me and make a full statement.

"I want to know exactly what happened at that house in Thousand Oaks when you were there the first time. Then what you saw when you went back again. Now!" He kicked at the cot with his foot, and from the expression on his face, I could tell he wished it was me he kicked. I was his friend and I had held out on him, put his job in jeopardy, betrayed his trust. Talk about feeling awful. I wished it had been me he kicked.

The idea of being grilled by Sol for more hours was not my idea of a good time, but my alternative was not getting out until my hearing, which could take several days.

We sat in an interrogation room. This time I was on the wrong side of the glass while Sol did the questioning. I wondered who was on the other side, where I had sat a few days ago listening to Blaine's skillful approach.

Sol's was more direct. "I want you to tell me in minute detail everything you did and everything you saw, took, moved or heard. Leave out nothing...not a scent, a sound, or a word. Am I understood?"

"Yes, sir." I was determined to be a good witness and told him everything, including how my sisters had begged me to call him. This was my doing and I was determined to take full responsibility.

It was early the next morning by the time I made it outside. I was free. At least for the moment.

The sun was shining in my eyes when I saw a small, red haired woman, hands on her hips, a large black poodle sitting at her side. Both were silent next to a Mini Cooper. Neither one seemed very pleased to see me. My only greeting was a perfunctory: "Get in the car."

I got.

The ride home was like sitting in a vacuum, probably a first for Callista. No way was I going to break the silence. When we arrived at the house, I looked around and realized how much I missed the place even though I had only been away overnight; but it was an overnight that could be stretched out into a few years. My immediate need was to call my attorney and have him recommend a good criminal lawyer.

Crime was not my guy's specialty.

Still no words out of my sibs. After a long shower, I changed into old jeans and a sweat shirt. The kitchen seemed to be the place to go.

Wrong.

Standing behind the counter were both of my dear sisters, feet apart, arms crossed in front and faces wearing expressions that could have frightened Count Dracula. It was left to me to say the first word. I resorted to my old faithful. "What?"

"Did you know we were in the Sheriff's Office and grilled for hours as accomplices?" Belvidere started the conversation.

"...uh...no."

"Did you know we might also be facing charges of evidence tampering, obstructing a homicide investigation, breaking and entering at the Eichler house, accessories to murder after the fact, aiding and abetting?" Callista followed with her two cents.

"...ummm...no."

"Did you know we will be called as witnesses to testify against you if you are brought to trial?" This time the question was in unison. I always wondered how they could do that.

"Oh...shit no!"

"Can you imagine what Mom and Dad will say when they get home and find out all their children are jailbirds?"

"Were you both in jail too?"

"Not in cells, in interrogation rooms...different ones."

"Okay, bad enough. I'm so sorry you have no idea. You both have my sincere apology. I thought I was doing the right thing by our client. I was wrong—should have told Sol everything right from the start."

"You got that right." Callista angry I never wanted to see, but she was in my face. "Sol is so mad at me for not telling him—I'm not sure he'll ever forgive me. He won't talk to me and won't pick up when I call him...won't even answer my texts."

There was a shine of tears in her eyes that broke my heart. When I looked down, her fists were clenched. Her voice was hard as she continued. "I was interrogated by someone named Blaine. Sol had nothing to do with it, but I'll bet he was looking through the one-way glass...the bastard!"

My eyebrows raised. Never before had she said anything bad about Sol...ever! I sent a silent prayer to the Big Dog in the sky for them to forgive each other. Me...well, I was getting what I deserved.

Belvidere glared at me. "Blaine was kind enough to whisper that we get separate lawyers and split the cases if we get charged. We've already hired our own criminal attorneys, Callista and I. You'll have to get one too...makes the state go through three separate trials. You have any idea what they charge?" Her voice had changed to icy steel.

I shook my head...no idea.

Callista took up the cry. Needlessly spending money for attorneys was not her idea of an appealing use of our fees. "Well, Mr. Smart Guy, compute this—we'll be paying at least three times seven hundred dollars an hour...for as long as it takes.

"Belvidere and I voted. This is your pile of ka-ka and all the legal fees come out of your share." This time Callista's foot stomp wasn't invisible as she turned and left me to face the wrath of Bel.

Expecting more yelling, I was surprised when Belvidere looked at me. Her dark eyes were filled with sorrow rather than anger. Silent, she turned around, and shrugging her shoulders, walked away.

I was left standing alone in the kitchen.

The oven timer rang, breaking the silence. Three chicken pot pies Callista had baked for lunch were ready. I turned off the oven and put the pan with the pies on the stove top. I took one and put it on a plate, figuring I better eat something while I had the chance.

When I bit into the pie it felt like sawdust in my mouth.

CHAPTER THIRTY-TWO

Dr. Landsworth

When I came back to the home office after slinking out for a good workout and a spa lunch as penance, my sisters were in the kitchen devouring a container of triple chocolate gelato. I had to horn in quickly before there was none left.

There is a family addiction to ice cream as the cure-all for excitement, sadness, jealously, and getting over anger...you get what I mean. When there was nothing more left all three of our muzzles were sticky with sugar and cream. We took time out for a shower before reconvening to go over our various discoveries the day before. I could tell they were still miffed at me, but they were trying to be rational.

I related my meeting with Mrs. Freedhoff. Both my sisters had ah-ha looks on their faces when they heard Moroney had been lurking around when Carlos went missing.

While there was nothing linking her to any crime, we were sure Moroney had committed at least several. Who knew what her involvement could have been with Carlos. I admitted the truth to myself and my sisters: finding out this information had been the catalyst for my confession to Sol.

Belvidere and Callista had been seated in the waiting room of the Landsworth office. A television playing a looped series of promotional videos for Landsworth's new line of vitamin based diet and wellness products was their only entertainment. Basically, the products all contained vitamins mixed with several exotic forms of herbal, root and berry extracts. The main ingredient—an elixir made from a root found in the Andes.

When combined, the pitch claimed results mimicked mammalian chorionic gonadotropin, the hormone pregnant mammals produced to turn fat into nutrients for the fetus, and androstenedione, or andro, the hormone produced by the adrenal glands in mammals.

Landsworth's products were all based on this exotic herbal combo.

The advertising called the root an amazing discovery, a way to safely enhance performance without the deleterious side effects of steroids.

After watching the promotional pieces, Belvidere fired up her tablet. A few minutes of sleuthing on the internet turned up exclusions to the Anabolic Steriod Control Act of 2014. It clearly provided "that a substance shall not be considered to be a drug or hormonal substance that is considered to be an anaboloic steroid if it is: (1) an herb or other botanical...etc," Landsworth's products sounded sexy and enticing, but since they contained only herbal and vitamin ingredients, they were no more than over-the counter supplements under the purview of the FDA, not steroids or drugs under the DEA regulations. Cima was right.

While they were still in the waiting room, Callista had suddenly let out a loud yip, and Bel turned back to the television. There was Carlos, giving a recommendation for several of the products. It was the first time they had ever seen him out of uniform and a ball cap. Callista had nudged Belvidere's ankle. Belvidere understood. "Yes, he is very handsome. No wonder all the women like him." Callista gave a low growl in response.

Belvidere's meeting with the doctor was uneventful but informative.

"So, Ms. Pudel, how can I help you? You surely don't need anything for weight loss, you are one of the finest looking specimens of womanhood I've seen lately." Bel started to turn feisty until she realized his statement was said with deadpan professionalism. He was gay. No other man would consider being seen in public with a Lily Pulitzer bow tie and bleached blonde hair. She looked down on the top of his head. He couldn't be more than five foot three or four, and she was wearing high heeled boots. Actually, he was sort of cute, she thought. In a Callista-like way. She repressed the urge to pick him up and give him a little cuddle, as if he were a little man-toy. She stopped in time. Scaring him wasn't part of the plan.

She had put Callista down on the floor and looked the doctor in the eye, not easy as she had to scrunch down to his height. "Don't worry, my dog is perfectly trained, she will not soil your office."

The doctor swallowed, clearly intimidated. "I am sure you have trained the little darling to perfection. However, the state health laws don't allow me to permit a dog on my premises, other than a service animal, of course, but why don't we overlook the law this one time, shall we?" He put a hand on his pristine lab coat and struck a pose.

Yes, gay. Callista stopped sniffing his shoes and trotted over to sniff in an open bottom file drawer. She obviously had discovered all she needed to know about the good doctor.

Landsworth looked at the little dog near his files.

"She does not chew anything either. Sit, Callista." Callista sat, and turned an annoyed muzzle up to her sister. The spikes on her collar glinted in the bright overhead lights.

"That is quite an interesting collar for such a little dog." The doctor said. Callista bared her teeth and growled. The doctor jumped.

"She was a gift. I don't like little dogs. I would have preferred a pit bull." Belvidere was enjoying her part of tough athlete, playing it to the hilt.

"Oh, I see." The good doctor shrank back a bit. Callista kept the game going with a convincing snarl.

"So Dr. Farnsworth, oh, sorry, I mean Landsworth, what would you suggest as a regimen to give me an edge. I've been chosen to compete in a television contest, one of those American Ninja things requiring exceptional physical abilities. I'll need every bit of strength and endurance I can muster. My friend, Carlos Etcheveria, suggested I speak with you—you are highly recommended by him."

"Umm, yes, Carlos. We've had our difficulties these days. He did so well using my vitamin and herbal hormone line that he's been suspended by the league. They can't seem to understand all the new discoveries in medicine today and what they can do to help athletes perform. But that's a discussion for another time. Let's get back to your situation, shall we?"

Callista had her nose out of the file drawer and was examining several stacks of flyers piled on the floor in a corner of the office.

"Ms. Pudel, if you would please remove your outerwear, and put on the gown I've left for you on the chair, I'll be back in a few minutes. I'd like to examine your musculature and bone structure to come up with the right combination of nutrients. I tailor a plan specifically for each of my athletes." He offered a moué and a sly wink as he slipped out the door to the hallway.

Once he left the room, Callista took several flyers and other papers in her mouth and handed them to Belvedere who stashed them in her big handbag. Callista then jumped on the stool the doctor had vacated, and up on the examination table. "Push his computer over closer to me so I can get to it while you undress."

Belvidere changed into the gown while tiny paws moved over the computer keys. Callista gave a few grunts, moans and snarls. Belvidere took off Callista's collar and plugged the tiny flash drive hidden in the leather lining into the computer. Callista pushed a few more keys and the information was downloaded into the flash. A short knock on the door announced the doctor as Belvidere stowed the flash back into the collar and Callista jumped from the computer onto her lap. As the doctor entered, Callista vaulted back on the floor and sat next to Belvidere's oversize handbag.

"I see your dog is not only well behaved, but also very attached to you." The doctor gave her a wide grin to show he also liked dogs. "Now, if you will please lie back on the table we shall proceed."

An hour later they exited the posh reception area while yet another celebrity extolled the value of the doctor's vitamin and hormone supplements from the television loop. Callista trotted along on her leash and Belvidere toted a large shopping bag filled with close to a thousand dollars worth of supplements—a month supply only. There would be no discussion. That bill would soon be on their expense account.

The moment they arrived home, Callista popped the flash drive into her office computer and the whole story was revealed. Two web addresses seemed to her like odd combinations to be corresponding: 'Fantasy Baseball Team All-Stars' and another called 'Daisy Designs For Cats & Dogs.'

By the time I joined them, Callista was bursting with information. She had hacked into e-mail accounts under each name. How she had figured out both web sites were bogus was typical Callista.

I couldn't help smiling as I listened to her explain her thought process. "When I checked the history on Landsworth's browser, Daisy Designs stood out."

I listened as she continued. "There was no way Landsworth would have Daisy's Designs For Dogs & Cats on his office computer when all his other files were strictly business related. There had to be another reason. The web site opened with professional photography of dogs and cats in various attire—pretty nice designs, several party dresses, a smoking jacket you'd look good in." She nodded at me, knowing full well I do not like the idea of clothes for animals. She smirked when she continued, "...a party dress with tulle ruffles that would look great on me. Nothing for Belvidere, unless the black leather motorcycle jacket with spikes modeled by a pit bull came in her size."

Belvidere threw her a nasty look from across the room but kept her muzzle shut. She was used to barbs from her little sister and generally ignored them. This one was deserved, she had insisted Callista wear the spiked collar to the doctor's office, and not just because it had the secret compartment for the flash drive.

"After a little more work with the help of a program I'd been given as a present—remember the boxer-poodle mix named Bosco...hacker by profession? Anyway, I had Landsworth's password and was into the Daisy e-mail accounts. It didn't take a genius to figure out Carlos was the owner of the Fantasy Baseball site Daisy corresponded with regularly."

Carlos and Landsworth had set up proxy servers for their correspondence through the bogus web sites, but my sister is a pretty good hacker and traced their messages. I listened while she continued.

"I've made copies of the e-mails for you both to study in detail. Landsworth had originally given Carlos illegal amounts of the anabolic-androgenic steroids, but Carlos had a negative reaction to them. Then Landsworth heard of a recently discovered Andean root that claimed similar results. Bingo! Whether it was in his mind, or actual enhancement, Carlos was performing better. If the combination worked on his system, maybe it would work on other athletes."

Belvidere opened the shopping bag and lined up the products they had bought. Nine bottles stood across the kitchen counter like soldiers at attention. As Callista continued, Belvidere began to silently read the instruction pamphlets for each product.

"If the products actually worked, they were sitting on a goldmine. A legal way to provide athletes with performance enhancements without any of the nasty side effects like 'roid rage or limp dicks."

Callista stopped for a moment to giggle. "There was a lot of correspondence about that, by the way. Carlos and the good Doc were carefully monitoring sexual performance. Carlos was sure his was enhanced.

"In any event, they joined forces to create and promote a new line of legal supplements they could market everywhere. Landsworth had a good practice, but not enough money to finance this type of under-taking, so Carlos and Cima got together to help bankroll the project." Callista was gleeful about having put all the pieces together.

So was I. "All right, I get the picture. So that's how Cima got in-volved with the whole enhancement investigation. But how did they get from selling vitamins to enhancement drugs and the DEA investi-gation? Aren't vitamin supplements overseen by the Food and Drug Administration and outside of the purview of the Drug Enforcement Administration?"

"Yes. They planned the whole thing as a scam. It was Cima and Carlos' idea. Carlos wanted to take a little time off from the game. Af-ter playing for eight years he was burned out. He'd breach his contract if he just walked in and said he wanted time off. But, if he was 'outed' for using enhancement drugs, he'd be suspended during the investiga-tion. He'd test clean so he wasn't worried about breach of contract or being kicked out of the game permanently.

"While the investigation went on, he'd have time off. Actually, he wanted to spend more time with both the Cimas, Felicity and Mrs. Freedhoff—seems he's a family man at heart."

"You mean they planned the suspension?" I felt I was trying to make my way out of a labyrinth this was so twisted.

"Yes. Carlos outed himself. He convinced Landsworth to make an anonymous call to the DEA from a burner phone. I can't wait to show you the e-mail, the poor doc was terrified. Anyway, he dumped the phone in the ocean afterwards. Within a week, Carlos was paid a visit by the DEA. He invited them in and suggested they test him. He handed them all the supplements he was taking and the investigation went on from there."

"Weren't they afraid of the bad publicity?"

"No. They wanted it. Cima had someone tip off the media. Free publicity—the reason for the whole scam. Think of the fortune they'd have spent to get the coverage Carlos received from the investigation. His name has been blasted daily from every television and headlines on every paper in the country. Now he'll be the spokesman for the new products and there isn't a living soul in the country who doesn't know who he is...and his stats show the products worked."

Damn, I thought. They were good! It skated the line for disaster, but if it worked, they'd all make a fortune.

Belvidere and I poured over everything on the counter to see what the good doctor had recommended. We read the labels, the inserted directions, and puff pieces so veiled it would be impossible to say they hadn't lived up to their claims. Callista was at her computer and unusually silent as we pawed and sniffed through the bottles and pills. Then she shouted, "I've got it!"

"So what have you got?" Belvidere asked before I could get the words out.

"I've got SEC filings on Edgar, the Securities and Exchange Commission website. Dr. Landsworth is part of a public offering—a new company selling a line of herbal enhancements and vitamins. The business will start with a multi-level marketing scheme. They've begun the paperwork for the initial offering. Here, look, he's already got filings on-line. And check out the Board of Directors."

Carlos—a director. Of course. For a moment I thought he'd be a bad choice with a police record, but he hadn't been charged with anything and actually, his record was clean. The Baseball Commissioner suspended him, but it was only a token. Even the publicity was good. When the vitamin/herbal hormone combo enhanced his performance sufficiently to cause an investigation, it had proved the supplements delivered what they claimed.

All the pieces of that puzzle fell into place. Carlos cooperated fully with the DEA because he knew they couldn't prove there were any illegal hormones in products Landsworth gave him. All they'd found were herbal supplements and vitamins The end result absolved him of any wrongdoing, and the case was dropped.

Landsworth was never going to be indicted. The whole thing would go away by the time Carlos' suspension was over. A tempest in a teapot stirred up solely to make Landsworth and Carlos a lot of money, and Cima along with them. They had taken a big chance and it seemed to be working. But where was Carlos?

"What a convoluted plan. I don't think they've crossed the line into anything actionable, certainly not worth any legal proceedings."

"I've skimmed through almost all the correspondence. There is no indication of any conflict between Landsworth and Carlos. They were just partners working together." Callista said.

"Are there current e-mails from Carlos?" This might be a trail we could follow.

"Only from Landsworth. Looks like Carlos stopped e-mailing about the time he went missing. Landsworth has tried to contact him every day since then asking him to reply. There are some papers Carlos has to sign for the SEC filings."

It was time call Sol. He was going to know about every move we made, even if it bored him to death.

The information gave me a new glimpse into Carlos—not only was he a charmer, he was also a cunning and smart risk-taker. No wonder Mrs. Freedhoff liked him so much.

Landsworth had no reason to do Carlos any harm—instead of being a detriment, Carlos was a crucial element to their scheme. I was pleased with this information for another reason, it confirmed what Cima told me.

But where the hell was Carlos? So far, all I had found out was that everyone who was supposed to want him dead was actually looking for him—and not to do him any harm. Who had a motive?

I don't remember much about that night, other than lying in bed, wondering where Carlos could be and who could have wanted him gone.

But those thoughts were pushed aside by the constantly repeating worry of figuring out how many hours it would take to keep us all out of jail if Sol made good with his threats. How would I pay legal fees at twenty-one hundred an hour? The worst part of the nightmare was, I couldn't blame Sol. I brought this on myself.

In the morning, I woke coiled up in my sheets like a mummy. As I disentangled myself from their confining folds, I had to appreciate the aptness. If I couldn't fix this problem, as far as my family was concerned, I'd really be dead.

CHAPTER THIRTY-THREE

Another Piece Of The Puzzle

Belvidere called her part bloodhound friend to find out what he'd need to track Carlos the day he disappeared. She gave me a list of possible items to collect.

I went back to the Freedhoff mansion and left with Carlos' toothbrush, a tee shirt with sweat stains Gupta found stuffed in the back of his closet, and a pair of well-used workout shoes. There would be plenty of scent for her friend from the shirt and shoes. The toothbrush I sealed in a baggie for DNA in case Sol might need it.

I explained to Mrs. Freedhoff what we planned to do. Without asking for an explanation as to the 'why', she gave me permission to bring in a team to search the grounds.

Mrs. Freedhoff had also received a call from Sol. She could send someone to pick up her money. The bag was still needed for evidence, but the money had been checked for fingerprints and scanned. It was no longer needed. Gupta would pick it up later in the day.

I called home to let them know we had permission to search the grounds around the mansion and down the old road to the docks below. Gupta told me it was the side of the estate where Carlos liked to run.

By the time I arrived back home, Belvidere had reached Sol. She was the only one of the family who appeared to not be in the shithouse with him. I listened to their conversation on speakerphone.

"Antonio has permission from Mrs. Freedhoff to search the property, especially the areas where Carlos usually ran."

"Who are you using for the search? Orvill?"

"Yes, he's agreed to come and help us out. I'll pick him up early tomorrow morning."

"Okay. He's a good choice. I'm going to leave you to it, but ask him to give me a call when he's finished. If he finds anything, he'll know what to do." There was a short pause. "I trust him." Emphasis on the 'him.'

I heard the phone go dead on the other end. Crap! I got that message loud and clear.

Both sisters gave me dirty looks. I wondered how long it would take me to get out of the doghouse with them.

At dawn the next morning, Belvidere's Range Rover rumbled its way back into our garage. The back door opened and a soulful looking fellow entered with her. She introduced him as Orvill. He stuck out a rawboned hand, gave me a more than hearty handshake, and tipped his wide brimmed Stetson at Callista.

The fellow was tall, at least two, maybe three, inches on me, and when he walked, all his extremities seemed to have a mind of their own as to what direction they chose to move in. I'd heard the expression 'loose-jointed' before, but this was the first time I'd seen it in action. I raised my eyebrows at Belvidere as they walked in the office.

"Orvill is the friend I told you about. When he flips, he's a blood-hound-poodle cross." She tossed the information at me nonchalantly.

Okay, if she said so, but it was a new cross-breed on me. I knew all about goldendoodles, labradoodles, yorkiepoos and maltipoos. What would that cross be called? Bloodydoodle? Doodle-hound. Bloody-poo...gross! I gave it up.

The genetic combination did explain Orvill's demeanor. His face was long and mournful. Once he took off his hat, dark rust and brown hair couldn't seem to make up its mind if it wanted to curl or stick out straight all over his head. 'Straight' might be winning, because he had tried to slick it down and several cowlicks refused taming.

I had to admit he was well built—broad shoulders tapered to narrow hips, tight butt and a long torso. A well-defined six-pack was visible through his army-green tee-shirt. Slim fit extra long Wranglers and well worn Ropers. Clearly a country boy, but also a fine looking stud. Wonder where Belvidere found him? She probably won't tell me.

When Orvill spoke, his deep voice was as mournful as he looked. "Bel, she tells me you need to see if some trace is left from a few weeks back. Pretty hard by now with the rains we've had, but if who you're looking for passed any spots rain didn't hit, I might get a scent. I've also trained as a cadaver dog, so if there are remains anywhere in the vicinity, don't you worry, I'll find them too."

I liked that he got right down to business. "Sounds good to me. We have a good paying client so let me know what your rates are and we'll have a deal."

"Oh, don't you worry none 'bout that. Bel and me, we go way back. She's promised me a romp and a rack 'a ribs at our favorite barbeque joint later on, so I think we're more'en even." The sad look disappeared as a radiant smile crossed his face. I was almost blinded by large white teeth and eyes that twinkled as he looked at her. Uh-oh! If that wasn't love, I don't know what was.

Interesting. Now I see. They go way back? They romp? Our favorite barbeque joint? He called her 'Bel.' I looked over at my sister, who, for the first time in memory, had turned bright red. You are so busted baby! Now I know where she's been going all these years.

But why haven't we met him before? He didn't seem to have anything wrong with him. No sign of being a criminal, gang member, drug dealer. Maybe a retired bull rider was the worst I could come up with.

"So, Bel, where did you and Orvill meet?" I couldn't restrain a little snarky smirk. After all I'd been through, it was time to give a teeny bit back.

Orvill took over. "I'm surprised she hasn't brought you and little sister along. We've been taking western swing lessons for the last few years. Before that, we did a little line dancing, and before that, the two-step." He shook his shoulders and stood a little taller. "We're in training now for a swing competition. You'll have to come and cheer us on." A true country gentleman, Orvill had put one of his extra-long arms around her shoulders. He was going to save her? My tough sister who saved everyone else?

My big sister Belvidere—western swing?—line dancing?—two-step? Next a swing competition? No way! The woman always seen in black spandex and leather with a touch of bright colored silk? In a billowing western skirt and fancy dress boots twirling around a dance floor with Orvill.? It was impossible to picture. Had Callista known about Bel's secret life without telling me? Was my Parisian-cum-Matrix-urban-chic-leather-wearing sister actually a shit-kicker in disguise?

"Let us know when and where the competition is. We'd love to go, wouldn't we Callista?" The look I threw her was far from brotherly. Had she been holding out on me? But her eyebrows raised and she shrugged her shoulders. She was either a better actress than I thought or this was news to me too?

I turned back to Orvill. We had business to attend to, but Belvidere was going to have a lot to explain later. "Has Belvidere given you the shoes and tee-shirt?"

"Yes, there's plenty of trace. Let's hope the weather hasn't washed any trail away."

"Here is a new surveyor's map of the Freedhoff properties. Off to the south side of the mansion and down the cliff is a level area. Originally a dock, it had a warehouse for offloading merchandise shipped in from South America. The Freedhoffs were merchants in the import-export business in the 1800's. When the Long Beach and San Pedro ports opened, they ended the dock's use. It's become a ghost town of old offices, the warehouse abandoned, unused machinery for winching goods off the ships and loading onto ground transport. I've been told Carlos liked to run down the pier to the end. It's still standing and in fair shape. The rest is falling into ruin."

"How big is the whole area?" Orvill asked.

"From the survey, the area is about ten acres, buildings included."

"I've done bigger. I should be able to cover it in a couple of days, depending on the building's condition and if I can get around easily. I try to avoid cave-ins so I'm glad you and Bel will be with me." He smiled again, aiming it at her—this time she returned the favor.

"Our collars all have mics attached and I've got an extra one for you. Callista will not flip, she'll have a walkie talkie in the Range Rover and be our command post."

"Sounds to me like you have everything covered. Do the police know anything about what we're doing? I'm not keen on illegal searches."

"The police know, and we don't need a warrant—we're employed by the owner of the property and searching at her behest. You and Sol know each other, he's asked you to call him when you're finished."

"Sounds like all the bases are covered. Let's go to it then." Orvill let out a growl and a halfhearted bark as he turned into the biggest bloodhound I'd ever seen, outweighing my poodle body by at least twenty pounds. His black and rust colored coat had a glossy sheen, wavy and long, the only place I saw the poodle influence in him. Even with the typical drooping eyes, long face and longer ears, he was a formidable looking animal. I was beginning to understand what Belvidere saw in him.

CHAPTER THIRTY-FOUR

The Dock

We drove in Belvidere's Range Rover, Callista pulling the seat as far forward as it would go and putting a pillow behind her back. Large SUVs aren't the preferred vehicles for the height challenged.

The gate at the estate was already open for us and, rather than head for the house, we turned left across the manicured grounds to a dirt road running down toward the ocean through several twists and turns. The area was heavily wooded, the road practically overgrown. Tall trees spread branches draped with vines, creating a leafy roof overhead. Dense underbrush bordered each side of the deeply rutted road. Nature was making a fierce attempt to keep civilization at bay, reclaiming any encroachment on the silent forest.

I understood why Carlos liked to run there. It was probably cool in summer, and in winter offered solitude, a place for contemplation of the pitfalls in one's life. It was where I would have chosen to run too.

As we jounced further along I reflected on all I had learned about Carlos, the man and his sentiments, his childhood, his business acumen, and his prowess as an athlete. I found myself hoping he was safe and sound someplace; casting his lure into warm waters far away from where we were heading. But I couldn't get the empty, twisted feeling in my stomach to go away, no matter what fantasy I made up for the man.

Callista steered the Rover down a steep bumpy incline and the road ended abruptly. A large open area, once the back apron of the wharf shed where cargo was loaded onto waiting wagons for distribution, spread in front of us. Now the space was surrounded by rotting wood and broken rusted machinery. We parked, turned on our mics, tested the reception and began our search.

Orvill took the lead. We were to stay far enough back to not interfere with the scent trail he was tracking. Belvidere was in front of me, keeping at least ten yards behind Orvill's tail as it wove in and out of the long underbrush that was once the staging area.

Orvill was following a grid he created in his mind, and we followed in the paths he already trod. I found it tedious business, but neither of them showed any signs of flagging.

After about an hour, his tail stopped wagging, stood straight upright and didn't move. Belvidere whispered to me. "It means he's got something. We can get closer, but we have to keep to the previous tracks he made."

"Over here, check this out." He announced, nudging a plastic bottle with his nose.

"What have you found?" Belvidere asked.

"I found his scent on this water bottle. The wind must have tossed a board over it. It means he was here, but no time frame."

"Do you think the buildings might be of more interest? At least some area would have been kept out the rain." It seemed logical to me.

"Okay. It might be better than wasting more time outside."

The wharf shed was at least thirty feet tall, doors and windows gone from both time and vandalism. It stood empty but for some rusty machine parts and piles of blown in debris. Most of the tin roof had been ripped open to the sky, but places remained where the roof had held and the hard packed dirt beneath looked dry.

Orvill began to work his grid inside, tracking in straight lines from one side to the other. Belvidere and I sat on our haunches against what was left of a side wall, and watched his methodical pace. I felt certain, if there was something to find, Orvill was going to find it.

After a few minutes, I heard barking by the car. It wasn't Callista's high pitched yap, but it was familiar to me. Melissa? I left Belvidere and went outside.

Melissa and Callista were in conversation by the Rover when I got there. "Hi Babe! How did you find us?"

"How did you find my favorite running place is more the question? This is where I run all the time when you're not with me."

"So you're familiar with this area?"

"Well, like uh, ya! I, umm, you know, have been running here for years...like since I bought my house."

"Did you ever meet anyone else when you were running?"

"Sure, like, you mean Carlos? We ran together all the time. He always called me his secret blondie girl friend...not that he ever saw me as a real girl, so don't be getting jealous my poodle boy." She snuggled up to me and licked me on the cheek.

"You and Carlos ran together?" The coincidence was pretty amazing, but then, not so much when I realized how close her home was to the mansion. It never occurred to me before because I took different routes to each place. I do tend to compartmentalize my life—seldom letting one phase slide over into the others.

"Do you remember the last time you saw him?"

She looked off in the distance. I knew she was mentally calculating days by counting on her paws. I'd seen her do it before.

"It was about two weeks ago, I'm not sure exactly. When I felt like running with Carlos, I'd get up real early and come over here 'cause, I like, you know, had to be on his schedule. I watched him for a minute or so, like...you know, trying to decide if I was going to go over to him so we could run together.

"Then a woman came up to him. I guess she...like...had been following him a ways back. Carlos, he didn't look...like...you know, very happy to see her. I think they were, umm, fighting? He pushed her away, like he was real angry. She made this scary sound, deep in her throat, but...I donno...it like, reminded me of a rattlesnake...you know? I got out of there. Maybe she was his real human girl friend and they were having a quarrel. I didn't want to, intrude, and she was kinda' scary anyway. That was the last time I saw him. I've been missing him...you know...we had good times running. He'd talk to me about things, like I wasn't a dog, but, you know, as if I was a real person."

I felt deeply sorry for Carlos at that moment. Melissa's story and description made him more real to me than before. I understood this man, felt compassion for him too—a man who enjoyed running with a pretty dog—the only being he could truly confide in.

"Did you see where they were standing before you left?"

"They were near the shed, but outside...like over on the flat cement piece there." She assumed the stance of a pointer to indicate a space beneath the remains of a loading crane.

I ran back to the shed with Melissa behind me. After introductions, we told Orvill and Belvidere what she had seen. Orvill looked over at the crane with interest and went to check around it. He motioned to us to stay back in the shed where we had been and not move around.

He trotted around the crane, nose to the ground and then headed back into the shed and over to a pile of rotted wood and rusted debris. His tail straightened up again and he poked around for a minute or two before coming back to us.

"I've found something. There is a cadaver in the pile of debris over by the crane, and maybe more than one.

"It's time for you to call the Sheriff's office...tell Sol what I found." Then he flipped back to Orvill, and beamed his big smile at Belvidere. "If they want me to sniff around some more, I'll be happy to do so, but this is now officially a crime scene, and we need to leave without touching anything."

CHAPTER THIRTY-FIVE

More Than Met The Eye

While Orvill called Sol to describe his findings, I spoke with Mrs. Freedhoff. I knew our call wasn't going to be overheard on the new cell phone I had brought her. I was glad I had insisted she keep it with her at all times. Then I told her what we had found.

As her representative, I advised her to invite the Sheriff's Department to enter her property, and search anyplace they wished with no need of a warrant. She agreed to cooperate fully in their investigation. When I requested she not say anything to her family about our findings, or reveal the Sheriff's presence on the property, she had replied tersely. "I understand. Not even Gupta."

She asked to speak to Sol before he brought his team to the scene. I called him and set up a conference on my cell. As they spoke, I could hear her voice; firm, and probably how she had sounded when she managed her family corporation.

"Sheriff Jefferson, I suggest you bring in your team through the old trucking road leading directly to the wharf rather than through the estate grounds. If you have a survey at your disposal, you will find the entrance. A chain link fence and gate closes off the old road. You have my permission to break the lock and enter my property. Do you understand?"

"Yes Mrs. Freedhoff, I do. Thank you."

"If there is anything to be signed, Antonio is authorized to sign on my behalf."

"That won't be necessary, all calls are recorded so we have a record of your permission. Thank you for the offer. I appreciate your cooperation."

Sol requested the case as an adjunct to Bobby's murder since both were on the Freedhoff property. He arrived first. Sol greeted Orvill and the two of them walked the scene together, Orvill showing him his find. The two men had worked together on several cases when Sol needed to track a suspect or find a cadaver.

When the two men came back to the Range Rover, we filled Sol in on what we had learned.

Sol turned to Callista with an eyebrow raised. Belvidere and Orvill were standing side by side, looking very comfortable together. She gave him a 'not now' look and got back into the Rover. I looked at him and shrugged my shoulders. He hadn't said a word to me yet, and I knew he was still angry. I ignored the cold shoulder, and introduced him to Melissa. After explaining to him exactly who she was, I stood aside while she repeated everything she knew about Carlos, and the last day she had seen him.

I could tell the next time we all got together away from a crime scene was going be interesting. All the questions flying around would not be relating to any problems we might be solving, just the unraveling of a several personal secrets, mine included. I sighed. It was probably about time for all of us to come clean anyway. 'No More Secrets' was going to be my new mantra.

Later in the afternoon, one of the CSIs took Sol aside. When he came back, he shared disturbing news. "I was just informed there is more than one body in the pile of debris. The CSIs think they have found body parts to several men, probably four at least, might be more. They want to enlarge their search of the area—bring in a cadaver dog. Belvidere, can you take the Range Rover to pick up the cadaver dog you're trained to use? You can drop Orvill off at home or his store, if he'd like." Sol managed a straight face. He knew exactly what Orvill was.

Orvill and Belvidere nodded understanding.

"Can I go too? This is boring sitting around." Callista doesn't have much patience for crime scenes. I also saw she was upset over the cool looks she was receiving from Sol.

"Oh, like yeah! I'm bored too, can I go...please." Melissa had been quietly watching all the hustle and bustle outside the car. At one point her eyes darted over to a rabbit in the brush but she managed not to flip and sprint after it. I knew she didn't have much patience either and was probably hungry by now.

I imagined the four of them would stop for something to eat and kill the time it was supposed to take to pick up the cadaver dog and come back. I was right.

Callista asked before she got back into the Rover, "Can I bring you guys some food when we return?"

"Bring me whatever is convenient. You know I'll eat almost anything." Sol agreed.

"How long do you want us to take?" She whispered to Sol.

"Whatever seems reasonable."

She nodded and the four of them left.

An hour and a quarter later they returned with Orvill in bloodhound mode, two giant buckets of hot wings, two large bags of Subway heroes, several bags of fries, a large cooler filled with ice, soda and a six-pack of beer. Sol might be on duty, but the rest of us weren't.

Callista announced a loud "Da-dah!" and produced three platters of doughnuts. "Thought the CSIs might also need a little afternoon energy"

The little minx was almost right, but actually, they needed cheering up more. Digging through the debris turned up what appeared to be the remains of several different men, and they thought there might be others yet uncovered. Some of the remains looked like they had been hidden for at least six or seven years—the time the granddaughters had come to live at the mansion.

After autopsy and processing the remains at the morgue, they'd have more information. They knew they were uncovering the dumping grounds of a serial killer.

Orvill worked the front apron first. There had been little traffic there, so the scene was relatively fresh, but he found nothing. He then moved into the shed to Rembrandt the corners. That was where he found more disturbing evidence. The remains of dozens of small animals were neatly arranged in one corner. A little village sat in the dirt, made of whitened bones and skulls, remains used like building blocks. This was a testament to a calculating mind, not the dinner leftovers of a feral carnivore. Mrs. Freedhoff mentioned pets kept disappearing once Moroney came to live. What Orvill had found was the sad proof of her statement.

It reminded me of the little villages my sisters and I had built as children with our Lincoln Logs and Leggo sets. But a skillful sociopath had created this assembly of death. How many neighbors missed their beloved dogs and cats over the years? Now, at last, it would stop.

I felt a chill enter my heart when I remembered Melissa saying this was her favorite place to run. My trusting and beautiful girlfriend had no idea how close to a horrible death she might have come.

It was after midnight when we finally went home. Sol had called the station on his personal cell to request police radio silence about their find. The news media was to be kept in the dark for as long as possible. He was still on site with the CSIs, but they were going to quit for the night after posting officers around the crime scene.

Everyone in the Sheriff's Department was under strict instructions not to breathe a word to anyone, their families included, about what had been found. So far, the media had been silent.

I hoped we could keep it that way for at least twenty-four hours.

The drive home was quiet. We were deep into our own thoughts and I was sure none of them were pretty. We dropped Melissa off first. When I walked her to the door and kissed her, I kept my arms around her longer than usual, reluctant to let go. She had no idea how close she'd been coming to danger. Probably running with Carlos had kept her safe...but after his disappearance...? It made me sick to even think about it, but I didn't want to frighten her.

"Please, pretty please, do not take any runs in the forest near the wharf any more. Go to the park, run with the foxes near the cliffs, but not there. Okay? Will you promise me?"

"No problem my poodle-boy. Like I needed you to tell me? Just sitting in the car all day creeped me out. I like to have fun when I run...you know...not go to scary places. I haven't been near that place since I saw Carlos argue with the woman. Something...like, I don't know...something...told me to keep away, like an icky feeling, but to-day, I don't know...something else made me want to see it again."

I breathed a sigh of relief. My girl did have some smarts after all, or at least some good instincts. I kissed her and whispered in her ear. "When this is over, I owe you a night out, a great dinner, a good run and lots of hanky-panky...just you and me. Okay?"

"Sure okay...like what did you think? Of course. But sometime I would like to go out with your sisters. I really like them. Orvill too, and Sol. You okay with that, poodle-boy?"

"Yeah, I'm okay with that. I know they all like you too."

Orvill had brought his car to our place while the women went for food. After we arrived back home, he took out his keys and started for the garage. Belvidere stopped him. "Hey, where you going you big hunk?" She struck a seductive pose.

My sister? Belvidere?

"I thought I had to, uh, had to go home?" He looked a little confused, but a smile was sneaking around the corners of his mouth. "Don't I?" His eyebrows raised in hopeful question.

Was it a pleased or pleading look? I wasn't sure.

Belvidere linked her arm in his. "Come on in. I'll show you my room. There are no more secrets in this house, so why not enjoy the night?" She tossed her long hair over her shoulder.

Callista and I laughed out loud as the two of them walked away, but they didn't seem to care. I could have lit the entire house with Orvill's smile.

The next morning there were five for breakfast. Sol showed up first, waking Callista up at six-thirty. Melissa only woke up before ten AM for a run, so she was a no-show. And then I realized with a shock, she had no idea where I lived. It was time for a lot of things to change, and that was going to be at the top of my list.

Then I remembered something else to disclose. I left the room and came back with a small Derringer in a plastic baggie. When I handed it to Sol, he looked at me with his eyebrows raised again. "What is that?"

I sighed and tried to look sheepish. "It's the gun I told you about. Belvidere found it in the Eichler house when we went back to search. When we found Gabriel stuffed in the freezer. Belvidere said it was wedged behind a chair cushion."

"When I found it, I thought it looked like it had fallen back there out of a pocket, rather than if it was tucked away or hidden." My sister to the rescue.

"Damn you Antonio! What else are you not telling me?"

"Nothing...and I've told you about the gun. I just don't happen to carry it around with me to give to you. Here it is. This is the first chance I've had to hand it over." I was getting a little annoyed. How long did I have to play submissive? The game was pretty stale by now.

"Yeah. Thanks...for nothing. You've fucked up the chain of evidence...again."

"Okay, but think of all the leads I gave you, the license number of the truck with the porn, the lead to the bodies yesterday. This gun couldn't have been the murder weapon, the bullets are too small.

Come on Sol, give it a rest, let me have a hall pass." I looked around for some help, but both my sisters had turned their backs on me and were giggling. Great. I'm threatened with arrest again, and they laugh.

Then Orvill came to my rescue. He knew Sol was being a hard ass. "Hand me the baggie and let me sniff it."

Sol yelled at him. "Just what I need, you screwing with the chain of evidence too."

"Hey, back off! Then you hold it for me to sniff. I won't leave any trace on the baggie."

"Oh, all right." Sol took rubber gloves out of his pocket and opened the baggie.

Orvill flipped and extended his long snout towards the gun. "It doesn't smell like anything other than it's been cleaned fairly recently. This gun hasn't been fired for a long time."

"You sure?" Sol and I said in unison.

Orvill flipped back. "I'm pretty sure it's a new gun. I smell people on it, but it hasn't been used in a while."

Belvidere intervened. "Just in case we hadn't told you, Orvill owns a chain of sporting goods stores...guns, ammo, hunting and fishing gear. He's a licensed gunsmith and knows what he's talking about."

Sol calmed down. He had worked with Orvill and knew his reputation. I felt it was safe to share my plan with him.

"Look, Sol. I've an idea I think will work. Moroney knows I've got her gun. She's asked me several times to return it, but I've been reluctant to give it to her."

"Sounds like a smart move to me." Sol was easing up but there was still a small twitch at the corner of his mouth.

"I have to make a report to Mrs. Freedhoff today, and while I'm there, I have a plan. When do you think the CSI's will be finished with the crime scene?"

"They'll be working it for several days at least, what do you have in mind."

When I finished telling him, we came to an agreement.

I called Mrs. Freedhoff and made an appointment to meet at noon.

Then I went with Orvill to his main store. I needed to make a few purchases and was glad to have his expert advice.

CHAPTER THIRTY-SIX

Crack Shot

Parking the Beemer once more under the porte cochère at the Freedhoff mansion, I was sorry for the news I was bringing. I'd grown fond of Mrs. Freedhoff and did not look forward to causing her distress.

Gupta greeted me as usual, but instead of his usual bright turban, he was wearing a white one. I knew white was the color the Sikhs wore to funerals. He gave his little hand twirl as he opened the door and ushered me in. Mrs. Freedhoff had evidently broken her agreed confidence to let Gupta in on what we had found. I didn't think it mattered. He wasn't going to tell anyone or interfere with my plan.

We met once again on the porch overlooking the ocean. A space heater blew warm air towards the chaise.

I looked out to sea. No sun. A few seagulls were working the seaweed for baitfish. Rather than their usual soaring and plunging attacks, they seemed to be cruising overhead in a desultory manner, as if the pickings were slim and they weren't really interested. I wondered if they thought they were fooling the bait fish.

The fog bank was dense and dark, blotting out any trace of light, moving slowly as it threatened to bring its mist onshore. It wouldn't be long before it would be too damp and cold to sit on the porch.

Mrs. Freedhoff was swathed in the faux fur throw, her face almost as pale as the white fluff she was surrounded with. Today she wore a black hat, a stark contrast to her face and coverings. Blush, carelessly applied, stood out on her cheeks. She looked like a caricature of her former self. I felt an overwhelming sorrow as her frail hand reached out for mine. "I'm so sorry for your loss, Mrs. Freedhoff." I knew Sol had already spoken to her, both to question her, and to tell her he had identified the remains of her son-in-law. Dental records had been checked. There was no doubt Carlos had finally been found.

I watched as a tear slid down her cheek. Her eyelids were red and it was clear she had been crying.

She squeezed my hand. "You know, it's almost a relief. I've been living with a sick feeling in the pit of my stomach. Almost sure he was dead, I still couldn't stop hoping. And I felt a painful sadness —if he wasn't dead, why had he left without saying 'goodbye' to me? None of it made any sense. Now at least I can grieve for him in peace. It's a strange comfort to know he didn't just leave without a word." She wiped her eyes with her handkerchief. "I'm sorry, I've been a very poor hostess. Would you like Gupta to bring you something to drink? Coffee, perhaps something stronger?"

"That would be good. I think a coffee. Black please, with sugar."

"Is there anything I can bring you, Madam?" Again the hand twirl.

"Yes thank you. My usual."

As he turned to walk away, I could see he was also distressed. I was sorry, but I knew there was more sadness to come.

While Gupta was out of earshot, I filled her in on my plan. She listened silently and nodded when I finished. No words were needed.

On Gupta's return, I finished my coffee quickly. It was time to go. As we said goodbye, I held her hand for a bit longer than usual. "When you feel ready, I'd like to come and visit you, but on a friendly basis this time, no business. I have some people who would like very much to meet you. I think you might find you have a lot in common. Also, my sister, Belvidere would like to come and bring Callista. We don't pay enough attention to that little dog and she certainly enjoyed being snuggled by you."

"A stellar idea Antonio, I so loved having dogs in the past...but..." Her voice drifted off and I shuddered as I remembered the small village of bones...probably her beloved pets' last resting place. I tore the thought out of my mind and left.

As I walked across the entrance rotunda, Moroney slunk out of the shadows.

Oddly, she was wearing a pair of long blue jeans and a Grateful Dead tee-shirt. Her clothes were clean and rather baggy; not her usual attire. She hung back a few feet from me, not her usual physical assault either.

"Did you bring my gun back?" She bleated. "You said you'd bring my gun back." Her humming began at a low pitch.

"No, I did not. It had a defective hammer when I tried it, so I took it to a gunsmith for repair. But don't worry, you'll have it back soon. I want to apologize to you for the other night. It's just that I don't like surprises. I never react well to them."

She smirked a bit but said nothing. The humming slowed.

"Walk out with me to my car. I've brought you a present, something I think you'll like. My way of making amends."

The humming sputtered to a stop. Twisting her hands in front brought her breasts together. Thankfully, they were covered by the tee-shirt this time. She stepped out of the shadows to follow me to the car.

I opened the trunk and brought out a grey plastic case marked 'Luger,' opened it, and took out a large handgun.

"What is that?" The usual smirk was replaced by a half-smile.

"Like it? It's a Luger."

"Yeah. Can I fire it?"

"Sure, but not here, it's too close to the house. We could go to the porch where your grandmother sits and fire it out towards the ocean. I've never seen anyone under the cliffs there, but maybe you know a better place?"

She looked at the gun with longing. "I know a really good place. We can walk there, okay?"

Her eyes were glowing and she was humming again, but this time it sounded like an almost happy humming, or maybe gleeful.

Carrying the gun and case, I followed her along the old dirt road to the south of the mansion. There was a decided bounce to her step. When I looked towards the ocean, the fog bank had just reached the porch of the cottage. The bougainvillea would be pleased by the moisture. I hoped Gupta had taken Mrs. Freedhoff inside. The thought of her encased in more damp gloom was unappealing.

We walked steadily for about fifteen minutes. Through several of the turns but still a distance from the wharf, I stopped, reached down and pulled at my shoe. "Here, hold this." I said, and handed her the case with the gun while I bent over to fiddle with my laces.

She watched until I had my shoe off, hopping on one foot as if I was taking a pebble out. Then she took the gun out, looked at it, and pulled back the trigger.

"Hey," I yelled, "be careful, that thing is loaded."

Her humming got louder and louder as she took aim, chortling as she pulled the trigger. Red bloomed like a gigantic rose across my chest as the pain of the impact hit. She pulled the trigger again and I felt a resounding thump in my groin, red covering the front of my trousers like a balloon of blood exploding. I reached down to cup my family jewels and was hit again on the back of my neck, and in rapid succession, the side of my head, and then on my shoulder.

As she attacked, I heard hysterical laughter and giggles, louder and louder as the shots came faster and faster, the last hit my face and I was blinded as I fell to the ground, the sound of screaming loud in my ears.

"You fucking bastard, that's what you get for turning me down. No one rejects me, you got it? You're just like all the rest!" I felt spittle on my face as she leaned over me and continued. "But don't you worry little man, you're going to be in good company very soon." Her breath smelled like what I'd imagined a zombie's would be like, as if the world had rotted inside her mouth. I quelled the urge to retch.

She moved away for a moment and I thought she had gone. Then the sound of running feet and a sharp pain as she kicked at my back. The bitch kicked me like she was trying for the extra point. I thought I'd heard something snap, but maybe it was my imagination.

Her voice sounded like she was moving away again, but the tirade continued. "I've picked out a nice spot for you, right next to Carlos. You two will like being together, he was the worst fucker until I met you.

"You'll suffer like I made him. I enjoyed letting him bleed out...fun watching his life drain away. My favorite part, when they beg for help, telling me I couldn't do such a thing. They don't believe me until the light in their eyes goes out." She laughed, a high pitched cackle and kicked me again. "Just before that moment is when they finally begin to understand—I can do it! So start begging...now you bastard!"

The humming was interspersed with the guttural words making her hard to understand, but she got her point across.

"Carlos never saw it coming either...until I took the first shot to his balls. He screamed. I liked hearing it so I took my time with the next shots, just his arms, his knees. I laughed when he floundered around in the dirt...where he belonged, begging me to stop. Come on, tell me, why haven't you begged me yet?"

She kicked me hard and I curled up in the fetal position. It didn't stop her ranting. "I saved the last shot for his neck and laughed when his lights went out...the fun part until it's over."

Her excitement garbled her words but I thought they were clear enough to confirm what we suspected. All I could hope was my cell had recorded enough to put the bitch away for life.

But where was everyone? The plan was for me to stop about halfway before coming to the pier with the crime scene tape and the CSIs. I thought I had picked the agreed on spot to stop and fuss with my shoe. Maybe I picked the wrong place? Hard to be exact on foot when you're looking at a map with little indicators. My heart sank as I realized this could easily end up being my final error in problem solving.

All I could hope for was that she was so intent on shooting and kicking me she wouldn't notice I was covered with paint instead of blood. I wondered how long that might take. With every minute that went by my thoughts became more dismal.

The humming began again, a breathless and rasping low drone. The change in sounds frightened me. What if she had another weapon with her? A knife, another gun, a steel rod? Even a heavy rock dropped on me could crush my skull.

I had been gut shot twice, the breath knocked out of me. I gasped but couldn't seem to fill my lungs. It was a struggle to move.

Oh shit, I kept thinking. The plan had been to rescue me, but no one seemed to be coming. My next thought was to wonder how fast I could run as a dog in my condition. Would the paint still be in my eyes or would it stay with my human form like clothes when I flip?

I was on the edge of a flip to give it a try when I heard the sounds of a scuffle. The ringing in my ears from the head shot almost drowned the first noises out. Nothing could hide the earsplitting screeches that followed.

Feet grinding in the sand penetrated my momentary deafness. Someone was coming. The paint obscured my vision, I couldn't see who was approaching. When the steps closed in, I put my arms up in defense. Warm paws gently pushed my arms aside.

An angel looking a lot like an Afghan Hound was licking my eyelids once I could focus again.

A few feet away, Moroney lay flat on her back, wailing like a dying soprano banshee. A large black poodle stood on her chest, its jaws clamped around her gullet. Belvidere was shaking. I knew it wasn't fear, but the effort it took not to rip out Moroney's throat. The ancient wolf who resides within us wants to have its way. Protect the pack—

kill the enemy. Give no quarter.

Sol bent towards Belvidere. I heard his voice, softer than it had been for days. "It's okay, he's all right. Just had the wind knocked out of him. Let go of her." He reached out and softly stroked the black poodle's head. "I've got everything under control now." He whispered in its ear as he continued stroking.

The black poodle hesitated, then slowly released its grip and backed off. Sol turned Moroney over, forcibly pushing her face into the dirt. Roughly cuffing her hands behind her back, he read her the Miranda Warning.

Belvidere trotted over to make sure I was all right. When she looked down at me, I could have sworn her eyes were the golden color of the ancient wolves we poodles were descended from. Then she blinked and shining black poodle eyes surveyed me once again. No words were necessary. I heard her thoughts loud and clear. "Beloved brother, I've always got your back."

Melissa was sticking her tongue in and out like she had eaten peanut butter and couldn't get it off. I laughed and hugged her soft blonde coat, blotching it with more red paint. "Thank you for rescuing me. I'm sorry you got paint in your mouth."

"Faugh! That stuff tastes, terrible, like, you know...shit." The first time I had ever heard her say a bad word. I couldn't help laughing.

Belvidere and Sol had been in on my plan to make sure Moroney was the killer. I wanted to get a full confession from her and figured she wouldn't know the difference between a real Luger and the best paintball copy. I was right. She had gone for the bait I laid out for her.

Given the opportunity to kill me, she took it, just like when Carlos also refused her sexual favors. Rejection wasn't something she could handle, or maybe it was just her pleasure in the killing...either way, it made no difference.

Sol assured me my cell had broadcast the whole confession. The CSIs had recorded it as planned and were already making copies. We had her. The District Attorney had an open and shut case. All that was left was to identify the other remains Orvill had found. The information would at least bring closure to the families.

Other than being a little sore and ruining a shirt and a pair of old pants, I wasn't the worse for wear...well...maybe the shot to the groin might put me out of business for the night...or maybe not. I was confident the ringing in my ears would soon dissipate. I'd have an x-ray or two to see if the snap I heard was something important.

Melissa was looking at me with her soft brown eyes, her blonde topknot, black muzzle and grey streaked ears resplendent with the red paint that had rubbed off on her. My darling girl needed a bath and a good brushing. I was already contemplating a nice long hot shower together. Maybe I could flip too and convince Belvidere or Callista to take us both to the groomer, if we could figure out a reasonable explanation for all the red paint.

But first, I wanted to know how Melissa happened to be in the area after I had made her promise to keep away. Maybe I was a little rough with her when I asked. "How the hell did you get here? I told you to stay away from the wharf, to run someplace else for a while."

"Don't be mad at me. I was doing...you know...what you wanted. I promised to stay away from...like... the woods and the wharf, so I took my other favorite run, like...by the mansions.

"Then I saw you walking with the same woman I saw with Carlos. You know...the last time I saw him. I was afraid you might...like...get hurt too...like...you know, dead. That was when I followed you both, but...like...through the woods, not on the road behind you or anyplace where she could see me. When she started shooting you, I was going to get her, but Belvidere...she got to her first...already had that horrible woman by the throat. So instead...I ran to you...my darling poodle boy." She licked my face and then sputtered again as she tried to get more paint off her tongue.

How can you get mad at someone who loves and wants only to rescue you? And then I thought about sight hounds, bred to bring down much larger animals. They weren't as fragile as they looked. If Melissa had taken down Moroney, leaping at her with the impact of her speed and agility, she probably would have broken Moroney's neck. On second thought, maybe it wouldn't have been a bad thing. But I was sure, later on, when the thrill of the hunt and the kill wore off, it would have been very upsetting for Melissa.

Sol came over to help me up. Maybe he was offering peace?

"The Sheriffs are taking her in. She's screaming her 'kill the dog' mantra again. That woman has no idea how lucky she is to still be alive. After the first shots she took at you, Belvidere was after her, and then, out of nowhere came Melissa—and man, is she fast! I admit I had everything I could do not to flip and rip Moroney apart. No telling what would have happened if Melissa had gotten to her first. At the first sign of that woman's blood, there might have been all three of us tearing her to pieces...our control only lasts so long and then the wolf comes out."

He reached over and patted me on the shoulder and then scratched Melissa's ears. "Good girl. Now take him home and the two of you need a good shower, you're both covered with red paint...which I hope is the washable kind." He laughed as he walked off.

I smiled to myself. Sol was going to forgive me after all.

CHAPTER THIRTY-SEVEN

Whew!

A week later I was back at the Freedhoff estate. Gupta answered the door with a big smile.

"How is Mrs. Freedhoff?" I asked.

A voice from behind the big man answered. "I'm fine, thanks to you."

And there she was, standing in the entrance, dressed in a pair of slim black slacks, a black and gold printed silk over-shirt and a large smile. Her hair was styled in a simple bob and I noticed it now had blonde highlights. A little well applied make-up brightened her face and emphasized the beautiful bone structure I noted when first we met. Gone was the frail old woman—in her place, a spry octogenarian stood on her own feet.

"You look a little startled, young man. Haven't you ever seen an old woman up and about before?"

"I hadn't seen this particular beautiful lady up and about before. I must say, it's a rare pleasure."

A little more color came to her cheeks. "Watch out, Antonio, with that kind of charm, I just might forget how old I really am. You do know we cougars never give up." And then she laughed, a long, full peel of joy. The laugh was so pure I felt it cleansing the house of the evil miasma clouding it for so long. An exorcism couldn't have been more powerful.

"I've brought a surprise to cheer you up, but now I don't think you need it. You already look pretty chipper to me. When we are finished talking, you can have it."

I was gifted with a coy smile and a tilt of her head. "I'm loath to admit it, but having Moroney in the house was like an infestation of black mold filling the basement. She put everyone on edge and made the whole household miserable. Since she's gone, it's like the clouds have lifted and the sun has come out once again. My only sorrow is, it took Carlos' death to discover what she really was."

I noticed she took Gupta's arm when she walked, but her step was firm and she wasn't shaking.

Instead of the cottage, we sat in the spacious and elegant living room. Brocade chairs, Louis XIV the predominant epoch, created individual seating arrangements. Callista would approve.

We sat tête-a-tête, Gupta standing behind her when she began. "The best news first. Felicity signed herself into rehab for at least six months. The combination of Carlos disappearing and her suspicions Moroney was involved, put her over the edge when she thought I'd hired you to find Carlos.

"I've finally met her nice friends, Mr. and Mrs. Cima, who you had told me about. They were instrumental in getting her help. I'm very thankful to them. The odd thing is, we've all become quite close. A rather strange band of people tied together by mutual love for Carlos. I think he would have been happy to know of our bonding. He might even have thought of it as a tribute."

I didn't say anything, but the Cimas had also befriended Callista— Freddo playing Scrabble with her, Stella and Callista exchanging recipes.

Lately, Bel and I have arrived home to shouts of "zounds, zinnias and zygotes." We'd find Callista and Freddo hunched over a Scrabble board while Stella sat in front of the television watching re-runs of "The Real Housewives of New Jersey." Belvidere and I keep away. It's good for Callista to have her own friends away from all the paperwork of Pudel & Cie.

Sol keeps his distance when Cima's around. I think he's still a little suspicious of the man, although I heard through the grapevine Sol let Dr. Landsdown walk on a charge of selling illegal drugs after the FDA came back with their analysis of the enhancement vitamins—only herbal. The SEC offering was back on track as planned.

I turned back to Mrs. Freedhoff. "I understand you made a deal with the District Attorney on behalf of Moroney."

"Yes, and I thank you for walking my attorney through it. Moroney has been declared incompetent to stand trial by reason of insanity. I've been appointed as her guardian and conservator. Felicity will be my successor.

"The deal is: while she is kept under maximum security in a facility for the criminally insane, she will not stand trial. On her behalf, both Felicity and I waived all statutes of limitations, so, if at any time she is released from the facility, she will immediately be incarcerated in a regular prison and stand trial for murder in the first degree—for Carlos as well as all the other young men whose bodies were found in the wharf shed. God only knows how many of his other creatures she has harmed."

I saw her mouth tighten at the corners. I was relieved to know Moroney was going to be safely tucked far away for as long as she lived, and her family did not have to suffer the publicity and indignity of a lengthy trial.

Mrs. Freedhoff motioned to Gupta. He handed her a gym bag, this one a bright turquoise and I flashed back to his turban of the same color. She laid both her hands over the zipper as it sat on her lap. "Now Antonio, this is the rest of your fee and I hope you'll find it satisfactory." She passed the bag over to me. "Go ahead, open it."

I slid the zipper back and looked at stacks of new hundred dollar bills with their ugly blue tint. Note to self, never think of money as ugly. It is as beautiful as the things it lets you buy and do. This bag would bring my sisters and me respect, if and when our parents ever returned. Our first case—and we scored!

"It's seventy-five thousand, the balance of the hundred-thousand you returned, less your original retainer. Is that sufficient?"

"Thank you so much. It is more than all right." And I couldn't help myself, I'm not a hugger by nature, but I jumped up and hugged her anyway. I think she liked it.

We were at the door saying our goodbyes as she heard yapping coming from my Beemer.

"Excuse me for a moment, I almost forgot something." I ran back to the car and Callista jumped out and ran up to Mrs. Freedhoff, vaulting up into her arms.

"I know you liked Callista, so, I brought you a surprise." I went to the car to fetch a Gucci pet carrying case. Inside, a tiny black and white Pomeranian puppy peeked through the mesh. I took the pup out and handed her over to Mrs. Freedhoff.

"Meet Baby Doll. She's six months old, house trained, and has her first certificate from obedience school. She's also being trained as a licensed therapy dog. We thought you might enjoy her company." Baby Doll licked her on the nose and snuggled against her chest. "You don't have to worry about dogs disappearing anymore."

Mrs. Freedhoff didn't have to say a word. I watched as she held the tiny black and white body to her heart. Her smile said it all.

Callista hopped back into the car and I waved as we left. Callista stood with her paws on the back window.

Before I got to the gate, a familiar figure ran in front of the Beemer waving his arms. "Antonio, stop, stop!" It was Jonathan. I had forgotten all about him.

"Let me say hello to Callista before you leave." I opened the door and he jumped in the back seat.

After he had hugged her to his satisfaction, he turned to me.

"Thank you for recommending Pa for the job here. Pa's teaching Mrs. Freedhoff and Gupta how to use facebook and Twitter...and guess what? We have honking powerful internet all over the estate! Mrs. F bought tablets for me and Pa, the whole staff—she and Gupta have them too. Pa and Mom love it here! They keep saying this is a job sent from heaven, but I know it was you and Callista...my lucky charms." He finally stopped to catch his breath.

"I'm glad it worked out for you and your family. Mrs. Freedhoff is pleased to have you all here. She needs looking after once in a while and sometimes gets lonely. Gupta is happy with the way your Pa looks after the cars and drives, it gives him a needed break."

Jonathan leaned over and gave me a hug before jumping out of the car and waving goodbye. As I pulled off, he shouted, "...and if you need any more help in problem solving, remember...you can always call on me." Smart kid. I laughed all the way home.

When I drove away from the mansion, I shoved the turquoise gym bag towards Callista. We had the biggest month in the history of Pudel & Cie.—and Cima's fee was yet to be billed!

Callista was quiet, pawing her way through the stacks of money. Then she flipped, and I heard her chirping to Belvidere on her cell. Very little makes Callista happier than money. More to spend on her execrable decorating taste. I suppressed an involuntary cringe.

I stopped on the way to buy four red roses this time. Our family tradition for the alpha male had to be honored. Two problems had been solved. I couldn't let my sisters down this time.

CHAPTER THIRTY-EIGHT

Plea Bargain

The huge legal fees of my nightmares were greatly reduced. The Sheriff's Office took the credit. Capturing a serial killer was no small feat. But bringing closure to families of seven missing men once all the bodies uncovered at the site were identified was a major triumph. All because of my help.

I hadn't actually gotten off free, but the charges were reduced to a misdemeanor. I was on probation for a year, during which time I had to report to my probation officer regularly, and I had five hundred hours of community service. If I spent four hours every Saturday and Sunday it would take a hundred and twenty-five weeks to complete. Talk about learning a lesson! Maybe I could have it reduced if I behaved myself. Maybe? Maybe not. Maybe I could work more days.

All charges against my sisters were dismissed. It took our attorneys three hours to make the deal. Sol had spoken in my defense about how helpful I was in closing the open cases, putting myself in danger and arranging the search of the Freedhoff premises. To say I was grateful would be a massive understatement.

I was willing to take my punishment in stride as long as Callista was back in Sol's good graces. He finally understood she was not to blame. She and Belvidere had tried many times to convince me to tell him everything. But every dog knows the rules—fidelity to the pack comes first. Both my sisters were bound to stand by me as their alpha male and pack leader, even if they didn't agree with my decisions.

If Callista and Sol ever married, then he would take my place, but until then, I was still her alpha.

Sol came to the house the day I was sentenced.

Once again, I apologized.

This time, he laughed. "I figured getting paintballs smacked in your balls was almost payback enough. But I was convinced you learned your lesson when you stayed around to take your punishment.

"I know you could have flipped, you and Melissa chartered a plane for wherever you wanted to go, and just split.

"There was no way Melissa and her pet poodle would have been stopped from leaving the country, and you knew I couldn't do a thing about it. But you're all right. You stayed, no matter what the outcome. Showed character." He nodded at me, then reached over and slapped my shoulder. To me, that slap was more reward than a sword touch from a queen. I was forgiven.

Sol wasn't finished. "But don't be getting all happy. You still have those five hundred hours of community service. I've arranged for you to work them off at the Orange County Animal Shelter, cleaning cages and teaching, dog obedience and pet owner classes. That will keep you busy on weekends—maybe even out of trouble."

Maybe a slap on the back wasn't quite as good as being knighted, but I'd take work in an animal shelter over jail any time.

I might still be somewhat in the doghouse with Sol, but Callista and he were back together as usual. She forgave me the moment I said she could buy a Gustav Klimt drawing she'd had her eye on. The Klimt made up for my veto of a humongous Art Nouveau glass-dead-animal-diorama to put next to the round tête a tête monstrosity in the office. Enough already! At least the Klimt only took up a little wall space.

Belvidere was becoming accustomed to her relationship with Orvill being out of the closet. She even bought a king size bed for her room, complete with L.L.Bean linens. Callista and I were shocked when it arrived. Orvill now divides his time between our house and his cabin in Yosemite, and Bel usually goes with him.

I was still having a hard time trying to picture her in jeans and a flannel shirt, let alone country western two-step garb. Talk about my head exploding! But I was enjoying Orvill's company. It was good to have another man around the house to talk to.

It was going to take a while before Sol and I got back to our old easy companionship. My fault, I know, still...

CHAPTER THIRTY-NINE

New Arrival

Callista sent me to pick up several bags of ice for the wrap party she planned to celebrate the problems solved.

When I returned home, something was amiss.

A large, odd-shaped automobile was parked in front of the gate. No Cadillac Escalade this time. It didn't match the vehicles of any of our expected guests.

This baby was large, sharply angular and black. I know my antique cars—been a buff since I collected models as a kid. I was looking at a Rolls Royce. But no ordinary Roller—a 1924 Silver Ghost touring car with its tonneau pulled open to allow fresh air inside. It crouched against the curb like a big heavy cat ready to pounce; its pelt gleaming with golden highlights under the street light.

The right hand driver side door opened. A tall, broad shouldered man in a dark chauffeur's cap and uniform got out, and went around to open the passenger door.

A huge labradoodle laboriously climbed out of the car. Limping slowly towards our front door, his belly rolled like a ship in heavy seas while his legs moved slowly, as if every joint cried to be oiled.

Even with the dim lighting, I saw the white of his muzzle when he turned around. Nodding to the chauffeur toting a tapestry covered Gladstone bag, they slowly made their way up the walk.

My mouth dropped open. "Oh crap! Now we're really in for it."

« The End »

ABOUT THE AUTHOR

Alice Donenfeld-Vernoux has enjoyed a long career in the entertainment business: movies, television and New Media, as attorney, producer, studio executive, creator of over a hundred television programs, distributor, consultant and consistent exhibitor in the world entertainment markets.

Her novels, "Cave Dreams," a speculative romance, and "Out Of The Chute, contemporary woman's fiction, are both 5-star rated, and available in print and Kindle on Amazon.com.

Currently she is at work on several more novels following the adventures of Pudel & Cie.—following the three siblings as they paw their way to solutions in their family business.

In the works is her memoir, "Behind the Spandex, Globetrotting With Superheroes" spanning her career as executive both with Marvel Comics and Filmation Studios. As head of worldwide television and licensing for both companies, she traveled with superstars the likes of "Spiderman," Captain America," "He-Man and the Masters of the Universe," "Fat Albert and the Cosby Kids," "She-Ra Princess of Power," and "The Incredible Hulk,"—the first woman heading a global television distribution company.

She lives in Baja California, Mexico, and Laguna Hills, California with four rescue dogs, including—a black and a white poodle of course.

Thank you for taking the time to read "Moroney Baloney."

If you enjoyed the book, please consider telling your friends, or posting a short review. Word of mouth is an author's best friend and is always much appreciated.

As a reader, it is your enjoyment that fuels an author's inspiration to continue writing.

Alice Donenfeld-Vernoux

www.ingramcontent.com/pod-product-compliance
Lightning Source LLC
Chambersburg PA
CBHW032003170626
46807CB00006B/2624